THIS FIRE NEVER DIES

ONE YEAR WITH THE PKK

Fréderike Geerdink

Translated by Vivien D. Glass and Anna Asbury

LeftWord

First published in February 2021.
Digital print edition, February 2021.

LeftWord Books
2254/2A Shadi Khampur
New Ranjit Nagar
New Delhi 110008
INDIA

LeftWord Books and Vaam Prakashan are imprints of
Naya Rasta Publishers Pvt. Ltd.

leftword.com

ISBN 978-81-950310-4-7 (paperback)
978-81-950310-3-0 (ebook)

This publication has been made possible with financial support from the Dutch Foundation for Literature.

Nederlands letterenfonds
dutch foundation
for literature

I dedicate this book to all my jailed colleagues in Turkey.
Journalism is not a crime.

Contents

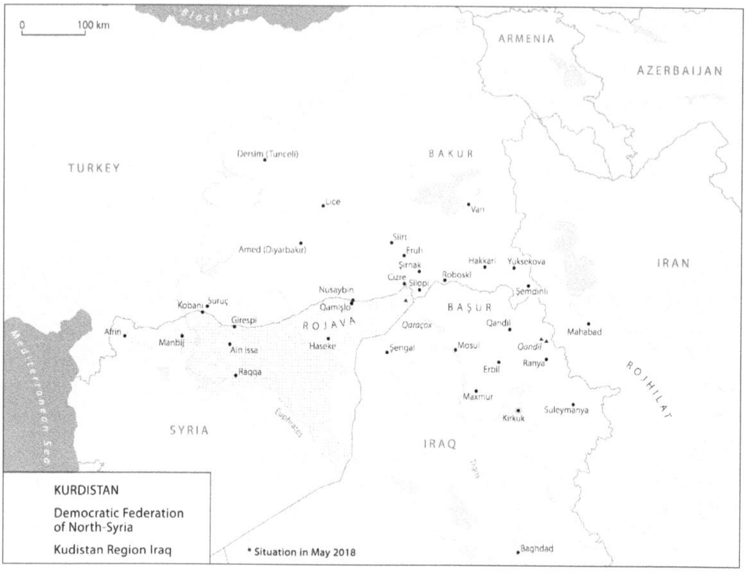
0 100 km
Black Sea
ARMENIA
AZERBAIJAN
TURKEY
Dersim (Tunceli)
BAKUR
Lice
Van
Amed (Diyarbakır)
Siirt
Eruh
Şırnak
Cizre
Silopi
Hakkari
Yüksekova
Roboskî
Şemdinli
IRAN
Nusaybin
Qamişlo
Kobani
Suruç
Girespi
ROJAVA
BAŞUR
Qandil
Mahabad
Afrin
Manbij
Ain Issa
Haseke
Qaraçox
Şengal
Mosul
Qandil
Ranya
Erbil
Raqqa
Maxmur
ROJHILAT
Kirkuk
Suleymanya
Mediterranean Sea
SYRIA
Euphrates
IRAQ
Tigris
KURDISTAN
Democratic Federation of North-Syria
Kudistan Region Iraq
* Situation in May 2018
Baghdad

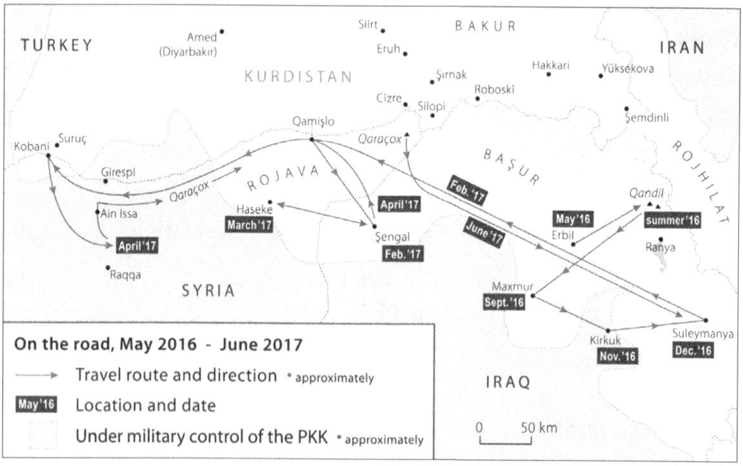
TURKEY
Amed (Diyarbakır)
Siirt
BAKUR
Eruh
IRAN
Hakkari
Yüksekova
KURDISTAN
Şırnak
Roboskî
Cizre
Silopi
Şemdinli
Qamişlo
Qaraçox
Kobani
Suruç
BAŞUR
ROJHILAT
Girespi
ROJAVA
Feb. '17
Qaraçox
Qandil
Haseke
April '17
Ain Issa
March '17
May '16
summer '16
June '17
Erbil
Şengal
Ranya
April '17
Feb. '17
Raqqa
SYRIA
Maxmur
Sept. '16
Kirkuk
Suleymanya
Nov. '16
Dec. '16
On the road, May 2016 - June 2017
Travel route and direction * approximately
May '16 Location and date
Under military control of the PKK * approximately
IRAQ
0 50 km

PREFACE

A Crazy Plan

The group of fighters had made tea in a large open field in the Qandil Mountains, near the Iranian border. The black pot was suspended over a smokeless wood fire, the sugar bowl was handed round. There was talking, laughter. The view overlooking the valley and mountains was spectacular, the autumn colours exuberant and the sky bright blue. A shepherd was driving his flock round the side of a mountain towards us. I heard the sheep's bells and a loud, rasping cough. A sudden desire to stay in the mountains overwhelmed me. But it was impossible. I was not a fighter.

A couple of hours later, the penny dropped. I may not be a fighter, but I am a journalist, I thought – what if I joined the PKK for a year and wrote a book about my experiences? Would that be doable, or was I mad to even think about it? I asked the PKK press man if we could have a word. 'Listen,' I said, 'I've got a crazy plan.' 'We love crazy plans around here, so let's hear about it,' he answered. 'In short: I spend a year with the PKK and write a book about it. What you think?' He laughed, and promised to discuss it with the leadership.

It was November 2015, two months after I'd been deported from Turkey for my work as a journalist. The deportation took me by surprise, though I realize with hindsight how incredibly naive that was of me. After all, I had been at loggerheads with the Turkish state for months.

The problems had started in January of that year. At half past twelve one afternoon, there was a knock on the door of my apartment in Diyarbakır, the Kurdish city where my office had been based since 2012, after I had worked from Istanbul for seven years. Opening the door, I found myself staring down the barrels of about five machine guns. The uniforms of the gentleman – and one lady – bore the acronym TEM of the Turkish counterterrorism police. They searched my apartment and took me to the station. I was suspected of spreading propaganda for a terrorist organization.

A few hours later, I was released, probably in part thanks to the efforts of the Dutch foreign minister Bert Koenders, who just happened to be on an official visit in the Turkish capital Ankara. Don't ask me why the police arrested me on exactly that day, or what went on behind the scenes. I don't know, and to me, it doesn't matter.

The only thing that matters to me was, and still is, my work. The incident distracted me from the task I had set myself: travelling around Kurdistan writing stories. This distraction was only increased when the state decided to press charges against me for spreading propaganda for a terrorist organization. I gave even more interviews to Dutch, Kurdish and international media as well as some small Turkish opposition media organizations; I had to arrange for a lawyer, outline a strategy and write my defence. I felt strong, fired up with adrenaline. My attorney Ramazan Demir counted on my being acquitted. Early in April, he was proved right.

Did I consider giving up my work in Turkey? Not for a second. It wasn't the way I conducted myself as a journalist that had landed me in trouble: it was the Turkish state's lack of democracy.

This is what I wrote about, in Dutch and increasingly in Turkish and English, and to make matters worse, I wrote from a Kurdish perspective, in the symbolic capital city of the Kurds. It was more than the Turkish government could stomach. My criminal file revealed that the prosecution had cherry-picked arbitrary pieces of my writing. You can't adapt to arbitrariness, even if you wanted to; in short, this left me with two options. I could carry on with what I was doing, or I could give up journalism. An easy choice.

From that moment on, my deportation from Turkey was a matter of time, though I didn't realize it – probably out of self-protection, as the knowledge would have paralysed me – until it happened, on 9 September 2015. I will give a full account of the incident later in the book. I have had to leave my life, which fitted me like a glove, behind in Diyarbakır. Taking nothing with me but myself, including my fighting spirit and my determination to tell the story of the Kurds. And in a flash of inspiration in that valley in the mountains, they led to this project, this book.

Not that I didn't agonize over the decision to actually see the project through. I wasn't worried for my safety: safety is a matter of risk assessment. I was more concerned about the journalistic integrity of the project. The PKK would be allowed to have no say on its contents. I would need to be given sufficient access to the camps and bases. If for any reason I wasn't able to do the work the way I wanted, I would call off the project prematurely.

And I didn't want to take the decision on my own. I spoke with various colleagues, one of whom said, 'Nothing would flow more naturally from your years of work in Turkey than this project. It would be crazy not to do it.' She was right. Shortly afterwards, my project proposal was approved by the Dutch Fund for Journalism Projects. The not-so-crazy plan could go ahead.

I was returning to Kurdistan.

Fréderike Geerdink

Amsterdam,
9 April 2018

CHAPTER 1

The Pool

Comrade Ronahî is lying on the large rocks on the bank of the rushing river. She's gasping for breath, coughing. Another guerrilla fighter is crouching beside her holding her hand, others are bent over Ronahî. Comrade Dilsoz, standing nearby, is panting; in his effort to save Ronahî from the power of the swirling water that was pulling her to its depth, he himself went under for several moments.

Comrade Hesen is standing in the river on his leg-and-a-half plus peg leg, looking around him; wondering if this might, after all, have been the wrong spot to block off the river with rocks and tree trunks to make a swimming pool for the fighters to cool off in the sweltering summer heat. Too close to the waterfall and its unpredictable undercurrents, perhaps? How could they have made such an error of judgment? Hadn't he built countless pools in his life?

It's around three in the afternoon on Saturday, 16 July 2016. Earlier, about twenty men and women spent several hours building the dam. Two comrades worked upstream, almost out of our sight, looking for tree trunks and lowering them into the river. The current carried them downstream, where they tumbled down the waterfall and were manoeuvred into place by the guerrillas waiting in the river. Others made a human chain from the bank to the work in progress. Dislodging large rocks, they handed them down the chain to the builders, who placed them on and in between the trunks. Still others filled large woven plastic bags with stones and dragged them to the dam through the water, where they were lugged into place by three or four men and women.

The sun is scorching, the water icy. The walnut trees on the riverbank provide shade. The roar of the water drowns out Comrade Adar's calls until she's only a short distance away. She's shouting something in Kurdish. I recognize the word, which is the same in Turkish, '*Darbe!*' Is that really what she means – darbe, a coup? A coup? 'Who says that?' I ask. Adar answers that it's all over Turkish television. The Turkish parliament has been bombed, the Bosphorus Bridge was occupied for hours; there have been lots of casualties but now soldiers are being arrested. The coup seems to have failed.

Ronahî is still as limp as a rag doll. She's helped to her feet and supported. Hesen and the others standing in the river wade towards the bank. I jog down the faint and narrow forest track after Adar to the camp, barely 100 metres downstream. In a corner of the central tent, a sturdy construction of about forty square metres and over two metres high, a television set stands on a couple of crates that have been transformed into a table by a cleverly placed tablecloth. CNN Türk, NTV, Habertürk, A Haber – we zap through all the Turkish stations. It's the same on every one.

The news reaches us almost twenty-four hours late. The attempted coup took place the evening before, on 15 July, and the stations are already broadcasting commentary programmes instead of news summaries of what has happened so far. We watch footage of chaos on the Bosphorus Bridge in the dark, where angry citizens are waving Turkish flags and dragging young soldiers out of their vehicles. At an army base, soldiers are kneeling on the ground in their underwear, waiting to be taken away for questioning. Prime Minister Binali Yıldırım is shown, surrounded by security guards; it's outdoors somewhere, but I can't tell where. Where is President Erdoğan? Are the reports of the parliament bombing true? Was the Chief of Staff General Hulusi Akar involved? I can't make head or tail of the reports; it already seems too late to catch up with the news.

I'm sitting cross-legged on the floor in front of the TV. Behind me are three other Europeans who, like me, are taking a Kurdish language course this summer. They don't speak any Turkish, and ask me to translate for them. As usual on Turkish television, especially in a crisis situation like this one, all the experts are on the government's side. When they talk about Fethullah Gülen, the Europeans don't know who that is. 'Well, then I can't explain any of this to you,' I say, inwardly irritated at such ignorance in people who have decided to come all the way up here to the mountains to join the PKK, apparently having done so little research into Turkish history they've never even heard of Gülen.

But how many high-ranking Gülenists can there be in the Turkish army? I wonder. Isn't this far more likely to be the work of the old-school generals, who never warmed to Islamic politics and even less to Erdoğan? And since when do Turkish coups fail, given the amount of experience the Turkish army has with this particular job? Did Erdoğan know about it?

I'm not going to find out from Turkish TV. I turn to Comrade Nûman, an experienced guerrilla in his late thirties who is always happy to share his views on all kinds of matters. But Nûman is talking to another comrade about something else, ignoring the TV completely. 'What do you make of it, Comrade Nûman?' I ask anyway. He shakes his head and says, with a shrug, '*Her şey bize bağlı* . . . It's all connected to us.'

Ronahî is lying under a blanket in a corner of the tent. She's shaking. Her thick, curly hair has almost dried, her face is pale. Her head is propped up with a large pillow so she can see the TV screen, but her eyes are closed. The other fighters seem to have lost interest in the coup as well.

BLUE WATER

When I arrived at the PKK camp six weeks ago, a female guerrilla gave me a new name, a nom de guerre: Avaşîn. Such names are mostly a security measure, but mine is also easier for many of the Kurds to pronounce and remember than my Western one. Avaşîn means 'blue water'. It is the name of a region near the Turkish border, but there is also a river called Avaşîn. At the source of the Avaşîn, another river rises, which I am told is not as clear, as sparkling, as refreshing or as enchanting as the Avaşîn, but dark and murky. Do I know the Avaşîn? Haven't I visited the Yüksekova district, which the Avaşîn runs through? Aren't I that Dutch journalist who was quite recently kicked out of the country after reporting from Yüksekova? That makes Avaşîn the perfect name for me, especially since my eyes are *sîn*. My eyes aren't blue, but one thing I do remember from earlier Kurdish lessons is that, when it comes to eye colour, sîn can also mean green.

I picked my surname myself. The choice was an obvious one. During this year I'm spending with the PKK, I'm called Avaşîn Amed, after the Kurdish name of the Kurdish capital Diyarbakır – my beloved home base until I was expelled, the fortress of the Kurdish resistance and the city I lost my heart to.

Amed has been destroyed. Or, to be precise, a part of its historic centre Sur has been destroyed. Just like Amed is the heart of Kurdistan, Sur is the heart of Amed. The war raged from late

2015 until the spring of the following year. The Turkish government thundered in and flattened everything.

In the guise of Comrade Avaşîn, I enter a different world, without knowing at the time how fundamentally different it really is. It's a world I thought I, Fréderike the journalist, knew quite well, having followed the PKK closely for many years and interviewed its highest-ranking commanders at their headquarters in the Qandil Mountains. And that was not all. During the last three of my nine years as a Turkish correspondent, I was based in Diyarbakır. I travelled extensively through Kurdish territories, generally called the Southeastern Anatolia Region but known among Kurds as Bakur, which means 'north' – in other words, northern Kurdistan. In all of these towns, villages and hamlets, I got to know the Kurdish people; the reality of their everyday lives, the contempt and denial of their identity they have been subjected to for decades and which they continue to fight against tirelessly and unwaveringly. I learned about their history, their dreams, their dead.

I heard the slogans. Slogans that are chanted at every demonstration, funeral, holiday and remembrance day. *PKK halktır halk burada*, the PKK is the people, the people are here. *Bê serok jiyan nabe*, no life without the leader.

With this reality fresh in my mind and the eyes of a journalist closely following the daily news and its insanity in search of the stories behind it, I arrived in the mountains in early June 2016, the adrenaline still coursing through my veins.

The year that had just passed had been long and intense. It had started with the Turkish general elections on 7 June 2015, which I watched from my home in Diyarbakır. When the results were announced, the city was plunged into euphoria. The left-wing Peoples' Democratic Party (HDP), an alliance of Kurdish and Turkish left-wing parties and social groups which had originated in the Kurdish movement, had swept an astonishing thirteen per cent of the vote. With this result, the party had not only reached the electoral threshold of ten per cent with ease, but also – and this would prove crucial for later developments – stripped Recep Tayyip Erdoğan's AK Party of its majority in parliament.

That evening, there were riotous celebrations in the streets surrounding the HDP head office. People were beside themselves with joy. There was music, large circles of dancing men, women and children, bonfires and fireworks, slogans, banners and flags, balloons, honking cars, faces that shone with ecstasy but which still had amazement and incredulity written all over them. A party that had come from the Kurdish resistance was to send over eighty representatives to the parliament in Ankara? Really?

Three months later, I was expelled from Turkey. In short: Erdoğan didn't acknowledge the HDP's victory and was pressing for new elections. He deliberately reignited the conflict with the PKK, which had been on the back burner ever since a mutual ceasefire had been declared in 2013, in a bid to attract the nationalist electorate, and smothered the Kurdish euphoria in death and destruction. I was reporting on the renewed war and the struggle against it when I was collared by the police and, escorted by two officers, put on a plane from the east of the country to Istanbul and from there to Amsterdam. Scram, nosy parker.

My last journey through Bakur is still vivid in my mind. I was taken from Yüksekova to Hakkâri and back in an armoured military vehicle – don't ask me why. Inside the vehicle, music was playing at full blast – blaring nationalist aggression from which there was no escape. I tried looking up at the stars through the window on my right, but it was too small and had bars. I continued to stare out into the darkness all the same, refusing to have anything to do with the soldiers around me, avoiding any kind of contact. I was their prisoner. But though we despised each other, we were connected by a potential common fate: at any given moment, PKK guerrillas hidden in the mountains around us could detonate a roadside bomb that would tear our bodies to shreds. It wouldn't be the first time that happened on this road. Now! I thought, holding my breath. Now! Now! Nothing.

Today, I'm back in Kurdistan. In the heart of the struggle no less, witnessing it first-hand.

WATERMELON

Here I want to continue with the sort of journalism about the Kurds that in Turkey, and especially in the south-east, I practised with the greatest love: telling the stories of ordinary villagers and city residents. Not that I've never interviewed a local or national politician, but reporting on how ordinary people are affected by war and the increasingly crumbling democracy have always been more appealing to me. Why wouldn't I apply the same tactic with the PKK and YPG/J? I had now interviewed the leadership a couple of times, but how did the 'foot soldiers' of the armed forces really see the situation? What were they fighting for, and why? What was their daily life like?

As a non-embedded journalist you don't get to see that. I remember that in autumn 2015, long before I began my year with the PKK, I found myself on a PKK base at the front near Kirkuk.

I interviewed the commander and spoke with a couple of fighters. After an hour or so I was told that I had to leave. Might I take a quick look inside the barracks? No. Was there time for an extended interview with a couple of fighters? No. They had another job to do, their time was up. What kind of job? Just a job, a task, and that was that. But I was curious about the bigger story. That was what I was after now.

My first appointment is with Cemil Bayık, the vice president of the Kurdistan Communities Union (KCK for short), the umbrella organization which the PKK also belongs to. Simply put, he and Besê Hozat are the highest in rank after Abdullah Öcalan, the leader and founding member of the PKK who has been held on the prison island of Imralı in the Sea of Marmara south of Istanbul since early 1999.

I have interviewed Bayık, whose code name is Comrade Cuma, several times before. He wishes to welcome me to the PKK and discuss some of the things I can do in the year ahead. The conversation never gets very specific, simply because the constantly changing security situation makes planning very difficult.

He has, however, outlined the first ten weeks for me, as he tells me over a plate of watermelon chunks. I'm going to language camp. I was already aware of its existence, having met a German guerrilla on a previous trip to the Qandil Mountains who had learned her excellent Kurdish at a PKK course. Now I'm to take the same course. I'm looking forward to it. I started learning Kurmancî, the most commonly spoken Kurdish language in Turkey, when I lived in Istanbul years ago, and continued my frantic attempts to master the language in Diyarbakır. For various reasons, all my efforts ended in failure and deep frustration; hopefully, an intensive PKK course will yield better results.

The only snag is that inside the language camp, strict security measures prohibit any form of communication through the internet or telephone. Comrade Dalyan, one of the two guerrillas who conduct PKK communications with the foreign press, confiscates my phone with an almost malicious glee. 'We're cutting you off from the outside world, Comrade Avaşîn,' he grins; I laugh with him, while inwardly suppressing a rising panic. If there is important news, surely I must know all about it so I can observe the way in which the guerrillas deal with it? Besides, if something important happens it might make sense for me to conduct my research at a different location, but how do I find out about it if I can't communicate? I keep my doubts to myself. If I have to spend ten weeks in isolation, so be it. It is, after all, a small price to pay to improve my Kurdish.

As it turns out, we're not completely cut off from the news at language camp. There's a television set that shows the seven o'clock news every evening on SterkTV (*sterk* is Kurdish for 'star'), a station affiliated with the Kurdish movement. To avoid being bombed the minute we switch on the TV in our outdoor camp under the trees, the set is hidden away in a kind of living room sunk into a hillside. Every evening, we climb to the entrance of the structure.

The design of the 'living room', whose ceiling is just under two metres high, is of a baffling ingenuity. All you see from the outside is a blanket hanging from a crossbar attached to a tree trunk. Going through it, you find yourself in a low tunnel about a metre long, concealed in the hillside, with two more blankets on a crossbeam at its other end. You take off your shoes in the hall, duck under the crossbeam and go inside through the blankets. The room measures approximately twenty-five square metres. Its walls are made of piled-up sandbags and support the tree trunks and another layer of sandbags that form the roof. The outside is completely covered with a plastic sheet and strewn with twigs, leaves and sand, and the whole thing blends seamlessly and invisibly into the hillside the living room is built on.

The cable from the satellite dish is buried in the ground, and the power cable runs invisibly to the village, several kilometres up a hill, which supplies our electricity. Power services in the Kurdistan Region being unreliable, the electricity usually only comes on in the evening. We sometimes wait at the entrance of the living room and watch the distant village. The moment we see the lights go on, we go inside – without the energy-saving light bulb, the room is in complete darkness.

The living room is the only place in the camp where electricity and artificial light aren't strictly forbidden. There are stringent rules to prevent any light from escaping. For instance, anyone passing through the two blankets and the little hall at the entrance must take great care not to open both the blankets at once. You lift one first, then let it close again behind you before lifting up the second.

We take off our shoes, by the way, because that's just what you do when you go indoors anywhere in Kurdistan. Inside, the room is spotless. We regularly shake out the rugs and cushions we sit on, and the walls and ceiling are completely covered with plastic sheeting to keep sand and dirt from seeping in. The plastic is translucent. The size of the occasional spider, creeping down the outside of it, is terrifying.

SterkTV news usually opens with reports on the progress of the war against ISIS in Syria. In the summer of 2016, the battle for the city of Manbij is still raging, and the advance of the Syrian Democratic Forces (SDF) is given ample airtime every day. The SDF is a collaboration of the YPG (the People's Protection Units, a mainly Kurdish militia in Syria), Arabic militias and a number of smaller groups of Assyrians, Armenians and Turkmens among others. This is usually followed by an update on Kurdish demonstrations in European cities such as Stockholm, Strasbourg, Frankfurt, Vienna, Arnhem and The Hague, demanding that Öcalan be released from prison as soon as possible. There is also Turkish news, mostly about the Kurdish movement and the HDP, and finally some short foreign news items. These give me occasional glimpses of events that are probably causing turmoil in Europe; an attack with a truck in the French town of Nice, the British voting for Brexit.

The news forms a natural part of my language training, as all broadcasts are in Kurdish. I understand the broad outlines, but the details escape me. It's not really a problem – until the coup.

On the day after the army's failed attempt to seize power, the developments in Turkey are still the main topic on SterkTV. Then the battle for Manbij starts dominating the news again, and the coup and its aftermath is only covered in a short item, if at all. It is not enough to quench my intense thirst for information. Increasingly, I skip the evening news, to the bafflement of my fellow camp members: a journalist who doesn't watch the news? 'I already know what's on SterkTV tonight,' I say. 'The SDF have almost seized Manbij, the demonstrations for Öcalan's release continue unabated, and in Turkey, Kurds are arrested and murdered.'

ICE AGE

The guerrillas hardly ever talk about the coup. They keep busy doing their homework in their *Superman* and *Ice Age* jotters, reading their exercises out loud or sweeping the floor of the *kamelya*, a clearing in the woods that's the camp's central meeting place. It's constantly becoming dirty: grains of rice and strings of spaghetti, fallen leaves, twigs and other litter which must be carefully swept out and down the slope into the river. A meditative task which I often take upon myself.

Hardly a word is said about the coup. Only the small group of foreigners discusses the situation, but show such ignorance about Turkey in the process that I turn away from such conversations in irritation. The Italian woman gushes that it would be fantastic if the PKK started invading army bases, like the one in Diyarbakır. I tell her this is an unrealistic fantasy. Based for the greatest part in the mountains, the PKK has no easy way of reaching army bases in the heart of the city, and they have no heavy weapons. 'They would, if they seized some from the enemy,' she counters with little concern for logic.

I suddenly can't stand being in the language camp a minute longer. I want to return to civilization. I want to study dozens of sources and analyses, I want photos, videos, reports. I don't even know yet whether the story about the air-raid on the Turkish parliament is true, for goodness' sake. It really gets to me, and I get grumpier every day. But leaving is not an option. I've completed more than half the course, and my Kurdish is improving.

Besides, if I insisted on leaving the language camp now, it would take at least another fortnight before I'd actually be able to get away. Comrade Zagros, who's something like the head of foreign press communication, is not within range of the language camp walkie-talkie. I could of course write him a note in my best Kurdish, entreating him – politely yet urgently – to come and fetch me as soon as possible. I would then fold the note into a tiny square, write his name and department on it (Comrade Zagros, Dept. of press matters), wrap it in Sellotape and take it to the base camp of the 'language department', about a fifteen minute walk downstream from our camp. They would give it to a passing comrade headed in Zagros's direction, who would in turn pass it on, and so forth until it would finally reach Zagros a week or so later. He would then have to find time in between meetings with other foreign journalists and all of his other duties to pick me up. By that time, it would be late July or early August, only about three weeks before the language camp ends. I conclude that staying is the only sensible thing to do. '*Sabir*, Comrade Avaşîn,' my teacher Mizgîn advises. Patience.

Three days after the coup, on 18 July, we are suddenly summoned to the base camp. There's a '*kar*', a task, for us to do. I ask the camp commander if I need to go as well, and am told I do. I suspect we will be asked to carry bags of flour to the oven, weed the vegetable and herb patches or take fresh supplies of oil and tomato paste from the subterranean storage spaces to our camp.

Comrade Hêlîn and I leave for the base camp together. She is walking in front when she suddenly turns round and says, 'I can tell you now. Comrade Cuma is coming to talk to us about the coup.' I'm thrilled – exchanging views with him about the developments in Turkey is exactly what I need to get up to speed.

Comrade Cuma, aka co-leader Cemil Bayık, is already there when we arrive at the base camp. We are given a warm welcome by two of Bayık's personal guards. Bayık has plenty to say, reminiscing about the period he and Öcalan spent in Lebanon together in the 1990s. One by one, the others arrive and shake Bayık's hand, happy and surprised to see him here.

The details of his talk are lost on me as the whole meeting is held in Kurdish. I concentrate on every word. It helps that I've interviewed him several times before and am fairly familiar with the PKK's way of thinking. Bayık condemns the attempted coup in the strongest terms; the PKK advocates a fundamental change of the Turkish system, and coups have been a part of exactly this system for decades. In other words, something as undemocratic as a coup can never lead to more democracy, which is the PKK's goal.

He also places the events in a wider context. According to Bayık, the coup actually began a year earlier, with the elections of 7 June 2015; the first elections since the founding of the AKP in 2001 in which the party did not get a majority in parliament. The HDP was directly responsible for this by winning thirteen per cent of the vote – if it hadn't reached the ten per cent threshold, all HDP votes in the districts with a strong HDP presence would have gone to the second largest party, the AKP.

Ever since that moment, the co-leader argues, there has been a coup in Turkey. Not a traditional one where the army seizes power in one day, but a gradually executed takeover, in which Erdoğan slowly and irrevocably extends his grasp by taking more and more control over all national institutes, and criminalizing, persecuting and imprisoning anyone trying to resist.

Then we're allowed to ask questions. The young Comrade Rojda poses the question that is uppermost in all the guerrillas' minds: 'How is the leadership?' The Kurdish term is '*Serokatî*'; it refers to Öcalan, whose real name the guerrillas hardly ever use. Cemil Bayık explains that he doesn't know what Öcalan's circumstances are exactly but that the organization will do its best to find out. It is true that they are worrying; after all, the Kurdish question, and by extension Öcalan, always form a part of the political dynamics in Turkey. There is no knowing where the loyalties of the prison guards and commanders on Imralı Island lie. Was, or is, Öcalan's life in imminent danger?

I grasp the opportunity to ask a question in my rudimentary Kurdish about the TV footage from Turkey I've been watching in the past few days. SterkTV was broadcasting reports on commanders being arrested in army bases for alleged involvement in the coup. They were forced to kneel on the ground in their underwear. 'Did their humiliation make you chuckle a little too, even if just in private?' I ask. 'The army commanders are your enemies, after all.'

Interviewing Bayık on previous occasions, I never had the impression there were questions that couldn't be asked or weren't appreciated. Whatever I asked, I always got an in-depth reply, and this time is no exception. No, he didn't laugh, he says without missing a beat, and adds, 'Did you see how they were treated? That many of the prisoners are being abused and tortured, and that there were many casualties? How could we ever find that amusing? We are opposed to coups, and to the cruel and inhuman treatment of anyone.'

Chatting after the session with Comrade Hêlîn, who has been working as a journalist for the PKK-affiliated press agency Firat, I tell her I felt my job as a journalist compelled me to ask the question. She looks at me, eyes wide with incredulity. 'But how could you? People are being tortured, how could a guerrilla ever laugh about that?' The other comrades in our circle agree unanimously with Hêlîn. 'Comrade Cuma's response was interesting enough,' I explain, 'but your reaction has taught me just as much. That's what makes it such a good question. Thank you all.'

They shake their heads at me, bewildered at my lack of understanding of what the PKK stands for.

UPSTREAM

Life in the language camp follows a stringent routine. At 6 AM we are woken up by the comrade on the last watch of the night. The watch duties start at 10 PM, and each watch lasts an hour. The comrade on the last shift makes the rounds of all the single-person tents, shouting a cheerful '*Rojbaş!*' – Good morning! Breakfast is at six thirty, prepared by the same comrade. He or she begins at 5 AM, at the start of their shift, with the top priority task: cranking up the enormous, petrol-fired tea brewing contraption to make sure the tea is ready on time.

At seven thirty sharp, the lessons begin. We are divided into two classes of six students each. On some days, the comrades go out before the lesson to gather firewood for the kitchen and shower fires, and though I am regularly and emphatically told I needn't join them – because of my age, I suspect, being in my forties while my fellow camp members are in their early twenties or thirties at the most, though no one ever confirms this – I quite enjoy the physical exercise some mornings.

We follow the track up from the kamelya and walk upstream along the river. Sometimes we encounter civilians on their way to tending their fields and orchards. At 7 AM the temperature is already rising, but fortunately, the many enormous walnut trees turn the area into an oasis of shade. As it turns out, balancing bundles of twigs under your arm or on your shoulder without them poking out on every side like a bunch of Mikado sticks is quite a feat, let alone making the descent back to the camp with them. At every step, you risk slipping on a twig, a mouldering walnut husk or a stone. I'm impressed by the incredible ease with which some guerrillas complete this task, sometimes even carrying unwieldy tree trunks on their shoulders, sashaying into the camp with their harvest and depositing it on the woodpile in the kitchen with an elegant flourish.

The camp has two outdoor classrooms. In mine, a whiteboard is suspended between a young fruit tree and a pole securely driven into the soil. During the lessons, the camp's only walkie-talkie is hanging from a nail. My teacher Mizgîn has sole responsibility for the camp's safety. The hum of the device and the conversations between other camps in the area are constantly audible in the background, and Mizgîn is always on the alert to pick up any of the various codes used in emergency situations. Among other things, the two- or three-digit codes warn of drones in the area (if there are, the walkie-talkie needs to be switched off because the device can be detected by the drones and give away a camp's location), or of F-16s taking off from the army air base in Diyarbakır. The fighter jets can reach our area in under twenty minutes and wipe the camp from the face of the earth with a well-aimed shell.

At 9 AM there's a twenty-minute tea break, and immediately after the lesson ends at eleven, we have lunch. The comrade on cooking duty leaves the lesson between sixty and ninety minutes early to cook lentil soup, bake potatoes or prepare spaghetti with a generous dollop of lightly baked tomato paste. The large, charred pots and pans balance on iron bars that are supported by piles of bricks and cemented into place. Building a fire is an art. The trick is to pile up the sticks and twigs in such a way that they touch as little as possible to let in a lot of air while not making any smoke. Smoke can betray us. Some comrades are very good at it. I love watching the flames of the large fires lick the pots without the faintest wisp of smoke curling up through the air.

After lunch, we have some free time until supper at 6 PM. Some comrades go to their tents to do their homework. My tent, exposed to full sunlight from early afternoon, is too hot to spend even five minutes in, so I often join others to do my homework elsewhere in the camp, on a large plastic mat underneath the trees. The mat is kept in place with tree trunks on all sides. Shoes being prohibited on the mat, we leave them in an orderly row along the edge.

One unchanging feature of the camp is the sound of the river rushing past us down below. One morning during lunch, we hear children's voices coming from a distance upstream. From the edge of the camp, we can see them: boys from the nearby village, who have come down here for a refreshing plunge. They have built a dam with tree trunks and rocks – doubtless with the help of grown-ups – which blocks the flow and allows them to play safely in the water.

Two of us go up to them and ask if they would mind coming later in the day from now on, to give us an hour or two after lunch to use their pool to cool down. Sharing the pool with the lads would be a violation of the moral code – just like the male guerrillas in our camp won't bathe with the women. In this way, we respect the conservative values of the society to which the mountain-dwelling PKK belong; and not just because the guerrillas, coming as they do from Kurdish communities, share these values, but also because it is a way of guaranteeing our own safety. Trampling the norms of Kurdish society underfoot would make its members more inclined to accept bribes from the Turkish army to pass on the exact location of our camp. For the same reason, we women don't wear tops with bare shoulders and aren't allowed in the places where the men sleep and shower, nor are the men allowed in the women's part of the camp.

As our swimming pool is visible from a track further up, one of us always takes up position on a hillock that looks out on the track. The moment she spots any men approaching, she calls out,

'Men!', and as instructed, we let our bodies, dressed only in our underwear, sink into the water to hide our nudity. I'm in fits of laughter every time this happens, but the others are genuinely alarmed: a man, a man!

Most of the women can't swim, so the German Comrade Ronahî and I teach them whenever we have the pool to ourselves. We use swimming aids made of empty Coke bottles tied together with string. Now, comrades, swimming is done horizontally, not vertically. Don't spread your fingers or they won't push against the water, keep them together. And move your legs like this – no, watch me, like this! I enjoy doing a couple of strokes of front crawl against the current before letting myself float downstream again on my back, my arms crossed behind my head and my eyes shut. The roaring water is icy cold. So cold that I can never suppress a scream of shock when I jump in. So cold, I am frozen stiff for a full hour afterwards and covered in goosebumps for the rest of the afternoon; even my bones seem to be shaking. Lovely.

On some afternoons, there is another 'task' you can volunteer for. We set off to gather leaves, and later, back in camp, bundle them into piles and put them in large white tins. The guerrillas can use them to cook *dolma* (stuffed vine leaves) next winter. Other times we find brambles or a solitary peach tree and return to the camp with enough fruit to last a couple of days.

Once every two or three weeks, we bake bread. There are three baking teams: each language class of six people make up one of them, the members of the base camp the third. To get to the oven, we walk along the river for a bit, over a bridge, past some fields and across a few orchards. The walls of the baking hut are built with sandbags, just like the living room, and its roof is made of beams, sheet plastic and more bags. Inside is a wooden workbench and a domed oven made of cement with a metal flue pipe that sticks out through the roof. We mix the dough in huge metal bowls, using water we have fetched from the river and heated in a large black pot on a smokeless fire. First we roll the dough into balls, which we smack into flat loaves between our hands – I get better at it every time – and sprinkle with water. Our team's baker-in-chief, the petite but incredibly strong Mizgîn, slides them into the oven and keeps the flames blazing.

Meanwhile, the comrades who have stayed behind in the camp make sure the shower water is hot when the baking team returns, sweaty, white and covered in bits of dough. We wash our clothes, take a shower and arrive fresh to our supper with oven-warm bread. The rest, dozens of loaves that will last us two or three weeks, is packed into a freezer that is hidden away somewhere in a subterranean bunker.

LAST GLASS

After eating supper and doing the dishes, we clamber into the living room for the seven o'clock news. We often stay on for a bit afterwards, chatting and doing our homework, though I make sure I'm in my tent at 8 PM. Round about that time, the sun goes down, and on moonless nights the darkness is so complete I can't even find my way from the living room to my tent without falling flat on my face at least once – not even if a female fighter walks with me, holding my hand. I also visit the toilet before eight; the path leading to it has a deceptive turn where you can bump into a tree, and two steep slopes I find tricky enough to negotiate in broad daylight. I drink my last glass of water of the day during supper so I won't have to find my way to the toilet again before the morning light.

We live in a parallel world. A couple of dozen kilometres to the north, in the south-east of Turkey, a war is raging against the Turkish state. A couple of hundred kilometres to the west, the SDF is making mincemeat of ISIS, metaphorically speaking. And what are we doing? We write grammar exercises on a whiteboard under the trees (I am a guerrilla, you are a guerrilla, he/she is a guerrilla, we are guerrillas, you are guerrillas, they are guerrillas), pick blackberries and roar with laughter in the river.

But this parallel world, I'm slowly beginning to realize, is just as much part of the PKK as the other. I can get worked up all I want about being cut off from the outside world, but often enough, that is simply part and parcel of being a guerrilla. If I want to get to know their world, I will have to let go of mine, the fast world of journalism, and immerse myself in theirs: a world of slow revolution.

The slow revolutionary world of the PKK. If there's one thing I hadn't expected, it is this. I'm even starting to find the way that I and all those other journalists and news analysts with me have closely followed the PKK for years a bit ridiculous. Take the time that, during the so-called peace process – the lengthy ceasefire between the PKK and the Turkish state that started in 2013 and lasted until the summer of 2015 – HDP co-leader Selahattin Demirtaş made an impassioned speech in parliament, and all of us immediately started producing comments and columns interpreting his words and comparing them to Cemil Bayık's last statement. How much mutual irritation is there between the HDP and the PKK? we wonder. Erdoğan shoves a law through parliament, or the army kills a young Kurdish activist demonstrating against the expansion of army infrastructure in the south-east of Turkey, and we all fall over each other asking ourselves how this will impact the peace process.

The fighters meanwhile, or at any rate those who are not on the front line of the war, are busy doing their homework, picking berries and baking bread. And even those who are directly on the front line don't let everyday political and social dynamics get to them too much. A guerrilla fighter has one job, and that is what he or she focuses on. Whether it be planting a roadside bomb, freeing a town or village from ISIS or conjugating verbs in Kurmancî.

Not just that task is sacred, but so is life in the mountains. Whatever happens, the fighters are unperturbed. Even when there is a security threat, everyday life goes on as much as possible. This is brought home to me one afternoon when, after our lessons and swim, we notice drones in the air. Drones are the greatest threat of all because there's simply no telling whether or not they've detected the camp. We take all possible precautions – make smokeless fires, avoid clearings in the woods, walk underneath the trees whenever possible, never hang brightly coloured towels or clothing out to dry, don't use any artificial light, the Internet, or telephones. Comrade Mizgîn has even forbidden putting up two flags with the image of the Serokatî in the classroom – the flags were bright yellow and would have been too great a risk. Even so, we can't control everything. All it takes is one villager who gives us away to the Turkish army. The drone will then only have to record our coordinates, and once those have been passed on to the army base in Diyarbakır, a shower of bombs will inevitably follow.

When there are drones, we have to disperse. You have a choice of staying where you are or going to your tent. I stay in the kamelya to read. A short while later, Comrade Newroz passes me on her way to fetch water and Comrade Hêlîn appears shortly after. I don't understand. Have the drones gone already? I ask Hêlîn. 'Ages ago!' she laughs. I did hear them earlier though, or didn't I? I heard the buzzing of those overgrown bees often enough on my travels in Bakur to know what a drone sounds like. But here, I often find it hard to tell. Just now I spent at least half an hour listening intently, but the river makes too much noise, and the echoes coming from the mountains and even small hills are deceptive. If I turn my head to the right, I think I can hear it. If I turn it to the left, the sound changes completely and I'm suddenly unsure.

'Sit down, Comrade Avaşîn,' Hêlîn says, 'and listen.' We sit down on the long tree trunk bench and drink ice-cold water. 'Those drones,' Hêlîn explains, 'may well be a military threat, but above all they're a psychological weapon. The Turkish army uses them to intimidate us and disrupt our normal life in the mountains. We won't allow it. Safety is our first priority, but this is our life and we want to be in control of it.'

Her speech makes me feel safe – the guerrillas won't let some drones and F-16s send them into a panic. They know what to do in a real emergency, and the rest of the time, they try not to let Turkish warfare tactics get to them. The trees are a perfectly good protection against drones. The language camp was built in this remote part of the mountains exactly because it gets bombed relatively little – a great advantage for the language lessons, which benefit from peace and quiet and would suffer from having to move at a moment's notice all the time.

All through the summer, we only saw Turkish bombers pass overhead four or five times; once during the day, the others times at night. The emergency instructions are quite straightforward: planes flying over very close by and low to the ground mean red alert, in which case you leave your tent and quickly climb as far up the mountain as you can. If bombs start falling, you immediately lie down flat on your stomach. It is crucial never to put your fingers in your ears to block out the noise, or clench your jaws; the shock wave caused by an exploding bomb is so strong that the air pressure tearing through your body can cause internal bleeding. You can avoid this by keeping your ears and mouth open so the air pressure can escape from your body. To make sure you don't shut your lips reflexively during a bombing, you place a stick between your teeth and bite down on it.

Of course, none of this is any help if the bomb falls on top of you or very close by. Then you die. But I feel safe in my tent. If planes wake me up, all I do is reach out for the biting stick next to my bed and doze on. See if I care! One morning, at the call of 'Rojbaş', I'm not even sure whether there had really been any F-16s the night before or if I'd imagined them. I haven't imagined them, I learn from the conversations I hear as I join the others for breakfast.

WATERFALL

One afternoon, I have a long conversation with Comrade Nûman. In his late thirties with twinkling eyes and a slightly balding head, he's been a member of the PKK for more than half his life. The past few years, he's dedicated himself to writing a history of Kurdish art and literature, and while he's working on the last book of his trilogy at the language base camp, he sometimes drops by the teaching camp for a chat. Nûman is ever so slightly notorious: once he starts talking, the words keep cascading from him like a waterfall and you can hardly get a word in edgeways. If he starts his monologue in Kurdish, I usually withdraw from the conversation after a short while because I can't keep up. But when we're alone, we blithely ignore the golden camp rule – 'No Turkish in the language camp!' – and chatter away for hours.

In the Neolithic Age, that's when it all began. The history of modern man, which of course is also the history of the Kurds. That is when the seeds were sown of what has become Kurdish culture. On the one hand, I find his habit of leaping thousands of years back in time to make a point about, say, the famous Kurdish epic *Mem û Zin* a bit tiresome. On the other, however, the broad perspective Comrade Nûman offers me forces me to reflect on my own limited view.

I confide in Nûman that when I moved to Diyarbakır in the summer of 2012 and the rumours of an imminent peace process kept getting louder, I already envisaged a private dream of mine coming true: becoming a peace journalist. Once the Kurds no longer had to fight for justice, how would the activist identity they had been forced into change? Once the Kurds were in control of their own land, how would they treat religious and ethnic minorities? I finish by saying how deceived I felt when, after the euphoric elections of June 2015, the peace process quickly fell prey to Erdoğan's craving for absolute power.

While I'm sharing my thoughts, the new perspective is already dawning in a corner of my consciousness, and with it, a realization: peace in Kurdistan won't come in my lifetime. For peace to come to Kurdistan within the thirty-five years or so I am statistically likely to have left would be too much of a coincidence. Besides, the PKK aims for a higher goal than simply striking a deal with the Turkish state: overthrowing capitalism and eliminating the concept of a nation-state, beginning in the Middle East. A tall order, if ever there was one.

But far from disheartening me, Comrade Nûman's history lessons actually kindle my enthusiasm about the time I'm living in. Just imagine for a moment that the PKK does manage to realize its ambitions, many generations after ours when the movement might not even exist anymore and other organizations will have taken over the baton, and people will point to the period we live in as the years when it all began. And I, a freelance journalist from the Netherlands, am part of it! Some of the men and women who founded the PKK in the 1970s are still alive today. I talk, I live with the fighters who were involved from the very beginning. The man who has committed the entire ideology to paper is still alive, albeit in prison. Who knows, I might still get the chance to interview him. How's that for coincidence!

I do realize that expecting the PKK to turn around the history of mankind is something of a megalomaniac thought. But Comrade Nûman is not alone in his firm belief that this will happen – it is the general conviction of all guerrillas. So if I want to understand the fighters living here, really understand them, I could do worse than to subscribe to their ideals. This perspective suddenly gives me a different view of the coup, too. The breaking news stories, the reports, the footage and analyses I miss so much, what do they actually matter? In fact, the coup is nothing more than a ripple in the bloody and still relatively short history of the Turkish Republic, which will only celebrate its first centenary in 2023. I struggle to accept this perspective – Journalist Fréderike is not that easily silenced. But Comrade Avaşîn Amed can learn to live with the isolation.

Portrait

Comrade Hesen Teeters but Never Falls

Comrade Hesen rolls up his right trouser leg. 'Look,' he says. 'Artificial.' I had already heard that he had been injured in battle years ago, but hadn't expected him to have a prosthesis. Nor would I have noticed it from the way he walked, though it has become more obvious after this revelation. He almost loses his balance sometimes, especially on an uphill path, and there's a stiffness to his gait. Sometimes, he uses a walking stick.

Hesen is one of the teachers at the PKK language camp where, in the summer of 2016, about a dozen fighters and five foreigners are taking Kurdish lessons. He doesn't teach a class of his own, but in the afternoons, he gives three of the five foreigners extra lessons. As he finds it difficult to stand at the whiteboard for a whole hour, he sits down for a break halfway through.

After one such extra lesson, I ask him for an interview for my book. He was injured at just seventeen, a year after he'd joined the PKK. I want to know what it was like for a young fighter like that to be shot out of action so early on, and how he has managed to reshape his life in the PKK, physically and mentally. 'I've never talked about it with an outsider before,' Hesen says. 'Let me think about it.'

A couple of days later he tells me he agrees to the interview, but only if Comrade Hacer, the language camp commander, allows it. Hacer gives her permission. I ask Hesen when would be a good time for him. He answers, 'There's no hurry, is there, Comrade Avaşîn? We'll be here for weeks. Let's leave it for a little while.'

In the middle of the kamelya, the central part of the camp, there's a long table made of twelve vegetable crates tied together, topped by pieces of cardboard and covered with a sheet of plastic. It is flanked by the two halves of a long, split tree trunk resting on sandbags at either end, which seat at least eighteen people. The tree trunk's too low for me to sit on comfortably, except for one slightly higher spot above the largest bag. But Comrade Hesen can't sit down on the tree trunk at all, as his knee won't bend far enough. One morning, a new chair has suddenly appeared at the head of the table. Sawn out of a tree trunk, it is perfectly smooth and stable. Made by Hesen, who pitches in with his carpentry skills whenever needed. I'm usually at the breakfast table before him in the mornings, and pinch his chair for a bit. When I spot him making his way unhurriedly from the men's camp, I switch to my own spot above the sand bag. True to camp etiquette, Hesen tells me every time to stay seated, as the tree trunk chair isn't his property. I won't hear of it.

One afternoon after lunch, I decide not to push him for the interview again. Instead, I just ask him how he lost his leg. It happened in 1997, he says. Two comrades and he wanted to attack an army post in Uludere district, in south-east Turkey close to the Iraq border. 'I stood on a landmine and BOOM!' he says, miming the explosion with his hands. The army sometimes places mines around their territory in the evening as a line of defence, he explains, removing them again in the morning. Luckily for the army – and unfortunately for Hesen – it worked.

Hesen cuts across his right shoe with his hand to show how much of the foot had been blown off. The flesh went black. 'They had to take off my foot,' he says, 'or I might very well have lost the whole leg.' Two fellow fighters held him down, a third one did the sawing. Fast, to limit the time he'd be in pain. 'Aah, aah,' Comrade Hesen says, without raising his voice too much but half laughing and half grimacing at the memory, in answer to my question whether he screamed.

After the explosion, they should have gone south, to the Iraqi part of Kurdistan. Iraqi Kurdistan was already virtually autonomous at the time – its autonomy was later established in the constitution of Iraq in 2005 – and Hesen would have received treatment within a couple of hours there. But the battle between the PKK and the Turkish army having reached one of its many climaxes, the Turkish army kept the border hermetically sealed. So they had to go north – staying in one place is never an option for a guerrilla army unit. Taking cover during daytime, they walked to Siirt Province, dozens of kilometres away, at night. Hesen: 'Sometimes, there was a mule we could use. Then my friends would tie me to a stretcher made of tree trunks and fasten it onto the mule. Other parts of the journey, one of my comrades carried me on their back.'

Somewhere on the way, they severed his foot at the ankle. The wound was cleaned with river water, salt and eau de cologne ('Aah, aah'), and bandaged with rags. By the time he arrived at the hospital in Mosul, Iraq, eight months later in the spring – once the snow had melted and long journeys on foot were possible again – the stump was clean. 'But cutting the bone had damaged it so much that my lower leg had to be amputated,' Hesen says. Did the doctor know who he was? 'No. I had a forged identity card. I said I was a shepherd who'd trodden on a mine during work.'

A few days later, I ask Hesen if he has time to carry on our conversation later that day. 'Not today, Comrade Avaşîn, I'm too busy. But then there's no hurry, eh?' 'There's no hurry,' I confirm, 'not to worry. I'll just ask again later.'

Comrade Hesen is reading a book in Kurdish, titled *A Graveyard in Diyarbakır*. I ask if I can borrow it when he's finished, to practise my Kurdish. He hands it to me a few days later. I do my best to read it, but soon give up – practically every word is new to me, and most of them aren't even in the dictionary. When I return it, Hesen explains the book is not exactly light reading, as it was written almost a century ago. The Kurdish that the writer used is pretty archaic. 'So how come you can read it?' I ask. I knew he'd grown up in Turkey, where Kurdish isn't taught at school. Did he take the PKK Kurdish language course in the past? 'I taught myself Kurdish,' he answers. 'Simply by reading, reading, reading – old Kurdish literature among other things.' Of all of the ten or so language camp staff, Hesen speaks Kurdish the best. The teachers and students can ask him anything, he always knows the answer.

The rest of the time, Hesen does his own thing. He's the camp's builder as well as the language expert. I'm told he has built pretty much everything here. Having arrived a week into the course, I unfortunately didn't get to see the camp's construction, but one of my fellow foreign students tells me, 'When we arrived here, Hesen said this would be a good spot for the camp. I didn't get it – all I saw was a wood on a pretty steep slope. A camp, here? But a week later, there it was.'

I get an impression of how that must have gone when an area of forest near the men's camp needs to be cleared to make space for a large tent. It's also on a steep slope. Comrade Hesen is hard at work with a circular saw and a pickaxe, chopping tree trunks to pieces, breaking away rocks and calmly issuing instructions to others. Nothing about him suggests that he's half a leg short. He teeters slightly sometimes, but he never falls over.

In the camp kitchen, I watch him take the circular saw to huge tree trunks dragged there by others, sawing them into logs for the kitchen fire. He climbs up the pile of timber, selects the best angle for the saw to bite into the wood and pushes down the blade. His work is calm and accurate.

A week later, I ask again, 'When will we have our talk, Comrade Hesen?' 'Not yet, Comrade Avaşîn.' 'So when?' 'I don't know, but not just yet. But I promise you, we'll have done the interview before we leave here. You can sit me down on a chair on the last day if necessary, and we'll talk. Honest, I promise.'

A couple of days later, a group of us are chatting after lunch. I ask Hesen, 'What was it like for you to join the PKK? Were you sent into combat straight away, even though you were just sixteen years old? They've stopped doing that, after all.' He answers, 'There was no other option. They couldn't send everyone to the training camps in Lebanon, and there weren't as many of us in Qandil as there are today. The headquarters was located in Damascus, where Öcalan was, but for many fighters signing up, there just wasn't room except in battle. I was assigned to a unit, and an attacking army isn't going to spare you just because you're underage.' Heval Hesen bellows with laughter, mimes exploding bombs with his hands, 'Boom, boom, boom, oh, not you, you're sixteen.'

He grabs his tablet to show me some photographs of the time. On one underexposed image, he points to the youngest member of the group. Taken in the couple of months that he was still an intact PKK fighter.

I want to know what made him join up, and how a young fighter reconciles himself to the fact that he will never see combat again. During breakfast, about a week before the end of the language lessons and my departure, I ask again, 'Today, Comrade Hesen?' 'I'm about to leave, Heval Avaşîn. But don't worry, it's just for three or four days, then I'll be back.'

I ask where he's going. 'To the camp for new fighters, to teach. I always give them a few lessons on life in the PKK. About how hard it often is, and that there's absolutely nothing romantic about it. That it's a dirty war, despite our freedom in the mountains.' A little later, he leaves, on foot. He's carrying his walking stick and wearing a black scarf with red and pink flowers around his head to shield it from the blazing sun. An hour's hike away, there's a car waiting to take him to his destination.

It's the last day of language camp. Comrade Hesen returned two days ago, at nightfall. I saw him walk down the path past our field from my tent. He looked exhausted. The next day, I didn't ask him for the interview, thinking I'd sit him down on a chair on the last day, as he himself had suggested.

But on the last day, he's not here. There's a graduation ceremony, there are speeches, guests, singing, dancing and theatre, chicken, rice, salad and Coke, but no Hesen.

After the party, I'm picked up by Comrade Dalyan, who is to take me to my next destination. We're going via the language base camp, a fifteen-minute walk through the woods. 'I was to do an interview with Comrade Hesen,' I tell Dalyan. 'Do you know him?' 'Yes, I know him,' Dalyan says. 'He wanted to be interviewed? How extraordinary. He doesn't like talking about the past.' 'He agreed to do it,' I say, 'but each time I reminded him, something or other prevented it.' We cross a suspension bridge over a river. Dalyan says, 'Good bridge, isn't it? Hesen made it, did you know?'

At the base camp, I find Hesen sitting on a plastic chair at the long wooden table. He pours tea for us. I say, with a laugh, 'We were going to talk, Comrade Hesen! Why are you here, why didn't you come to the graduation ceremony? You've missed the party.' He says, 'I was on watch duty today. We could have talked here, Comrade Avaşîn. But you weren't around.'

CHAPTER 2

No Life Without the Leader

'I lose myself. I fall in love with my leader. When I listen to the leader, I fall in love with him; when I read the leader, I fall in love with him. This is love. The leader is, of course, a man. Physically speaking, he's a man. But his spirit is representative of all things living in nature. His spirit, thoughts and feelings represent women, men, the old and the young; they represent a pigeon, a bird, a tree, water. He is more than just a human being or a man. He manifests himself as a man, but his spirit, his soul, are so rich, his thoughts are so rich, and this reality . . . that is our love. The love we strive for.

'The men at home, our fathers and brothers, have given us nothing. They haven't fulfilled us, haven't given us satisfaction. The leader does fulfil us. Through the leader, we are born. When you have eaten, you are full, and in exactly the same way, the leader satisfies us when we listen to him. This is love.

'A man, a woman who love each other and come together only to separate again commit the greatest violation of what love is. To do this is to curse love. Love is life for as long as you feel it and educate, develop and nurture yourself according to its ideology.

'We can't be with the leader, he is not among us. Many days, hours and roads separate us from him. Perhaps we will never be able to see him, to meet him, but we live with him nevertheless. We follow his path. That is our love. That is the love of a Kurdish woman, Comrade Avaşîn. As members of the PKK, we live under trying circumstances – the fighter jets of the enemy, the mortar bombs, the spies – but we can endure them all because the leader is love. A love that keeps you going is true love. But a love that takes away your life, wears you down, is not true love; then, even using the word "love" is a disgrace. A disgrace.

'I become enchanted. When I listen to the leader, I am flying, I no longer feel the ground underneath my feet, Comrade Avaşîn. That is the feeling the leader inspires in us. I am flying. We are flying.'

I listen with bated breath as Comrade Nuhayla sings the praises of Abdullah Öcalan. She is a short, experienced and confident guerrilla whose long, straight red hair is loosely gathered in a strip of fabric that keeps coming undone, and which she patiently keeps tying again. She launched into her ode spontaneously at the end of the morning, after reading a text by Öcalan to a group of female fighters for at least an hour and a half. She wanted to explain the text to me, but was so full of what she had just read that she interrupted herself mid-sentence, no longer able to suppress the urge to declare her love.

'Through the leader, we are born' – a short sentence which could hardly say more. It is a summary of everything Öcalan means to PKK fighters, and in part to the whole Kurdish community. It sheds a new light on conversations I have had with older fighters in particular. Take Comrade Serhat from Van Province: when a fellow student at Istanbul University whispered into his ear twenty-five years ago that he was a Kurd, not a Turk, he couldn't believe it at first – nor did he want to believe it. Or Comrade Cuma, aka Cemil Bayık, the second-in-command of the PKK after Öcalan, who wasn't aware of his Kurdish identity when he was young either, and didn't speak a word of Kurdish.

A man pushing eighty I met in Maxmur in Iraq confided in me with some bitterness, 'I was a Turk until I was fifty, a nationalist Turk even, a supporter of Atatürk.' How he found out he was Kurdish was not something he wanted to tell me. Just hearing the question moved him visibly. He did say, 'One year after finding out I'm a Kurd, I left Turkey. I can't tell you exactly why, but I was in danger. And I still can't go back, even though my children and grandchildren live there. Two of my daughters have become PKK fighters. They are doing what my generation failed to do. They are fighting for our people.'

Before the PKK was founded, Kurds didn't exist in Turkey. The word Kurd was banned, and so was Kurdish music. The Kurdish language, considered a Turkish dialect at best, was forbidden; there was no such place as Kurdistan, and the Kurds were called 'Mountain Turks'. The denial of a Kurdish identity in Turkey was, and still is, taken to such lengths that the above bans have never explicitly been written into the law, since something that doesn't exist can't be prohibited. Instead, everything in Turkey is simply Turkish, from its language, art and culture to its history and people. Anyone who dares to behave in a non-Turkish way can be silenced by separatism and terrorism laws, or by laws that prohibit insulting Turkey, the Turkish army, the father of the nation Kemal Atatürk, or 'Turkishness'.

Turkey has a watertight system for keeping all things Turkish – or supposedly Turkish – in line, which is inextricably linked to the time in which this system came into being, a century ago in the year 1923. When the First World War was over, the Ottoman Empire was among its losers, and the region we know as Turkey today was plunged into chaos. To the Ottomans, the Treaty of Sèvres, the 1920 peace agreement between the remnants of the Ottoman Empire and the allied winners, was deeply humiliating: Anatolia was divided into zones controlled by the British, the Italians and the French, and the Greeks, Armenians and Kurds were allotted large swathes of land. The Turks were left with a relatively small piece of land surrounding Ankara. It was Mustafa Kemal (only later named Atatürk, Father of the Turks, by the Turkish parliament), a successful general in the Ottoman army, who refused to accept the treaty. He assembled objectors and troops in a bid to turn the tide of history.

Kemal's plan was ambitious: he would drive the allied troops out of Anatolia in order to force them to rip up the Sèvres Treaty and return to the negotiating table. Then he would create a country for the Turks, based on a model that had become increasingly widespread across the West in previous decades: a modern, secular nation-state.

The Kurds, whose land had been part of the Ottoman Empire since the early sixteenth century, joined Atatürk's struggle. It should be noted that this wasn't the choice of the Kurdish people as such, but of powerful Kurdish sheiks, clan leaders and landowners. It may seem confusing that they went to battle against the Sèvres Treaty, which after all promised them a country of their own, but under the circumstances it was understandable. The Sèvres Treaty determined that part of what is now considered Kurdish territory in south-east Turkey, i.e. the Bitlis, Muş, Ağrı and Van Provinces, be allotted to Armenia. On top of that, the Armenians were supported by Russia, a strong military power that the Kurds were no match for, not having an army of their own. Fighting for the promised Kurdistan was therefore not an option – nor did they even aspire to a country of their own. They didn't consider themselves Kurds, but Ottomans; for though nationalism was on the rise, it hadn't yet led to a strong sense of Kurdish identity, just like there was no coherent Turkish identity in those days.

The Kurdish support of Atatürk's war was simply a continuation of their relationship with Ottoman rulers in the past centuries, in which, far from being subordinate to the sultan, they governed their own territories autonomously – to the extent that they didn't pay taxes and their young men didn't serve in the Ottoman army. The sultan benefited from this situation too, as it meant he didn't have to keep a whole contingent of Kurdish clan leaders under control and that he could rely on the Kurds to protect the remote mountainous corners of the Empire against invasion.

In the middle of the nineteenth century, Istanbul started to undermine the Ottoman alliance with the Kurds. The empire rapidly lost ground. Sultan Abdülmecid I tried to halt this process by centralizing power, and one by one, the Kurdish territories were taken over by the Ottoman army – often with a great deal of violence. By fighting with Atatürk against the Sèvres Treaty which the Ottoman rulers had signed, the Kurds were hoping to regain their former equality. The Turkish 'war of independence' against external occupiers, which began in 1919, worked out successfully for Atatürk's army and in 1923 the Sèvres Treaty was replaced by the Treaty of Lausanne. It is unclear what plans Atatürk had for the Kurds. He didn't deny their existence and had no problem using the word Kurdistan. But once the Allies had been defeated and the Sèvres Treaty replaced by the Treaty of Lausanne, he needed a single people to populate the Republic of Turkey. He started forging the population, a hotchpotch of ethnicities and cultures, into a unified whole with a strong identity, and a history, mythology, language and culture of its own.

The Treaty of Lausanne indirectly provided a blueprint for who should and should not belong to this, the Turkish, people, by stating that minorities in Turkey would get the right to organize their own education and use their own language – but only if they were non-Islamic minorities. The Greeks, Armenians and Jews therefore enjoyed these minority rights, while all others were considered Turkish from that moment on. In one fell swoop, this robbed the Kurds as well as other, smaller ethnic groups like the Laz, the Circassians and Arabs, of their right to exist.

The Alevi also got the worst of it. Alevism is an Islamic denomination based on a liberal and humanist reading of Islam. They were expected to fit in with the one religious denomination the state made available to them: Sunni Islam.

Naturally, many refused. From the founding of the republic until the thirties, one rebellion after another broke out in Kurdish territories, and there was opposition against the Turkish army's violent crackdown on any expression of Kurdish identity or autonomy. A little research reveals the names of these bloody incidents – Koçgiri in 1921, Sheikh Said in 1925, Ağrı in 1930, Dersim in 1937–38 – but the Turkish state has done everything in its power to cover them up. Until the 1960s, the east and south-east of the country were inaccessible to foreigners. Even today, important archives including those on the mass murders in Dersim are still kept under lock and key, and the atmosphere in universities and in the media does not exactly encourage research and publications on Kurdish opposition in the early years of the republic.

A FAMILY WITHOUT IDENTITY

But no one can ignore the PKK. Its founding has put the Kurds back on the map. Take that last 'K' in their name itself, the Kurdistan

Workers' Party, 'there where the Kurds live'; no longer denied or simply called 'the East', but by its real name, after six decades of such severe oppression and assimilation that the Kurds themselves were hardly aware of their own existence anymore – hardly dared to be aware of it, let alone live it.

Many older guerrillas talk about the fear that lay heavily on their childhoods like a stifling blanket. A fear which, as the fifty-year-old Comrade Elif Ronahî tells me, meant they grew up 'without an identity'. Comrade Elif lets me in on her story in a large women's camp in the Qandil Mountains. We're in a wooden cabin in the forest, seated on long flat cushions and leaning against soft pillows. We left our shoes on the threshold so as not to stain the spotless, colourful rugs.

Elif grew up an Alevi in Kahramanmaraş, a province inhabited by Turks and Kurds whose Kurdish population consisted to a large part of Alevi. She was in her early teens in December 1978 – a month after the PKK had secretly been founded in the village of Fiş in Diyarbakır Province – when between 110 and 150 Alevi were murdered in the Maraş Massacre, a week-long pogrom carried out by nationalists and religious conservatives. Elif did not even realize she was a Kurd as well as an Alevi until her older sister took her to a meeting somewhere in the nearby Gaziantep Province. All kinds of social topics were discussed, often in the presence of the now legendary co-founder of the PKK, Kemal Pir, among others. It was in 1979 and 1980, a couple of years before the PKK carried out its first attack against the state. Elif: 'Inspired by the meetings, I started asking my parents questions. Why had they never told us we were Kurds? My father said, "Because that could mean your death." In the meetings, we had also talked about Allah. I told my father that I did not believe in Allah. He locked me up in the toilet and wouldn't let me out until I'd say I believed that Allah existed and promised to stop talking about Kurdistan. I stayed in there for three hours. Then my mother whispered to me, "It's alright if you don't believe in Allah, just don't say so out loud. And only talk about Kurdistan with people you trust." After that, I was able to tell my father what he wanted to hear. He was terribly afraid. Living without an identity was safer.'

The PKK members soon felt like family to Elif. She was impressed, not just by the discussions, but also because she saw people from the meetings accompany Alevi children on their way home from school to make sure they wouldn't be beaten up by other children. 'I wanted to be one of them,' she says, 'but they thought I was too young for most activities. They did let me deliver notes, however, or pretend to be a "daughter" in a house disguised as a family home that was used as accommodation for PKK members.'

Violence was ever-present. In the 1970s, right-wing and left-wing groups fought each other to the death in street battles and endless vendettas. Besides notes, Elif started delivering small weapons such as revolvers between comrades. The military coup of 12 September 1980 ushered in even grimmer times. 'We felt powerful. Did you know we already called ourselves "Apocu" at the time?' she asks, referring to the Turkish term meaning 'follower of Apo', that is to say, 'follower of Abdullah (Apo) Öcalan'.

Elif was born. A girl in a family without identity, she emerged as a young woman fighting for her Kurdish and Alevi identity, fighting for her existence. And even though most Kurds are now aware of their ethnic identity, I've heard similar stories from young guerrillas, too.

TREKKING THROUGH THE MOUNTAINS

At the beginning of my stay in the language camp, I'm having difficulty making contact with young Comrade Arjîn. I know she comes from Bakur, the part of Kurdistan that lies in Turkey, but she doesn't seem to understand my Turkish; when I'm struggling with her Kurdish, she does nothing to help me out in Turkish. Every conversation I try to strike up with her ends in incomprehension, an apologetic gesture, raised eyebrows and a smile.

I try to pry out of her where in Bakur she comes from – it may well be a place I visited during my journeys through the province, and that might help to break the ice.

'Botan,' Comrade Arjîn answers. It's a region, including the Turkish Şırnak Province and part of Hakkâri, Siirt and Van Provinces, which I'm very familiar with. But she won't tell me the exact spot. It takes me a surprisingly long time, but after a couple of weeks, the penny drops: Arjîn understands my Turkish perfectly, but she flatly refuses to show it or act accordingly. The Turkish language belongs to the life she led before joining the PKK. That life is over now, making her exact place of birth irrelevant. She wants to leave behind everything that is Turkish about her.

In this light, she is lucky never to have attended a Turkish school. She hasn't been force-fed Turkish history, unconditional love for Atatürk, Turkish nationalism, the national anthem and undying love for the Turkish flag. Not that there wasn't a school in the village (or town, who knows?) she grew up in, but her father was a herdsman, and from the age of about six, Arjîn accompanied him almost daily on his treks through the mountains and valleys. Perhaps the family couldn't afford to send her to school, perhaps they thought a girl didn't need to go – Arjîn is vague about the reason for her lack of formal education. What matters to her is that she's now getting an education that is more suited to who she really is.

Though Kurdish was the language she spoke at home, Arjîn could neither read nor write it. Her Kurdish is contaminated by Turkish, most of which she picked up from the TV. Many Kurds aren't even aware that the Kurdish their children learn at home and on the street isn't a pure form of Kurdish. The same thing is also happening outside of Turkey – in Syria and Iraq, Arabic is seeping into the language, and the native language that is passed on verbally in Iran is obstructed by Persian.

We have heated arguments about it in class. As one of the purists, I don't think we should use the word '*mutfax*'. Mutfax means kitchen, but it comes from the Turkish word '*mutfak*', Kurdified by exchanging the 'k' for an 'x'. The real Kurdish word for kitchen is '*xwaringeh*'. And so, as we correct each other's homework on the whiteboard, I keep pointing out my classmates' use of the word mutfax to them, reminding them of the oath we took at the beginning of the course. We did, after all, swear to protect the Kurdish language. The Kurds agree with me, if a little sullenly – they are also used to saying mutfax. But the Italian woman in my group shrugs it off. 'If they say mutfax here, I'm saying it too. Surely the point is that we understand each other?' 'But,' I argue, stumbling over my words as I raise my voice, 'aren't we supposed to learn Kurdish here, not mangled Turkish?! Wouldn't that give the Turks exactly what they want, namely the destruction of the Kurdish language?' Mizgîn decides that xwaringeh is Kurdish and mutfax is not. Comrade Cîya offers a critical remark: 'You're right, Comrade Avaşîn. But why are you shouting? There's no need.'

Comrade Arjîn is only too happy to banish all Turkish words from her vocabulary. She does her homework with great care and seriousness, as in fact does everyone. Once a month, all students, teachers and coordinators from the base language camp come together for a big meeting, where everyone can voice criticism, give compliments or share whatever is on their mind. During one of these meetings, held in a beautiful clearing in the woods where we sit on chairs and on rocks, on roots or in the fork of a low branch, leaning against the trunk of a tree, Arjîn stands up to speak. She says, 'I just can't believe I'm holding a pen and writing in my own native language.'

Arjîn is born.

Similarly, you could say that the Kurdish people have been brought back to life by the PKK, by Öcalan. A PKK fighter would put it differently. They would say that you can't differentiate between the people and the fighters. The fighters come from the people, they are the people. The PKK was able to grow because its earliest members gave people a wake-up call, making them aware of their identity and of the assimilation and oppression they lived in. It is a continuous cycle of becoming aware, summoning strength, fighting for the rediscovered self and defending the life that has risen again from a state of death-like oblivion.

HEROES AND HEROINES

It follows that the birth of Elif and the birth of Arjîn are an intrinsic part of the birth of a people. But this new beginning is also linked to another concept that is important to the PKK: vengeance. And not just in the violent sense of the word. Of course fighters take revenge the 'traditional' way, by carrying out attacks on military targets. Revenge for the bombing of a camp in which many people are killed. Revenge, also, for the mass murders of civilians by the state, such as the Roboskî bombing that killed thirty-four Kurdish civilians in late 2011, or the attack on a peaceful demonstration in Ankara in October 2015, in which over 100 people were killed and for which the entire Kurdish political movement, including the PKK, holds the state partly responsible.

But above all, revenge means developing yourself in a manner that is radically opposed to everything the system stands for. Reclaiming what the state took away from you. Learning your own language, studying your own history and its Kurdish heroes and heroines, calling your native land by the names that do it justice, not those that the nations of Turkey, Syria, Iraq and Iran gave to your towns, your mountains, your rivers, valleys and plains. That is why Comrade Arjîn comes from the Botan region and not Hakkâri Province. That is why I am called Avaşîn, without knowing – or wanting to know – what name the Turkish government gave this river. And that is why I should correct my earlier story about the woman who gave me my name: talking of the city from which I was expelled from Turkey, she didn't say Yüksekova, but Gever, the Kurdish name of the town.

The lighter isn't working properly, but the dozens of candles stuck to the edges of the enormous rectangular cake need to be lit all the same. It takes a while, but then they all burn. A couple of hundred fighters and an equal number of civilians chant a slogan, '*Bê serok jiyan nabe, bê serok jiyan nabe, bê serok jiyan nabe!*' – no life without the leader! Children and adults blow out the candles and a fighter slices through a marzipan portrait of Öcalan's face on top of the cake with a large, shining knife. Elsewhere in the 'Leader's Garden', four more of these whoppers are being sliced. The slogan comes from all around.

It's 4 April 2017, the day on which Abdullah Öcalan was born sixty-eight years ago. The date is even more important than 27 November 1978, the day the PKK was founded; after all, there would have been no PKK without Öcalan. I suppose that last claim is debatable – you could argue that the time was simply ripe, but this is neither the time nor the place. This is a time for celebration.

The 'Leader's Garden' is not a real garden – nothing much grows at all in the Şengal region in north-west Iraq, bone-dry and arid as it is. The garden is actually a structure, a broad staircase carved into a hill on which long rows of photographs of fallen fighters are displayed in square light boxes mounted on pedestals. There is a portrait of Öcalan on the arch of a gateway at the foot of the hill, and another at the top. Lights go on in the evening, making the brightly coloured green, yellow and red flags behind the fighters' faces shine in the darkness. The night is otherwise pitch black as this area is barely inhabited.

Beside the hill is a fenced off plot of land with all kinds of animals: rabbits are hopping about, there are peacocks, goats and a duck pond. On the left, where the ground rises, there are barracks, a storage shed and a kitchen. This is where the fighters stay who guard the large checkpoint on the thoroughfare that runs past the garden. The checkpoint is painted in PKK colours and an enormous portrait of Öcalan is hanging from a structure above the road. The verge between the road and the 'garden' is planted with saplings. The soil surrounding each slender, flexible trunk is wet, as the saplings have only just been placed into the soil and sprinkled with water. It's surreal to think that PKK fighters and sympathizers – let's just say those who love Öcalan – have planted new life everywhere this morning, all the way to Europe. This was Öcalan's birthday wish, and it has come true.

LINKED LIKE A CHAIN

The PKK hasn't been in Şengal for long, only since August 2014. That summer, Şengal became famous overnight as the native country of the Yazidis, a religious minority whose villages and towns were overrun by ISIS. The other Kurdish troops, the KDP Peshmerga from Iraqi Kurdistan, should have protected the Yazidis with their lives, but the peshmergas fled. Thousands of Yazidi men were murdered and an equal number of women and girls kidnapped by ISIS, to be sold on slave markets or given to fighters as 'wives'. Kidnapped Yazidi boys were forced to fight for the ISIS jihad. In an attempt to save at least some lives, a couple of hundred PKK fighters arrived from Qandil as quickly as they could. They're still here when I'm there in spring 2017.

Wherever I go in the Şengal region, I encounter Öcalan. He's on the walls of every army base, in the halls and classrooms of an educational centre, at all the checkpoints, in the office of a huge storage room full of rice, vegetables, fruit, pens, pots and pans, socks, shoes and blankets. And this despite the fact that people here hardly knew about the PKK before the 2014 tragedy, as I find out talking to civilians and Yazidis who have joined the YBŞ (the Şengal Resistance Units, a local militia force set up by the PKK). So why put up Öcalan all over the place? Can't the Yazidis be helped without him? Do they need him to defend themselves?

I put the question to Comrade Ekîn. She was a member of the very first group of fighters to arrive from Qandil in Şengal, several days after the mass murder of Yazidis on 3 August 2014. Ekîn suffered a head injury in the November Şengal offensive in 2015, and is still recuperating in special accommodation for injured female fighters, a stone's throw from a PKK clinic, which is nothing more than an abandoned building with a few examination tables, a chemist's and some dentistry equipment. 'The local people didn't know us, but then we didn't really know the Yazidis either,' Ekîn remembers. 'I grew up in a Muslim family in Istanbul. I'd heard of the Yazidis before, but didn't know much more than that they had different rules and regulations about food and drink, and that theirs was a very closed culture. Most of the PKK fighters arriving at the time were the same. Only once I was here did I start to realize the Yazidis are an oppressed people.'

Ekîn paints a gruesome picture: 'The mass murder of 2014 wasn't the first the Yazidis endured; according to their own count, it was the seventy-third. As a result, they have developed a fatalist mentality, and they are certain that there are more mass murders to come. They have lost all confidence. As a people, they are uneducated. Not one of the powers that ever governed over them has given them the education they need to know who they are and see their own strength. On top of that, their hierarchical clan system has been used by outsiders to divide them. All of these aspects are linked together like a chain. We, the PKK, are trying to break this chain.'

In that respect, the Yazidis are comparable to the Kurds in Turkey – though it should be noted that a part of the Yazidis consider themselves Kurdish people in a minority faith community, while others see themselves as a separate ethnic group. Just as the PKK has opened the eyes of the Turkish Kurds, it is now trying to open the Yazidis' eyes and restore their sense of self-worth.

They provide education, sometimes in the form of courses at semi-official 'academies', but often in an informal setting. Early March 2017, I'm in a condolence tent at a refugee camp on Mount Şengal. In recent skirmishes between, on the one hand, the PKK, YBŞ and the YJŞ (Şengal Women's Protection Units) and the KDP Peshmerga on the other, a young woman has been killed. Men and women gather in separate tents to mourn. The tensions in the area have hardly subsided at all. President Barzani's KDP wants the PKK to leave the Şengal region. The violence that killed the young woman could flare up again at any moment.

'Let there be war,' one of the female mourners says. What she means is that, with the support of the PKK, the YBŞ and the YJŞ should stop merely defending themselves against the peshmerga, but that they should attack. Victory or death. But the female PKK fighters in the tent passionately object to the woman's wish. The experienced Comrade Engizek says, 'Armed battle can never bring peace. Weapons are for self-defence. A peaceful war is waged with education, demonstrations, marches and meetings, and by organizing the people. That is the kind of war the Yazidis must focus on now.'

The women listen, share their views and concerns and ask questions. The PKK members answer them, explain their own views, tell the women that they can – and must – rely on their own strength; as Yazidis and as women.

The conversation moves seamlessly to the role women can play in protecting the people and in peaceful warfare, and the position of women in the conservative, feudal Yazidi society. In that respect, the existence of the YBŞ has also broken through old patterns: since January 2015, the YBŞ has had a female counterpart, which in early 2016 was named the YJŞ. The men grumbled at first, but a poignant question made them change their mind: would ISIS have been able to enslave thousands of female Yazidis if women had been armed in August 2014?

Comrade Ekîn compares educating an oppressed people with raising a child. 'You teach a child to walk and talk, you're involved in every aspect of its development. In the Yazidis' case, this child is an entire people, a society. They have already been formed, by oppression. The most important thing we teach them is that unity is key – and possible, even with the existence of various clans. Only by standing strong together can they prevent new mass murders from happening in the future. Even when we, the PKK, aren't around anymore.'

According to Ekîn, the Yazidis' fatalist attitude is also to blame for the fact that only a part of the people still live on their native soil. She explains, 'With every tragedy, after each mass murder, more people flee. To Turkey, Syria, Europe. The same thing happened in 2014. Wherever they end up, they are assimilated; they lose their traditions, their faith, their culture. And because such a small number of Yazidis remain here, even those lose their identity. That's why we tell them to stay here, be strong, stand up for who they are, defend themselves.'

Ekîn explains that the YJŞ's existence is proof that the education programme is bearing fruit. 'At first, neither the men nor the women understood how it was possible for there to be female PKK fighters. How could they go through life unmarried? How could they carry weapons and go to war? Many Yazidis even drew the line at sending girls to school. But today, there is the YJŞ. If we managed that, how much more will the future bring?'

None of it would be possible without the PKK ideology. It is the reason Öcalan's portrait is everywhere; he symbolizes everything that has been achieved and can be achieved. Ekîn: 'We're not trying to turn the Yazidis into a kind of PKK. If that had been our aim, why would we have founded the YBŞ and the YJŞ? We want them to find their own strength. This aim is rooted in Öcalan's ideology, and his portrait symbolizes that.'

Ekîn also brushes aside my final argument, that the Yazidis' conservatism and the PKK's progressiveness will never allow them to see eye to eye, saying, 'Just look at the Kurds in Bakur. Three or four decades ago, they were just as conservative, just as powerless and just as divided as the Yazidis, because of their dominant clan culture. The PKK broke through this. The same has started happening here.'

There is one sore point which no PKK fighter in Şengal can help mentioning. Why did they come from Qandil and Syrian Kurdistan only when the KDP Peshmerga had been driven out and ISIS was already wreaking havoc? The fighters all refer to Abdullah Öcalan, who argued years ago that the guerrillas had an active role to play in helping the Şengal Yazidis. Where were we? Why didn't we listen to our leader? One of the fighters says, 'What happened in 2014 was our fault. We came too late.'

ETERNAL LIFE

There is a shortcut to discovering the meaning of the slogan '*Bê serok jiyan nabe*', 'no life without the leader'. It takes a bit more guts. You need to ask the question, 'If there is no life without the leader, what will happen after his death?' Of course you don't phrase it like that; using the words 'Öcalan' and 'death' in a single sentence is a recipe for shocked faces. You put it more delicately. 'Look, the leader is sixty-eight years old, and no one has eternal life. So what happens after even his life must finally come to an end?' Comrade Hêlîn, a thirty-year-old who joined the PKK when she was fourteen, explains that the '*serok*', the 'leader' in the slogan, doesn't refer to Öcalan the man, but to what has been created through him. 'The leader is an institution,' she says, during a talk we have in our classroom under the trees, on plastic chairs that soon stick to our wet behinds. We're sweating like mad; the afternoon sun always scorches down mercilessly on our few square metres of classroom through an open space in the foliage. Which, incidentally, is no coincidence: the open-air classroom was built on this precise spot because it is in the shade in the mornings. She goes on, 'The leader is the people, a philosophy, a history.'

I suggest that following a leader often ends badly, and she answers, 'But surely all leaders aren't the same? Isn't Erdoğan a very different kind of leader from Mandela?' 'And Öcalan,' I ask, 'is he more of a Mandela type, a moral leader, than an Erdoğan type, a dictatorial leader?' Hêlîn: 'The leader himself says that no organization can be led by a single person. He can only exist thanks to the people, to other leaders like Comrade Cuma, and to the women who are present in all positions of the organization. Öcalan stands for an ideological leadership, a practical leadership. We follow his path, educate and improve ourselves according to his ideology. Anyone can join the PKK, anyone can read Öcalan's books and glean from them what they want, in keeping with their own capacities and personality. This way, you grow into who you are.'

I'm not suggesting, by the way, that only women have taken Öcalan into their hearts. I meet thirty-one-year-old Comrade Botan in a PKK base in Kirkuk, Iraq. He asks me whether I've read *The Fifth Defence*, a volume in the series of books that Öcalan wrote. Taken together, the texts form the defence that Öcalan submitted to the European Court of Human Rights after being convicted of high treason by a Turkish court in 1999. No, I haven't read *The Fifth*. The book is only available in Turkish, and given that Öcalan is hard enough to read in English, I haven't attempted to tackle it yet.

Botan shakes his head. 'I've read *The Fifth* at least twenty times,' he asserts, 'and each time I discover something new, get a new association, fresh insight, see something I hadn't noticed before.' 'Don't you ever read novels?' I ask. 'Or other ideological works; philosophy, non-fiction?' Botan: 'Why should I, when the books of the leader have so much to offer me?'

Comrade Nûman, who's in his late thirties and has been writing books on the history of Kurdish art and literature for the last couple of years, has perhaps the most down-to-earth attitude when speaking about Öcalan. 'We owe Öcalan a lot,' he says. 'Thanks to him, we are free, freer than ever. Take the comrade who came here from Amed last week to give us a history lesson. Did you know that he's a historian? That he studied history in prison? He was locked up, but educated himself nevertheless, because he is free. We have Öcalan to thank for that.'

I talk with Comrade Nûman about how differently young guerrillas talk about the leader. About the things I notice. About the diary that an eighteen-year-old fighter showed me, in which she had written Öcalan's name and surrounded it with hearts and flowers. At the back of the diary, she'd glued a photograph of an elderly woman. No, it wasn't her granny; it was Öcalan's mother Üveyş. The young also have a habit of bandying about Öcalan quotes, beginning with the phrase '*Serokatî got*', 'The leadership said'. I tell Nûman that a young woman even used a 'Serokatî got' phrase to answer my query about cleaning the kitchen.

'Using "Serokatî got" is a sign of weakness,' Nûman says. 'The young haven't started thinking for themselves. It's understandable. You can compare them to newborn babies. They still feel a deep connection with Öcalan. It is up to us, the more experienced fighters, to slowly cut this umbilical cord and teach them a more mature and independent way of thinking. There's an important course that deals with this, called "The Essence of the Leader". It's a course you revisit again and again over the years and which is never quite the same because the comrades you meet there and the discussions you have with them are different every time. Just like, say, the social history course. It teaches you to think, for yourself.'

That is not to say he doesn't love Öcalan, by the way. He says, 'I love him because he has made my personal development possible. In the past twenty years, I've read all the great philosophers. Sometimes I didn't understand a word so I'd put the book aside for a while, and when I read the same philosopher again years later, it would all become clear to me. Without Öcalan, I wouldn't have had that opportunity. My love for him is like the love for a good friend.'

Many Turks would sneer at hearing the PKK leader described in such terms. Actually, that is putting it mildly. Many Turks seethe at such descriptions. To them, Öcalan is a 'baby killer' and a 'master terrorist'.

The term 'baby killer' was coined after the bloodbath of Pinarcik in June 1987. Pinarcik is a village in Mardin Province. Many Kurdish men there had been made into village guards, that is to say, members of the civilian militia paid and armed by the state to assist in the struggle against the PKK. Particularly in the first years after the armed conflict began on 15 August 1984, village guards were often the target of PKK attacks. They were, and still are, considered traitors and state accomplices, and the PKK sees them as legitimate targets because they are armed and therefore not civilians.

The story goes that the PKK had warned the men of Pinarcik several times in the days before the bloodbath to lay down their government-provided weapons. But the village guards refused to comply, at which a group of about thirty PKK fighters launched an attack on Pinarcik. Thirty people were killed, including six village guards, eight women and sixteen children. Photographs of the dead bodies made all the Turkish papers, especially one image of a dead baby, swaddled in a white blanket and with a bullet hole in its body. Öcalan the baby killer was born.

The monthly PKK publication *Serxwebun* [Independence], which is still published in Europe today, immediately ran a report on the massacre in its June issue of 1987. The killing was called a 'noble mission' in an article discussing various actions of the previous weeks. But though the terminology used is occasionally attributed to Öcalan, these words were actually written by some unnamed editor, not the leader. Öcalan was said to have ordered the attack, though there is no proof of this – nor is it very likely, given that he has was in Syria at the time, and it wouldn't make much sense for him to follow everyday events in Turkey, let alone give detailed orders for attacks on specific villages. A book by Murat Karayilan (a PKK veteran and now the highest commander of the HPG, the armed branch of the PKK), *The Anatomy of a War*, also discusses Pinarcik. He claims that it was the work of spies in the PKK, specifically a commander named Hogir, real name Cemil Işik, and that Hogir, who fled the PKK after the murders, was involved in other acts that led to the unscrupulous killing of civilians in the same period. That may well be true; the state has probably always infiltrated the PKK and attempted to bring discredit to the movement from the inside outwards. But it's simplistic to assume that's all there is to it. In those years the PKK did not distance itself from such attacks, not even Öcalan initially. It's true that civilian deaths are inevitable in a war, as a representative of the PKK in Europe said at the time, but targeted massacres are not.

Öcalan now no longer avoids final responsibility for what the members of his organization get up to. According to Aliza Marcus's book about the PKK, *Blood and Belief*, in 1990 Öcalan launched an investigation into internal killings in the PKK and into civilian deaths. In *Prison Writings*, a series of books he wrote after his arrest in 1999, he describes the various steps that need to be taken in order to prevent future suffering. One of them is an in-depth investigation into all crimes committed by the PKK and the state. 'This survey must involve a self-critical debate in order to determine which national or international legal standards should be applied to try the individuals responsible. [...] We will have to account for all the crimes committed by us or in our name.'

There can be no doubt there have been punishment killings and that civilians have been murdered – none of the guerrillas I spoke about it with has ever denied it. But according to those I have interviewed, the accusations that Öcalan has blood on his hands from personally carrying out executions, and that he gave orders to get rid of people who challenged his leadership, are nothing but malicious gossip and unfounded slurs. Comrade Hêlîn, for example, said, 'I've never met the leader but I *know* him, I grew up with him. He's not a murderer.' And, 'Öcalan is not our sole leader. During the long period he was in Syria, he appointed various local leaders. Is that the action of a man who wants to keep all the power in his own hands?'

Murderers in the PKK are traitors who don't understand its ideology, say today's fighters. According to the ideology, violence is justified in war, self-defence and in retaliation against an enemy, but not as a punishment of its own members. The PKK hasn't given any of its members the death penalty for years, no matter what their offence may have been.

So what is the truth? It won't be known until the Kurdish question is resolved. Only then, when a peace agreement has been reached, can a truth and reconciliation commission be set up, as has happened in post-Apartheid South Africa for example, and after a peace treaty was signed in Northern Ireland.

This topic often puts me in mind of an acquaintance of mine in Diyarbakır. One day, she tearfully confided in me that a niece of hers had been killed in the PKK. She was convinced it had been a punishment killing, in other words, that her niece had been executed after being involved in a conflict with her fellow fighters. She didn't dare expose the supposed execution, out of fear – justified or not – of repercussions from the PKK. My acquaintance was torn apart by this family matter; despite her fear, she was also an ardent supporter of the PKK.

I wrote this story down in a column, and soon received letters from PKK followers who swore by all that was holy that such executions of PKK members had been a thing of the past for many years. I think that is true today. But was it at the time the niece died, about fifteen or twenty years ago now? Nobody knows. When I mentioned this to Comrade Hêlîn, she said, 'There is a commission for justice in Qandil which investigates such cases. Why doesn't your acquaintance go there to find out once and for all how her niece died?'

My acquaintance's predicament is similar to the response of many Turks to the crimes committed by the state, except that those crimes are more thoroughly investigated and more is known about them – and that they surpass the PKK's in scale and brutality by a wide margin. There was the attempt to exterminate the Kurdish Alevi people of Dersim in the 1930s. Inmates of Diyarbakır prison being tortured to death in the 1980s. There were the thousands of Kurdish villages razed to the ground and the hundreds of as yet unsolved murders committed in the 1990s. The Roboskî air strike, which killed thirty-four Kurdish citizens in late December 2011. To Turks who see Öcalan only as a 'baby killer' and who support the state unconditionally, these crimes are all lies. And where the evidence that the crimes have taken place is overwhelming, they soon make up excuses: the civilians were rebels, the prisoners separatists, the villagers PKK supporters and the men and boys of Roboskî were assisting terrorists.

Only once a peace treaty has been signed can all the archives be opened up and can soldiers as well as generals, common guerrillas as well as high-ranking PKK officials, make full disclosure. And only then, once the fear of repercussions has also subsided, will civilians like my acquaintance dare to voice the suspicions that are troubling them. It is true the PKK has its own commission of justice already, but one day everything will have to be made publicly accessible and verifiable.

Finally, an amnesty law will have to be written, without which no peace process would be complete. Its scope will have to be negotiated and passed in parliament. Which crimes should be punishable, which should not? Who was responsible, who issued the order, who turned a blind eye? How much blood does Öcalan really have on his hands?

ASYLUM IN EUROPE

The man at the centre of all of this has been incarcerated on the prison island Imralı in the Sea of Marmara, about sixty kilometres south of Istanbul, since February 1999. He left Syria in 1998, after his presence in the country had almost started a war between Syria and Turkey and the Syrian authorities forced him to leave their territory. Öcalan expected to be granted asylum in Europe, but not a single European government wanted to burn its fingers on him. Passed on like a hot potato, he was flown all across the continent, until eventually, by way of Moscow, Athens and Rome among other places, he ended up at the Greek embassy in the Kenyan capital Nairobi. There, he was apparently told he would be put on a plane to Amsterdam, as the Netherlands had decided to grant him asylum.

The officers who picked him up and took him to the airport turned out to be Kenyan secret agents. At the airport, they handed Öcalan over to their Turkish colleagues. He was strapped into his seat, but after take-off the plane did not set course for Amsterdam in the north-west, but headed directly north, to Istanbul.

Among PKK members, 15 February 1999, the day on which Turkey arrested Öcalan, is known as 'Conspiracy Day'. The kidnapping was a collaboration of the Turkish intelligence services MIT, the CIA and probably the Israeli Mossad. In the same year, Turkey sentenced Öcalan to death. Under pressure from Europe, the sentence was later commuted from the gallows to life imprisonment.

Öcalan has been locked up in a single-person cell ever since. A young female fighter at a PKK uniform sewing shop in Iraq claims that he spends at least twenty hours a day just thinking, thinking, thinking. 'He never sleeps more than three or four hours a night, Comrade Avaşîn. It's all he needs,' she tells me while the presser foot of her sewing machine races across pieces of green fabric she is expertly sewing into cuffs. 'Don't you think he occasionally just sits and daydreams,' I ask, 'and that he needs a little more sleep than that, just like anyone else?' 'Absolutely not!' she cries indignantly.

As I was to find out in the months that followed, this seamstress guerrilla was by no means alone in her opinion. The leadership thinks, writes books and sleeps very little.

Meanwhile, I wonder how Öcalan is really doing. He lives in isolation most of the time. According to all international standards, solitary confinement is a serious form of psychological torture; in other words, you or I would turn into gibbering mental wrecks within a month, if not a week. Now, I'm perfectly prepared to believe that Öcalan is strong, and that developing new ideologies for the movement, which he has been doing since the mid-1990s, is keeping his brain active and healthy. I can imagine he draws strength from his great importance to the movement and the Kurdish people in general. But, I ask again, how is he really?

One of the first tangible signs that the peace process was in peril was that the regular visits to Öcalan by a fixed delegation of HDP members were suddenly suspended. That was in April 2015, and only Öcalan's brother Mehmet has made the journey to Imralı since. Photographs of the visits during the peace process have been made public, in which the leader, despite his grey-white hair, looks cheerful and healthy. There are no recordings. To what extent have the Kurdish movement's tactics during the peace process really resulted from his leadership? To what extent is he even still capable of leading?

And now that I'm at it, did he actually write the series of books he produced from inside his prison cell himself? The books did not leave the prison in the form of a neat manuscript, I read in a translator's foreword to one of Öcalan's books. His writing left Imralı on notes written by himself or by his lawyers and other occasional visitors who, after listening to him for hours, wrote down his words afterwards. Of course he has some books to read in his cell that have inspired his views on the Neolithic Age, the ancient Egyptians and the great philosophers of past decades, but he doesn't have an extensive library at his disposal. He depends on the state and his guards for everything he has.

In the time I was based in Diyarbakır, I once applied for an interview with Öcalan. Naturally, I already knew there was practically no chance the authorities in Ankara would even consider such a request, but I felt I owed it to my profession as a journalist to at least give it a try. It was early 2015. The Turkish state had just decided to prosecute me for spreading propaganda for a terrorist organization.

The charge against me was partly based on interviews I had conducted with PKK leaders, Cemil Bayık in particular. Prosecuting a journalist for interviewing anyone does not of course make any sense, and in my case, it was actually a pretty stupid thing to do. Had the state offered me an interview with Erdoğan or other AKP members closely involved in the peace process such as Yalçın Akdoğan, I would undoubtedly have been able to sell that interview in Dutch as well as English. That way, I would also have spread 'propaganda' for them. Denied not only this but also a meeting with the other important political player in this matter, namely Abdullah Öcalan, I was left with no other option but going to Qandil to speak to key figures in the peace process. But being a journalist, I couldn't just write that getting an interview with Öcalan was impossible – I had to try, first. How close did I get? The Ankara bureaucrats did not even answer my query as to whom I should submit my request to for an interview.

My wish to speak to him is, of course, as strong as ever.

On 9 October 1998, Öcalan was forced to leave Syria and initially fled to Moscow. The day is still commemorated by the fighters every year. On 9 October 2016, I was at a PKK base near the Iraqi city of Maxmur, whose commanders were holding a commemoration meeting. I had wanted to attend it, but for reasons that never became clear was not given permission. When I asked one of the commanders afterwards what conclusions had been reached at the meeting, she said, 'We will appeal to everyone to step up their struggle to free Öcalan'.

Freedom is a long way off for Öcalan. His release won't come at the beginning but at the end of the peace process; just as Nelson Mandela was only set free once it was beyond a doubt that Apartheid would be abolished, which happened less than a year later. I would like to make it perfectly clear that I am not comparing Mandela with Öcalan – the kind of leader Öcalan really is will only become apparent if and when he leaves prison alive. The PKK knows his release is not imminent, yet they continue to fight for it, just as the Kurdish diaspora in Europe and the US still demonstrates to that end. After all, Öcalan is the founder of the movement, the founder of the ideology they follow, the founder of their lives. They know that if he is freed, it means they are free. Öcalan's freedom is the freedom of the Kurdish people.

BACKGROUND

THE PEACE PROCESS IN TURKEY

In December 2012 Erdoğan, who was still prime minister at the time, admitted that the Turkish government was in talks with Abdullah Öcalan. Three months later on 21 March – Kurdish New Year – the peace process was officially launched. It was not the first time the government and Öcalan discussed a solution. Prime Minister Turgut Özal made overtures to the PKK in the early 1990s, but died before any actual negotiations were begun.

It was not the first time Erdoğan tried to initiate peace with the Kurds either. In 2009, he launched the 'Kurdish Opening', a process of democratization that was meant to resolve the Kurdish question. The initiative failed; neither did the peace process launched in 2013 lead to a fundamental structural reform.

A detailed account of the failure of each 'peace process' that was attempted in Turkey would fill volumes. The government was never fully committed to the 2013 peace process, as is evident from the fact that from the first it continued its expansion of army infrastructure. Protesting against this, the eighteen-year-old Kurd Medeni Yıldırım was killed by a police bullet in Lice, Diyarbakır Province, in June 2013. On top of that, the government expanded the village guard system rather than starting to dismantle it.

Meanwhile, the PKK had begun withdrawing its troops from Turkish territory to the Qandil Mountains – a process that at least some of the fighters underwent voluntarily, as I learned from talking to several guerrillas active in Turkey at the time. Öcalan called for them to leave and many obeyed, though they were free to stay if they wanted to. Many of the fighters were wary, with good reason. In 1999, six months after his arrest and two months after he was sentenced to death (later reduced to life imprisonment), Öcalan also called on the PKK to withdraw from Turkey. But on their way to northern Iraq, many of the guerrillas were attacked and killed by the army.

The battle of Kobani gave the final blow to the ailing peace process. 'Kobani is about to fall,' Erdoğan cried out hopefully during a rally in 2014. But Kobani didn't fall. The situation was unacceptable to Erdoğan: Kurds defending their territory – with American air support, to add insult to injury – and, after their victory, expanding their autonomy in northern Syria. And to make matters worse, the battle for Kobani had only bolstered the Turkish Kurds' confidence and strengthened their call for autonomy, the only possible outcome of a serious peace process.

For a while, it looked as if progress were being made. In February 2015, the 'Dolmabahçe Agreement' was presented in the Dolmabahçe Palace in Istanbul. The agreement, which had been reached through negotiations between Öcalan and the government and during which HDP members of parliament acted as mediators, frequently travelling to and fro between the prison on Imralı and the PKK headquarters in Qandil, consisted of ten areas of improvement that were needed to achieve a lasting peace. Though vaguely worded, they nonetheless clearly addressed pluralism, constitutional guarantees of freedom and identity, and a 'new constitution' to establish a 'democratic transformation'.

It is established beyond doubt that Erdoğan knew about this agreement – for something like this to come about without the permission of the most powerful man in the country would in any case be unthinkable. One month later, Erdoğan roundly rejected the agreement, and after another month, in April, Öcalan was placed in solitary confinement again. He has had less than a handful visitors ever since.

Looking at the broader picture, it becomes clear that the peace process keeps failing for the same reason: a lack of political will and courage. The then Prime Minister and now President Erdoğan is only prepared to talk with the PKK if he thinks it will strengthen his power, and any solution to the Kurdish question must lead to far-reaching decentralization. Turkey without the Kurdish question would be Turkey without a powerful leader. Any attempt to achieve peace that is based on power is therefore doomed to failure.

As the PKK co-leader Cemil Bayık told me in an interview, the PKK is still open to peace talks with the Turkish government. It does have a number of conditions it wants met, however, before it is ready to return to the negotiating table.

Firstly, there has to be a mutual ceasefire. Also, the government needs to enter into the spirit of such an agreement, which was not the case in previous peace talks. From the very beginning, the expansion of Turkey's military presence in south-eastern Turkey continued unabated, while the PKK started withdrawing its units from the country as agreed. When it became clear at the end of 2014 that the peace process was irrevocably doomed to failure, the PKK prepared itself to take up arms again.

The PKK demands that if negotiations are to be reopened, they must be overseen by a third, independent party, to prevent any confusion about which side may be frustrating the peace process. The Turkish government has always refused to permit a supervisory authority to be present at a peace process.

In its final demand, the PKK requires the Turkish government to make a sincere effort – though naturally, the sincerity of a negotiating partner only becomes clear in practice.

The last 'peace process' became the stage of twin power struggles. The first was about increasing AKP power, as local elections were coming up in 2014 and parliamentary ones in June 2015. For several years, Erdoğan had publicly hinted at wanting to introduce a presidential system. This would take an amendment to the constitution, which he would only be able to realize by way of a referendum, or directly through parliament if his party had enough seats. Erdoğan hoped that the peace process would further increase AKP support among Kurds, which had always been considerable. If the HDP in the south-east failed to reach the ten per cent electoral threshold, all its votes would automatically go to the second largest party – the AKP. The constitutional amendment would be in the bag.

But the HDP – or rather, its co-leader Selahattin Demirtaş – threw a spanner in the works. In the shortest election speech ever, he told Erdoğan on the eve of the June 2015 elections, 'We're not making you president.' Not only was the HDP confident it would reach the electoral threshold, Demirtaş's statement also made clear that his party would not cooperate with the AKP in parliament to amend the constitution to enable a presidential system. In the first months of 2015, the polls already showed that the HDP profited more from the peace process than the AKP. Erdoğan didn't see the point of seeing it through.

Meanwhile, a second power struggle had begun, between Erdoğan and the US-based Turkish preacher Fethullah Gülen. They had been allies between 2001 and 2012, the first decade the AKP was in power. In that period, the Gülenists, as Gülen's followers are called, were appointed to key positions in state institutes, especially in the police and the judiciary. The AKP and the Gülenists joined forces in an effort to weaken the Kurdish movement, among other things. In 2009, the so-called KCK trials began. Thousands of Kurdish mayors, administrators, human rights activists, lawyers and journalists were arrested and prosecuted for terrorism-related crimes. Some of the KCK trials are still ongoing.

In 2012, there was presumably a disagreement about how to tackle the Kurdish question – presumably, since the power dynamics between the AKP and Gülenists have always been obscure. The AKP wanted a peace process, but the Gülen movement opposed it. When the peace process was about to begin in early 2013, a public prosecutor summoned Hakan Fidan, the head of the Turkish national agency MIT, to the police station. The prosecutor, a Gülenist, suspected Fidan of having ties to a terrorist organization. Fidan, one of Erdoğan's closest confidants, did in fact have ties with 'terrorists': he was in talks with Öcalan, after all. The AKP rushed to push a bill through parliament to prevent Fidan from actually being prosecuted.

A month earlier, in January 2013, three Kurdish women were murdered in Paris, among whom one of the founders of the PKK, Sakine Cansız. A year after the murder – the war between Erdoğan and Gülen was now in full swing – Erdoğan held Gülenists in the secret service responsible. No one knows whether he is right. The investigation into the murders has been closed because the suspect has since died of a brain tumour in a French prison.

In December 2013, the war between Erdoğan and Gülen became official. Gülenist prosecutors launched a large-scale investigation into corruption in government circles. Erdoğan frantically started dismissing and transferring prosecutors, and was soon able to nip the investigation in the bud. For years, being a follower of Gülen had been a guarantee of a good career and prosperity, but that time had passed for good. The power struggle came to a head with the failed coup attempt on 15 July 2016. There is no conclusive evidence that Fethullah Gülen personally knew of – or even gave orders for – the attempt to topple Erdoğan. That Gülenists were involved, however, is beyond doubt.

'*Her şey bize bağlı*,' as Comrade Nûman said. 'Everything is linked to us.'

CHAPTER 3

The State is a Man

There's a large poster on the youth club house wall, showing six teenagers. Welat Kara, twenty-three years old, points at one of them, Sevgan. 'I was there when Sevgan died,' he says. 'We were hiding out in a house when fighting started nearby. He climbed out of the window and was immediately shot down by a tank. A few hours later, we buried him on the spot. We couldn't reach the graveyard because of the fighting.'

The six young people on the poster, one of whom is a woman, were all killed in the Şırnak urban war between March and June 2016. Şırnak wasn't the only town in Bakur in which heavy fighting erupted between the Turkish state and the YPS, a youth movement connected to the PKK, between the autumn of 2015 and the summer of 2016. The young fighters didn't stand a chance. They were killed in their hundreds in the narrow streets of the old centres of such towns as Şırnak, Silopi, Cizre, Silvan, Yüksekova and Sur, the historic centre of Diyarbakır.

I met some of the survivors of the urban wars by coincidence in Maxmur Camp, a refugee camp in Iraq that was set up over twenty years ago to house Kurds from Şırnak Province forced to leave Turkey in the 1990s. In those years, the fighting between the PKK and the government reached a fiery climax. The army burned down thousands of Kurdish villages. The villagers were given the choice between becoming a state-funded armed militia against the PKK, death, and leaving. Some crossed the border to Iraq, where then President Saddam Hussein allotted them a plot of desert near the city of Maxmur. There was nothing there except endless summers of scorching heat, scorpions, snakes and stones. A place to die, Hussein must have thought. But the Kurds decided to live. They built houses, schools, an open-air theatre and a clinic, and they set up their own government.

They maintained their connection with Şırnak, however, and when the urban wars broke out and it started to look like that city would also fall prey to violence, the young people of Maxmur started making plans in their youth club behind the theatre, on a plot of land next to the camp's main road. Should they join the fight or not? They should, a handful of them decided. Welat Kara was one of them. In mid-February 2016, they trekked north, crossed the border illegally and slipped past the many checkpoints and into the city in the dead of night.

The outbreak of the urban wars was a direct result of the failing peace process between the PKK and the government. To the mayors of various Kurdish towns, it seemed a good time to proclaim the autonomy of their municipalities. From now on, it wouldn't be the Turkish state that was in charge of the municipalities, where they had won the March 2014 local elections by a landslide, but the citizens themselves. The citizens were organized into neighbourhood councils – a great deal of time and energy had been invested in setting them up and training their members.

According to many politicians and experts inside and outside Turkey, the call for autonomy was fanning the flames – not least because it led to young fighters founding the YPS, the Civil Protection Units designed to protect the freshly independent areas. They diligently started digging trenches and putting up barricades. According to critics, the Kurdish movement should have anticipated that the state would not take this lying down, and is therefore partly responsible for the violence that broke out and killed hundreds of people in the months that followed. Human Rights Watch counted at least 338 civilian deaths in the affected cities.

I put the matter to Cemil Bayık during our interview in May 2016, at the beginning of my year with the PKK. Had the mayors and the YPS not simply provoked the state? Why had it been necessary for the wars to spread from the remote, sparsely populated parts of Kurdistan to the cities? Surely, they knew what to expect from the state?

Calling a proclamation of autonomy a provocation ignores the vital importance of self-governance for the movement, Bayık explains. He says, 'The aim of peace negotiations with the state was to establish a form of self-governance, which we believe lies at the heart of any solution to the Kurdish question. Erdoğan's rejection of the election results of 7 June 2015, in which democratic forces achieved an important victory, shows that he was no longer interested in finding a solution through parliament. The government reverted to war. What choice was there but to call for independence of the municipalities in which the democratic forces had won a majority?'

The 'democratic forces' he refers to are the HDP and the DBP, the Democratic Regions Party, a local sister organization of the HDP which is active in Kurdish territories. After the 2014 local elections, it gained administrative control of many municipalities.

The PKK and the Kurdish movement can't be held responsible for the government's disproportionate reaction, Bayık argues.

I counter that if civilians arm themselves with Kalashnikovs, machine guns and rocket launchers, and put up barricades, it's hardly surprising that the state responds with violence. 'Yes, there were trenches,' Bayık concedes, 'and the state used its duty to fill them and take down the barricades as an excuse. But in various places, attacks were launched before there were any trenches and barricades. Neighbourhoods that hadn't barricaded their streets weren't spared from government violence either. Do civilians need to die because trenches have to be filled?'

The young people I speak with in Maxmur tell me that the weapons the YPS used came from the PKK, and a PKK member in Istanbul I spoke to about the urban wars in the summer of 2015, very soon after they occurred, confirmed that. 'Kurds are always armed,' is Bayık's first argument; which holds true for Kalashnikovs, for instance, but not for machine guns and missile launchers. Bayık: 'Surely the young have the right to defend themselves? And what is one small missile compared to a tank, a helicopter, or an F-16?'

That the state violence was disproportionate has been recognized by Turkish and international human rights organizations such as Amnesty International and Human Rights Watch, and even by the UN. Hundreds of civilians were killed, including fathers, mothers, elderly people, children, and even infants. About half a million people had to leave their homes and towns to find refuge with family or in camps elsewhere in the south-east, or in the west of Turkey. The United Nations expressed concern about the situation in the cities and asked the Turkish authorities for permission to visit the stricken areas to conduct an independent investigation into human rights violations. Permission was withheld.

DEATH SNEAKING UP

In conversations with surviving fighters, I've found that some of the neighbourhood's inhabitants also watched the YPS's war preparations with concern, to say the least. Welat from Maxmur recalls, 'Some people begged us not to dig trenches or erect barricades. They feared it would lead to their houses and neighbourhood being destroyed. We explained to them that that would happen anyway, and that we needed to defend ourselves.'

Another survivor is Destan (not her real name), who fought in a different city, Cizre, where she grew up, although I meet her in Maxmur Camp. She was studying law in Istanbul and was in the middle of preparing an application to the European Erasmus student exchange programme to study at a Spanish university for a year when tensions started to rise in her native city. She says the barricading of city districts started with the discovery of a list. 'It named hundreds of people to be arrested by the government. Then my family called – my father and my aunt had been arrested. What else could I have done, other than go home and fight?'

Before leaving for Istanbul to become a student, Destan had been an active member of the youth movement in Cizre. She denies that part of the local population spoke up against the YPS barricades. 'On the contrary, the people were united,' she says. Then she adds, 'The barricades may well have made the situation worse, but that's just too bad. We, the people, have a will. A will to govern ourselves. We're not about to give that up, or the struggle that comes with it.'

The war of Cizre was one of the fiercest. In January 2016 especially, dramatic incidents came thick and fast. I remember being at a Kurdish conference at the EU Parliament in Brussels at the time, where one of the panellists suddenly interrupted the discussion to take an urgent phone call from Cizre. She wanted to share the call, from the co-chairman of the Cizre people's council Mehmet Tunç, with the audience through her microphone. The note of panic and urgency, and the sense of fast approaching death was audible as Mehmet Tunç's voice quivered through the hall, crackly because of the bad line.

'The situation is not what the media are making it out to be,' Mehmet Tunç said, referring to articles in the Turkish press which sketched the situation in Cizre as a struggle against terrorism. 'There's a massacre going on in Cizre. All the houses have been bombed, tanks have been deployed. [...] These people have been without enough food or water for sixty days. Only 10,000 are left of a population of 120,000. The people have been forced to leave. The same policies were used in the 1990s, when 4,000 villages were evacuated and their inhabitants forced to move to places like Cizre. By evacuating the villages, the government claimed to be finishing off the PKK. Now they are evacuating cities and again saying they are finishing off the PKK. Cizre is experiencing a tragedy. In this house alone, twenty-eight people have been injured. Five of the injured have died. The water has been cut off. If we go outside to fetch water, we are shot at by snipers. We don't go outside. One four-storey building has been completely destroyed by mortar bombs. The situation is very, very critical. So we say to you, our friends: please, stop these atrocities. It is in your power to stop this genocide. It is in your power to send a warning to the AKP government and put an end to the siege of Cizre. If you don't, you are accessories to this genocide.'

Mehmet Tunç overestimated the conference's power. There were a few members of the European Parliament, and the conference had been organized with the help of the EU Parliament's green party, but most of the attendees were academics, politicians, journalists and activists who concerned themselves with human rights in general and the Kurdish question in particular. There were also some heavyweights from the Kurdish movement such as the co-leader of the HDP Selahattin Demirtaş, HDP parliamentarians Selma Irmak, Dilek Öcalan (the great man's niece) and the veteran Leyla Zana. None of these people was in a position to issue warnings to the Turkish government or force it to call a halt to military operations in Kurdistan.

Meanwhile in Cizre, the HDP parliamentarian Faysal Sarıyıldız and a number of Kurdish lawyers were making desperate attempts to get the authorities to allow ambulances to pass to pick up the injured from the cellar and take them to hospital. They even tried to get an emergency ruling by the European Court of Human Rights. All in vain. A day later, the army set the cellar ablaze. All that was left of Mehmet Tunç and twenty-seven others who had still been alive were their charred remains.

The cellar where Mehmet Tunç died was not the only one in which disaster struck in those months. Fighters were seeking refuge in substructures of buildings, but so were civilians. A delegation of local journalists and politicians that was allowed to inspect the cellars afterwards, found part of a child's jaw, among other things. Elderly people died there, too.

The young fighter Welat Kara escaped death by hiding out in a cellar in Şırnak. The urban war was coming to an end and the young fighters had used up almost all their weapons and ammunition with no fresh arms supplies coming in – let alone food or drink. 'A fire broke out,' Welat recalls. 'Inside or out, it was hard to tell. The cellar quickly filled with smoke. I lost consciousness. When I came round, I saw six comrades lying on the ground around me, dead, blood coming from their noses.'

The survivors managed to escape from the cellar after dark. 'We were weakened by smoke inhalation and lack of food and drink,' Welat says. 'Every night, we walked a short bit of the way. Sometimes we'd find some *bulgur* [a kind of wheat] inside a house. We'd soak it in water for hours before eating it.' He grabs his left wrist with his right hand, slowly lifting his hand to his mouth, and says, 'This is how I had to lift the spoon to my mouth. I was too weak to do it with just one hand.'

The group managed to flee the city. Welat carried two hand grenades with him all that time, planning to activate them if security troops tried to capture him. 'Surrendering, falling into state hands, is unthinkable.' He adds, 'We were picked up and taken to the mountains, where we stayed for a couple of weeks to get our strength back. By July, we were back home in Maxmur.'

Eighteen-year-old Darya Taş was in the same cellar as Welat. She also managed to escape. It was not the first time she'd left Maxmur to join the fight: at sixteen, she went to the Şengal region to help the Yazidis against ISIS attacks. 'I wasn't allowed to fight then,' she says, 'because I was too young. So I taught Kurdish to children. This time, I wanted to go to war. How can I sit at home, watching the mothers cry on TV? How can I do nothing while the Turkish government is murdering people?'

Her stay in Şengal had motivated her so much that on her return, she and her older sister Evin (twenty-two) signed up for a PKK arms training camp in Qandil. She says, 'If there's one thing I learned in Şengal, it's that in Kurdistan, war can break out anytime, anywhere. As citizens, we need to be prepared. We have to be able to defend ourselves.' The training had not been enough to prepare her for the fighting in Şırnak.

Nothing could have prepared her for that. The YPS's weapons were nothing compared to those of the Turkish government. The fact that the YPS still managed to hold out for a comparatively long time with their Kalashnikovs, automatic weapons, hand grenades and light missiles is partly down to the layout of the districts. The streets are so narrow you can barely get through with a car, let alone armoured vehicles or tanks. On top of that, the YPS consisted mostly of local youths who knew the streets much better than the police and the army.

A STONE FOR AUTONOMY

Darya and Welat's families had barely expected to see their son and brother, their daughter and sister alive again. But Darya and Welat are not the people they once were. At the interview, Darya speaks softly, scraping the already flaky black nail polish from her nails. She won't – and can't – talk about her feelings, except to say that she doesn't sleep at night. Her sister Evin adds, 'She wants to be alone most of the time. It never used to be like that. She cries a lot.'

Welat talks about how he has changed. 'I used to enjoy my life. Not anymore. Now, I'm full of hate. Of course we, the people of Maxmur Camp, live here for a reason – the enemy has always been part of our lives – but it's different now. I lost three good friends in Şırnak. Sometimes I see their families in the street. They look at me, and I know they are wondering why I came back and their sons did not. I can hardly look them in the eye anymore.'

The difference with fighter Destan is striking. Though refugees, Welat and Darya grew up in a safe environment, a camp in which the approximately 12,000 inhabitants established self-governance, and where there is no violence. The camp is officially run by UNHCR, the UN refugee agency. Maxmur Camp is surrounded and protected by PKK bases. Öcalan's portrait is everywhere, and the refugees safeguard their own security with militias consisting of the young and the old, men and women. In Maxmur, supporting the PKK is not an act of rebellion: its society is based on the principles of the movement. Literally everyone supports the PKK.

In Şırnak, Welat and Darya witnessed violence for the first time in their lives. Destan grew up with it in Cizre. And while the shock of being faced with the reality of war still shows in Welat and Darya's eyes, Destan talks like a seasoned fighter and activist. Before going to Istanbul to study, she was involved mainly in cultural activities such as setting up language lessons. 'But if there was a demonstration or clashes with the police,' she says, 'I'd hurl stones and Molotov cocktails. Every stone, every fire bomb was carefully and deliberately aimed. One stone for education, one for my culture, one for autonomy. When the urban war broke out, there was no alternative other than to take up real weapons. As a people, we had to form a bloc of resistance against the bloodthirsty vampires. Rebellion was the only option. We had to write history. We could not bow our heads, we could not leave our friends behind in a bloodbath.'

After the war, once the government had regained control over all the districts, she left the city. Hiding in the back of a truck, she crossed the border into Iraqi Kurdistan. She was arrested and imprisoned for two months for illegal border crossing, but reached her destination, Maxmur Camp, afterwards. Now, she is waiting for a time when she'll be able to return to Turkey without running the risk of being locked up for life.

The Turkish press propagated the urban wars as a strike against terrorism. Whenever casualties were mentioned, the media published a flood of photographs showing armed youths, nipping discussions on the legitimacy of the war in the bud. The Kurdish movement, including the HDP, actively opposed the operations. No other political party or Turkish organization supported them, afraid as they were to be branded 'terrorists' themselves – that is, if they did not in fact believe that the army was justified in waging a war and made every effort to spare civilian lives.

But depicting the war purely as a struggle between the rebellious youth and the state is not entirely accurate, either. The fighters I spoke to in Maxmur told me frankly that their weapons came from the PKK. Darya had received basic training in Qandil – even if not specifically for the urban war. I asked Welat whether he felt more like a fighter or a civilian. He called the question academic, saying, 'We were both. We were Kurdish civilians defending our territory. We did so with weapons; being up against the state, we had no other choice. Does that mean I can't be a civilian?'

I ask Cemil Bayık about this too, putting it to him that some Kurds are angry because they believe the PKK brought the war to the city. 'Those Kurds have ties with the Turkish state and with [the Turkish security service] MIT,' Bayık counters. 'Of course, no one wants their house to be destroyed, no one wants to leave their home, no one wants to be murdered. They say that the residential districts wouldn't have been destroyed and that there wouldn't have been as many casualties if we hadn't brought the war to the city. But that's a hollow argument. The youths and the people joined forces to defend themselves against Erdoğan's genocidal policies. And what does the government say after murdering a child, or a pregnant woman? "We have eliminated a terrorist."'

But why would the AKP want to destroy cities? What do they gain by it? Bayık is just getting started. 'Because the cities were declared autonomous, because they were actually carrying out democratic projects,' he says, referring to the local councils operating outside state control. 'That's why the cities were targeted. And the state was able to do so because of the support of the

United States and the European Union, among others. They use the situation in the Middle East in negotiations about their own problems. The Turkish government deploys tanks and helicopters to destroy houses. The civilians have no choice but to flee, the young fighters stay behind. Then they say, "The PKK have occupied the cities, we must drive them out." No other nation will come to our defence, as actions taken by national armies are considered legitimate. Nothing the PKK does is ever considered legitimate. Tell me, what is the difference between what Saddam did in Iraq and Assad is doing in Syria, and what Erdoğan is doing in Turkey? What were we supposed to do after the government had cut off all roads to a democratic solution after the elections? Surrender? Never.'

A JUST PEACE

Surrender? Never. The struggle that has been going on since the mid-1970s cannot have been for nothing. All the sacrifices cannot have been made for nothing. Tens of thousands of people cannot have died for nothing.

Let us return to the start of the peace process, on 21 March 2013 in Diyarbakır. Two HDP parliamentarians had just read Öcalan's speech, in Kurdish and Turkish, to an audience of tens of thousands of people. With this speech, the PKK made its commitment public. The message was that from that moment on, the armed conflict would be over. The PKK would withdraw from Turkey and start to facilitate the search for a solution through negotiations rather than weapons.

I remember wandering through the crowd of people, who all seemed captivated by his words, and feeling bewildered. Bewildered, because nothing had in fact been achieved yet. I understood why Öcalan wanted to put this spin on things. Negotiations with the then prime minister Erdoğan had produced a mutual ceasefire, and now he needed the population of Turkey to enter into the spirit of the peace process. But what I did not understand was the euphoria I saw in people's faces, the spontaneous dancing that broke out everywhere, the atmosphere that seemed to suggest that the entire Kurdish question was now resolved. When I asked people how they could have gone from supporting armed conflict to not supporting it in the space of one speech, no one could give me a satisfactory answer. All they did was repeat phrases from Öcalan's speech and tell me they wanted peace at last.

That was exactly what I was worried about. 'Peace' is the magic word in Bakur. It's the one thing everyone wants. But when the government and Öcalan both talk about peace, do they mean the same thing? I doubt it. In fact, I'm sure they don't. And I'm equally sure that Turks and Kurds don't share the same views on what peace is.

When was the last time there was peace in Turkey? When it comes to the Kurdish question, many Turks consider the peace to have been broken on 15 August 1984, the day the PKK committed its first armed attack against the state. Two police stations were attacked, one near the town of Eruh in Siirt Province, and one near Şemdinli in Hakkâri Province. The date has been celebrated by the PKK ever since. On 15 August 2016, when I was attending the language camp, we were treated to a celebratory box of baklava from a nearby village, and two-litre bottles of Coke and orange soda.

According to the Turks, peace begins when the PKK violence ends. When no more soldiers return home in coffins. Incidentally, most of those soldiers are no longer the young conscripts they used to be in the 1980s and 1990s. Today, they are professional servicemen, specialized commandos. To the Turks, it doesn't matter much whether the peace is achieved by a lasting peace treaty or by the complete eradication of the PKK, although they would prefer the latter.

To the Kurds, peace means a lot more. A veteran in Kurdish politics, Ahmet Türk, often speaks of a 'just peace'. Justice. A Turkey in which not everyone has to be Turkish and a Sunni Muslim. A country in which all schoolchildren are taught in their native language and where ethnic groups are free to celebrate their own holidays, honour their heroes and learn the history of their people.

Such a situation has never existed in Turkey. For the Kurds, there has never been peace in the republic, not even before 1984. There has always been violence and genocide, there has always been assimilation and denial of their identity. No equality or justice, ever. The PKK believes that to achieve peace, the republic needs to be rebuilt from the first stone, so as to eliminate the faults in its construction.

AN INTERNATIONAL COLONY

Incidentally, this aim is not where it all started, on Monday, 27 November 1978. The house in the hamlet of Fiş in Diyarbakır Province in which the PKK was founded still exists. I visited it on 27 November 2013, nine months after the peace process began. The sound system was dismally bad. The crackling, distorted voice of MP Nursel Aydoğan echoed through the grounds, on which a couple of thousand people danced, chanted slogans, waved flags and drank tea. 'Thirty-five years ago!' Aydoğan shouted. 'Thirty-five years ago, Kurds lived without an identity of their own! But now! Now we live with our honour, our language, our identity! There are free Kurds!'

The bungalow was adorned with PKK flags. Inside the ramshackle building, the plaster was peeling from the walls. The room in which the 'founding congress' had taken place was decorated with portraits of some of its attendees at the time. Visitors took pictures of each other posing next to the portraits, flashing V signs. '*Bê serok jiyan nabe!*' – No life without the leader!

There were no police in sight that day, at least not at a visible distance from the festivities. There had been road checks on the road to Fiş, but thanks to the budding peace process, we passed them without problems.

In 1978, the aim of the PKK was an independent Kurdish nation-state. It was a time in which many African countries fought to free themselves of their European colonizers. UN treaties established every people's right to self-determination. The revolutionaries held the view that Kurdistan was also a colony, and that the oppressors – not just Turkey, but also Iran, Iraq and Syria – needed to leave.

It is interesting to note that the PKK originated in the Turkish left-wing movement in Ankara. Only after the very first years did the organization move its activities to the Kurdish south-east. Whether or not Kurdistan was a colony was a matter of lively debate on the Turkish left. The general feeling, based on theories on imperialism and colonialism, was that it was not; instead, the majority believed that Turkey was itself a 'semi-colony' held as it was in the iron grip of Western imperialism. A country that was not free itself could not, by definition, be a colonizer. Their solution for Kurdistan stems from that reasoning: if communism put an end to imperialism and freed Turkey, Kurdistan would automatically be freed as well. The followers of Öcalan, who called themselves the 'Kurdistan Revolutionaries' until the PKK was officially established, held a different view. To them, Kurdistan was a colony – an 'international colony', to be precise. In other words, a country occupied by several different nations – namely Turkey, Iran, Syria and Iraq.

That means that the PKK, at least in its founding years, was in fact a 'separatist' organization, as it was aiming for a separation from Turkey. But the group had not taken the decision to engage in armed conflict yet – on the contrary, it did everything in its power to stay under the radar as much as possible in the early years. In that regard, Öcalan had learned from the mistakes of other Kurdish groups, who he believed launched activities and openly turned against the state too soon. They were prohibited before they were well and truly established.

'Prohibited' was putting it mildly. In 1972, two leaders of the Turkish left-wing movement – well known at the time and nothing short of legendary today – were executed by the government. Deniz Gezmiş, the leader of the People's Liberation Army of Turkey (THKO), was twenty-five years old when he was hanged in Ankara in May 1972. He had been given the death penalty for intending to topple the constitutional order. Mahir Çayan of the People's Liberation Party-Front of Turkey and nine other revolutionaries were killed when they hid out with two hostages in a house in the central Turkish village Kızıldere, demanding the release from prison of Deniz Gezmiş and others. The government decided on an armed intervention. The only survivor of 'Kızıldere' was Ertuğrul Kürkçü, a member of parliament for the HDP until 2018.

Öcalan concluded from this that it would be vital to build up a strong organization before taking action. As a result, the first years were taken up mainly by living room meetings and discussion groups, recruiting new members and teaching them their ideology and tactics, as well as many self-criticism and reflection sessions. Meetings like the one in Gaziantep attended by Comrade Elif, whom I met in a women's camp in Qandil, when she was an adolescent girl in the 1970s. It laid a strong foundation for the Kurdistan Revolutionaries and later the PKK. Strong enough for the group to survive the military coup of 12 September 1980 and the unprecedented campaign of repression in the months and years that followed. Part of the leadership, including Öcalan, had fled to Syria just before the coup, and many others were locked up, some in the internationally notorious prison of Diyarbakır. Dozens of its inmates did not survive the severe torture, but it was also the birthplace of the first 'PKK Academy', where the prisoners debated, read and educated each other. Inside the prison cells, the PKK grew stronger.

In one of my interviews with Cemil Bayık I ask him about those early years. About the extreme violence that followed the military coup, and about the deaths of comrades who had been members from the very beginning such as Haki Karer, murdered as early as 1977, and Kemal Pir, who died along with three others in a hunger strike in Diyarbakır prison in 1982. If there had been a dormant will to fight the colonization of Kurdistan without violence in the PKK, the military coup put paid to it for good.

The 1980 coup wasn't the first time that a democratic route to change was cut off. Earlier coups in 1960 and 1971 had paralysed emerging democratic development. After every coup, more people dangled from the gallows, whether they were politicians, young activists or Marxist revolutionaries. Unions, political parties and cultural societies were prohibited. Everything a new generation built up after a coup was torn down again in the next one in an endless cycle of budding hope and repression.

'Do you know what Öcalan said?' Comrade Botan asks me. We're in the common room in between the men's and women's quarters of the PKK base on the outskirts of Kirkuk in Iraq. Against the wall, below portraits of Öcalan and of comrades fallen in Kirkuk, there are filthy old sofas and armchairs, sagging and pompous; we are sitting on plastic chairs, at one of the long tables, drinking tea. His bright, hazel eyes blaze as they look at me. It's so cold we're both wearing jackets and he has draped his dark green scarf loosely around his head. 'He said that even if a Kurdish state were presented to him on a silver platter, he would not accept it.'

A bit later he asks me a different, more personal question. Have I, he wants to know, ever considered joining the PKK? I answer, 'I've been writing about you for years, I'm staying with you for twelve months, so of course the thought has crossed my mind whether I should – or could – become a guerrilla fighter myself. But I don't think so. I don't want to be bound by an ideology, I cannot love a leader. It wouldn't work. I'm a journalist, that's the most important thing I identify with, and I won't give it up.'

Expecting something like this, he says, with an air of superiority, 'See, you can make that choice. We can't. We're Kurds, we must join, there is no alternative. We have to fight for our lives. You don't. You have the luxury of considering it, and deciding against it.'

He's right, there's a huge difference – but I also tell him I find his masculine stance unpleasant, even intimidating. Botan immediately admits to his 'shortcoming'. He tells me about his background. He comes from the Van region in the easternmost part of Turkey, a conservative area where traditional Kurdish clans still hold much of the power. Clans that are deeply patriarchal. Botan says, 'My clan is large and powerful, and my family occupies an influential position. I was born the eldest son of an eldest son in that family. Get it?' A little prince from the day he was born, destined to become a mighty clan leader. Botan continues, 'In mutual criticism sessions, my comrades point out to me that I tend to feel superior to the rest. I'm working on that.'

A RADICALLY DIFFERENT WAY OF THINKING

I'm staying at the Kirkuk base for a fortnight. I visit the front line against ISIS, where the PKK and the peshmerga work together keeping the jihadis at a distance. The front has been stable for months and the days are filled with keeping watch around the clock, making fires at night to stay warm and boiling tea, as well as the occasional armed clashes. On a hill overlooking a plain and two distant villages, a fighter explains to me how it works while I peer through a pair of infrared binoculars. 'The villages are still under ISIS control. The gangs [which is what ISIS fighters are customarily called] sometimes charge us over the field, but we always spot them. We shoot once to let them know we've noticed them. Then they run away. No, we don't aim at them. We don't let them provoke us. There's no need.'

I observe the group of fighters at the front as well as the ones at headquarters, over an hour's drive away from it. The men and women cook, wash, mop, get fresh supplies of clothes, scarves, shoes, fruit and vegetables and load ammunition into a truck headed for the front. Talking all the time, they pace up and down over the paved square in front of the barracks, hold educational sessions in which they read books silently or out loud, in groups or individually – mostly those of Öcalan. One day, they decide the walls of the women's quarters need a fresh lick of paint, and everyone joins in painting them.

At first, I thought Botan was the commander of the male fighters, but I was wrong. The leader turns out to be one of the least conspicuous men, a humble, quiet man in his twenties. Here, the people with the most bravado and those characteristics we call 'leadership qualities' in Western society are not given leading positions as matter of course. Just the opposite.

It comes down to this: the state is a man. Öcalan had this insight while residing in the Syrian capital Damascus in the mid-1990s. During my year with the PKK, I spoke to various guerrillas who spent several months in Syria with Öcalan. For each of them, it was a time of reading, listening, discussion and learning – and of course the regularly recurring volleyball games. Apparently, just being close to the leadership had an inspiring and strengthening effect. I am served up anecdotes on the Wise Lessons learned in Damascus. I hear the story of the young female fighter who never left the kitchen, cooking and making tea because that's what she'd been used to doing at home. Until Öcalan banned her from the kitchen and encouraged her to join the lessons and discussions. Today, the woman is the editor-in-chief of one of the party's European publications. Another one says, 'My greatest wish is to meet Öcalan again. But given the chance, I would offer my place to a comrade who's never had the good fortune of meeting him.'

But such stories don't interest me that much. I prefer concentrating on the radically different way of thinking that emerged in those years. The goal of an independent Kurdistan was dropped. Not because it was thought the aim was unfeasible or any other practical reason, but out of principle. After all, the nation-state was the source of all the misery the Kurds suffered from.

The PKK has always based its thinking on Marxism. I won't bore myself and my readers with lengthy explanations about which brand of Marxism exactly – the important thing to know is the fundamental criticism the PKK voiced on Marxism applied in practice. The USSR and other countries 'behind the iron curtain' were very far from being democratic. The workers had no say at all and the ideal of equality had vanished without trace. A similar thing happened in colonized African nations that had freed themselves of their occupiers, and where, more often than not, despotic, anti-democratic regimes took power.

In short, there was a hiatus between theory and practice.

According to the PKK's analysis, what made it go so disastrously wrong was the fact that the theory lacked a strong foundation. Since communism was created as a critique against capitalism, it is in fact rooted in the very same capitalist system it is trying to fight. To create a stronger base for the egalitarian theory, you have to look much further back in human history.

As we gather in a clearing in the woods, after the morning lesson, lunch and a dip in the pool, for the first of three lessons in Kurdish history, I have a premonition we're about to delve deep into history. One of the whiteboards has been dragged here from the open-air classroom, and a man in plain clothes (jeans and a T-shirt) is drawing shapes on it with a green marker pen. Recognizing the continents, I sit up and pay attention when he writes '10,000 years before Christ'.

Our teacher, who shook my hand with unexpected and baffling cordiality, could just as well have begun the lesson with the Big Bang theory on the origin of the universe. It wouldn't have been unusual in a PKK history lesson. But because we are given the concise version of what is usually a six-week course, the teacher skips the first part. He doesn't waste any time. Drawing an arrow from Africa to the Middle East to indicate where humankind originated and where it first migrated to, he then fast-forwards to the Neolithic Age, approximately ten millennia before the Common Era.

The Euphrates and Tigris rivers appear on the board, as well as the country between the rivers, Mesopotamia. Our teacher, K., talks about the Stone and Bronze Ages, then turns his focus mainly to religion. He poses a question about religion which he addresses to me specifically. I don't know the answer, having barely understood the question in Kurdish, and end up stammering and stuttering incomprehensibly in an effort to string together a Kurdish sentence telling him that.

I didn't take any notes during the three afternoon lessons in Kurdish history. Neither has anyone else, for that matter. The more experienced guerrillas have attended the full versions of this course before, some even more than once. The aim of the course is not learning to reproduce what the teacher says, but cherry-picking that which resonates with you at that moment, asking questions and initiating discussions you think are relevant. I try to follow the lesson as best I can and take pictures of the beautiful setting in which it is taking place, though the teacher asks me to make sure he is not recognizable on any of the photographs.

After the lessons, I approach him. I want to show him my pictures, to reassure him his face isn't visible on any of them. 'You don't remember me, do you?' he asks with a smile. I search my memory but draw a blank. We met a few years ago at a meeting of an organization in Diyarbakır, he says. It's possible, I did use to go there, but I don't remember him. He still lives in the city – a historian, he sometimes travels to Qandil to give lessons. It is not something he wants the Turkish authorities to know about, which is why he asked me not to take pictures.

I want him to tell me everything about the city, especially the old city centre Sur. We walk back to the camp, each of us carrying a couple of plastic chairs on our backs to return them to the classrooms. I hang on his every word as he talks about the parts of Sur that are still a no-go area and about how much the atmosphere of the city has changed. I want to talk with him for hours; he is my connection to the life I've had to leave behind.

In the kamelya, the tea is ready. We pour, switching back from Turkish to Kurdish, since that is the official language of the language camp. But before I know it, I've lost him to other members of the camp who have a stronger command of the language than me. My throat tightens, I fight against the tears welling up and only just succeed. Comrade Rojda, my next-tent-neighbour, comes up to me. 'Go back to your tent,' she says, 'I'll join you in a moment.'

For the first time, and the last, I cry about my deportation from Turkey. I'm sitting in the opening of my tent, Rojda crouching down next to me holding my hand. I try to explain what's wrong but she hardly speaks any Turkish. Besides, bawling about such a trivial incident feels disproportionate in the presence of this young fighter, just eighteen years old, who was forced to take up arms a couple of years ago to protect her village in Syria and who has seen dozens of her comrades being killed. She waves away my concerns, or at least the ones she can understand, as I am probably not making much sense, then tells me to go back to the kamelya in a minute and that she will have a word with Mizgîn, my language teacher.

I try to pull myself together again. I stumble downhill from my tent, to the burst in the water pipe and the piece of soap, splash icy water into my face, lather my hands and arms and rinse them, taking a couple of deep breaths. Back in the kamelya, I can see Mizgîn talking with the history teacher. He smiles at me, gets up, fetches tea and tells the people he was talking to that he is going to give me his full attention now. We talk. It is the closest I could possibly get to the life I was forced to leave behind. He knows the city better than anyone here, he knows the conglomeration of tower blocks where I rented an apartment and the park next to it, he knows the old cafe I used to enjoy sitting in, working and having a bite to eat. We find out we have shared acquaintances. We talk in Turkish while my language teacher Mizgîn turns a blind eye. K. assures me I don't have to worry about the city. It is true that a large part of Sur has been destroyed, but that doesn't mean the spirit of the struggle is history, too.

THE NEOLITHIC AGE

One thing that struck me about the Kurdish history course is that it focused primarily on the history of humankind in the part of the world that for centuries has been known as Mesopotamia. I had expected a more nationalist perspective, a narrative that would link the history of the people to that of the PKK. But the PKK itself was barely mentioned. All the conversations I had with guerrillas in the months that followed and everything of Öcalan's I read was permeated by that history. Sometimes I could hardly keep myself from laughing when I'd asked a question about PKK ideology and yet another fighter answered with, 'See, in the Neolithic Age ...'. But that's how important that period is to the PKK. It's the period their whole ideology is based on.

The religion that was often mentioned during the history course reflected Neolithic society. Crucially to the PKK, this religion mainly centred on goddesses, which leads to the conclusion that society was structured according to a matriarchal order. It was egalitarian, giving a central role to the community instead of individuals or a ruler.

There, according to the PKK, lie the roots of humanity, to which we are still connected. The further we drift away from them, the further we drift away from ourselves and the more we violate our true being. Today's society, and Western society in particular, could hardly be more removed from the living environment most suitable to human nature. Capitalism sets people against each other instead of bringing them together, its ruling class enriches itself, it impoverishes the people and destroys the earth as an ecosystem.

So where did it all go wrong? The metaphor of religion applies here too. While there were several goddesses in the Neolithic Age, they have gradually been replaced by male gods. Then those started vanishing too, until society was so hierarchical that its rulers themselves became personifications of god, just as the Egyptian pharaoh was god on earth.

The rise of monotheistic religions, I read in one of Öcalan's books, was not exactly a boon to humanity. In this book, he describes Christendom as well as Islam as essentially revolutionary religions that initially went against the spirit of their times. Unfortunately, both very quickly became useful tools in the hands of the rulers, and religion became a force against innovation and for the protection of power structures. Things got even further out of hand with the rise of capitalism and the nation-state. Those two, Öcalan writes, are inextricably linked. After all, the interests of capitalism and the nation-state are entangled, since both strengthen the powers that be. Both systems are fully aware of this and take great care never to undermine each other. They rule over the people together, while the people think they are free.

Patriarchy has supplanted Matriarchy. Today, female values are so completely out of favour that even women have started to believe they must adhere to patriarchal norms in order to be free. Women who get far in the ultimate patriarchal structures of capitalism or the nation-state are seen as examples, as trailblazers to freedom. Male and female guerrillas have asked me countless times whether the German Chancellor Angela Merkel is really considered a role model by Western women. In their view, she is a woman only in the physical sense. She has become an exponent of patriarchy, strengthening it rather than undermining it. In other words, searching for equality in oppressive systems is doomed to failure.

The PKK believe that communism never explored this issue in any depth. Since it wasn't based on the matriarchal society of the Neolithic, the liberation of women was never a central issue. There was no dictatorship of the proletariat. There was just an ordinary dictatorship, ruled very centrally by an extremely powerful government, with no respect whatsoever for people's individuality and making no visible effort to achieve real equality. The patriarchy carried out an experiment that was supposed to bring equality but never stood a chance of succeeding.

In that respect, the blunder of communism is quite similar to the blunder which, according to Öcalan's group, most Turkish left-wing parties made in the 1970s. Many leftist Turks believed that the liberation of Kurdistan would be achieved through the liberation of Turkey, while Öcalan and his followers chose to focus their efforts on the most heavily oppressed group, the Kurds. They had to be decolonized so they would be able to found a nation-state of their own.

With hindsight, this was just as big a blunder. Because, as the PKK says now, the most heavily oppressed group are not the Kurds, but women. Only when women are free can humankind be free.

Or, put more forcefully: as long as there is a single unfree woman, humankind is unfree, too. True freedom can only be achieved if we distance ourselves from patriarchal society and return to the female values on which matriarchy was based. Equality, care for the community, care for the environment. As I am told by many fighters, this insight is the outcome of the PKK's reaching maturity.

But are these all brand-new ideas? Had the things Öcalan committed to paper never occurred to anyone before? Isn't there a movement in Western feminism that has also been arguing that striving for economic equality and institutional power was not feminism but its opposite? These are all perfectly logical reactions to Öcalan's ideas, though they overlook one important point. Namely that the ideology Öcalan developed is rooted in the Middle East, and therefore fits into a Middle Eastern context first and foremost. Or rather that Westerners, who tend to feel superior to their fellow humans in the Middle East and consider Öcalan a bit of a latecomer as far as having insights goes, would do well to recognize that Western civilization is also rooted in the Middle East. At school we are taught that civilization started in ancient Greece, but that is not where Western culture originated. Its cradle lies in Mesopotamia and the surrounding lands. Without that civilization, the Greek one would never have existed, as many a PKK member will tell you and as Öcalan has written about extensively in his books. Westerners could find themselves by recognizing where their humanity is rooted.

A conversation I had about this with Comrade Batufa in a house in Maxmur Camp made a particularly strong impression on me. Its inhabitant was a female fighter who had been incurably wounded in battle and still needed regular medical attention – either at the camp clinic or at the hospital in Kirkuk. Others would occasionally stay the night, like me, or fighters who were passing through. Batufa was one of those fighters. She had come from Afrin, the westernmost Kurdish enclave in northern Syria at the time, and was on her way to Qandil. In Maxmur, she waited for a car to take her to her destination. A woman in her fifties with long, thick grey hair, she had been one of PKK's first members.

She started by explaining the Neolithic Age to me again, then we tried to find a link between that period, 12,000 years ago, and today. 'It's not that complicated, just simple biology, really,' she said. 'We all carry our ancestors' genetic material with us, no matter how long ago those ancestors lived.' 'So how can we be sure that what we carry with us is not just genetic material, but also matriarchal society's attitude to life?' I asked. 'How do we know that our craving for equality and care for the community have not been lost for good in those thousands of years, and recently under the destructive influence of capitalism, the nation-state, the patriarchy?'

Comrade Batufa asked me what I would feel if I saw a child starving to death. She asked me how it made me feel to know that now, as we spoke, Yazidi women were being sold on ISIS slave markets. 'It's unbearable,' I answered. 'Of course it is!' she said. 'But if you no longer had the seed inside of you that revolts against such consequences of the system in which you live, you would be fine with it. The fact that injustice cuts you to the quick proves that the seed is still alive in you.'

BEYOND BORDERS

These Middle Eastern roots are crucial to Öcalan's ideology. There has been a lot of talk in recent years about the national borders in the Middle East, drawn up about a century ago by Western powers, how these borders may need to be redefined. The concept which all this drawing of boundaries is based on, however, (i.e. the concept of the nation-state) is never seriously questioned. The idea that each people should have its own state originated in the West in the nineteenth century. From there, it was exported to the Middle East, but according to PKK ideology, the nation-state is an inherently alien concept in the territory where the Kurds live.

We call this territory Kurdistan, but Kurdistan is a point of view as much as a reality. The Turks refer to it as South-East Turkey, and many Kurds call it North Kurdistan. The Turks invariably call the Kurdistan Region in Iraq 'the north of Iraq', as the K-word still sticks in their throats. Yet others call the East of Turkey, which according to Kurds is part of North Kurdistan, West Armenia. Long ago, before not just the Armenians but also the Assyrians fell prey to genocide, a part of Kurdistan and Armenia was called Assyria.

And those are just the largest ethnic groups of this particular part of the Middle East. Historically, the Turks didn't even live there, they simply laid claim to it – occupied it, if you will. And what about the smaller ethnic groups in 'Kurdistan'? The Turkmens and the Arabs, to name but two? And the large monotheistic religions, all of which have historically been represented here? Not to mention the religions most people have never heard of because they have so few practitioners these days, such as Zoroastrianism? Or the religions we only know because they are threatened with extinction by a fresh genocide, like Yazidism?

The Middle East cannot be split up into nation-states. No matter where you draw the borders, communities are torn apart – just as Kurdistan was quartered when the borders of Iraq, Syria, Turkey and Iran were determined. Every time you give a country to one people, you are taking it away from another. Whenever you assign a religion to a country (there has been talk of dividing Syria and Iraq according to religious identity), another religion will suffer. Just as the Kurds and Alevis are suffering in Turkey.

What happens with the communities living outside the borders of the new country? If the Kurdistan Region in Iraq became an independent state, what would that mean for the Kurds in Turkey, Syria and Iran? Would they also be given a nation of their own? And if not, should all four parts of Kurdistan be fused together into one nation?

And what would happen to the Kurds in Istanbul, the city with the largest Kurdish population worldwide, and all the other Turkish cities where many Kurds live, such has Adana, Izmir and Mersin? What to do about the Kurds in Aleppo, Damascus and Tehran? Would they all have to move to their own country, and would the Turkmens emigrate to Turkey? Would the Arabs in the new Kurdistan have to leave the land on which they have lived for generations, just as the Turks had to leave the new Greece and the Greeks the new Turkey? Population exchange – a polite term for ethnic cleansing.

The Middle East deserves a solution that does justice to the ethnic and religious patchwork that it is. To achieve this, Öcalan's ideology advocates getting rid of the nation-state and replacing it with a system of grassroots democracy. That system has been named 'democratic confederalism'. It gives communities real sovereignty at a neighbourhood level. At a city or village level, those communities are all connected to discuss common interests. The cities are in turn connected to a canton, an administrative region, and the various cantons also meet to discuss shared interests. Revolving around diversity instead of around a single people, language, flag or religion – as the nation-state does by definition – this system guarantees that everyone's ethnicity and religion is respected. The nation-state will automatically become obsolete and only play a role on an administrative level. Old borders will fade.

In northern Syria, for example, they are already implementing this system in the cantons Cizire, Kobani and Afrin.* They? I could have written 'the Kurds', but then the system is by definition not meant exclusively for them. They initiate it, but anyone is free to participate. Everything is regulated by the 'social contract' – in other words, the constitution – jointly drawn up by the representatives of all ethnic and religious groups.

The social contract guarantees representation for all groups, and for women. There are three official languages, Kurdish, Arabic and Assyrian. The goal is to introduce the same system in Turkey. This effort is reflected in the name of the HDP's regional sister organization, the Democratic Regions Party (DBP). During the peace process, the DBP made some early attempts to implement the system by setting up neighbourhood councils, involving the people in the experiment and training men – and more importantly, women.

Incidentally, you may have heard that northern Syrian region referred to as Rojava, which means 'west' in Kurdish, i.e. West Kurdistan, just as the name 'Bakur' for the part in Turkey means 'north'. In December 2016, the joint administration decided to change the name Rojava to 'Democratic Federation of Northern Syria', two years later renaming it Autonomous Administration of North and East Syria. This is in strict keeping with the ideology,

* The canton Afrin has been occupied by Turkey since 2018. How exactly the north Syrian system works and how it will function in practice would fill another volume.

since naming a region after its dominant population would exclude other ethnicities. While the existence of the Syrian state is acknowledged, the intention is to expand the system to such a degree that it undermines the state's function as the dominant central power.

Living in Istanbul and later in Diyarbakır, I never read any of Öcalan's books, nor did I discuss his ideology in any depth during my conversations with PKK leaders. One important reason for this was that I wanted to make up my own mind about the Kurdish question, especially when I was offered a weekly column on the independent Turkish news website diken.com.tr (*diken* means 'thorn' in Turkish). I didn't want PKK ideology to cloud my thinking too much.

As a result, I continued to think in existing concepts. I knew the PKK was against a Kurdish nation-state and I had a basic understanding of why, but wasn't aware of the complete reasoning behind that fundamental choice. I used to joke that unlike the PKK, I was a separatist; especially in the summer of 2015, when the peace process failed. I could see the Turkish state and the Kurdish movement drifting ever further apart. Far from getting stuck in the twisted nationalism of the twentieth century, Erdoğan dreamed of going even further back in time, longing for a reign of Ottoman proportions. On the other side were the Kurdish movement and the HDP. The HDP is described as a 'pro-Kurdish' party by many journalists, though that doesn't do it justice. It is, more accurately, a collaboration of Kurds and Turks, supported by a wide range of groups facing discrimination and disenfranchisement, from Alevis and atheists to homosexuals and transgenders, greens and communists. Together, they fight for a joint, radically equal future. But how can two forces ever be united when they are drifting apart? A system of grassroots democracy – fine, I thought, but do it in Kurdistan, on your own turf. Nothing will ever come of it if you wait for the Turkish state to cooperate, so come on, take matters into your own hands!

What I didn't see was the wealth of diversity. People often say that the Kurds don't have a country because they are not united. To my mind, the reverse was true: the Kurds are not united because they don't have a country. Just look at Europe. Was Germany united before it was called Germany? Was Italy, before we started calling that great big boot 'Italy'? Only once you have a country can you start standardizing your language; only once you have a country, can you start teaching your own history in your own schools; only once you have a country, can you choose a national anthem, a flag, a capital city. Only once you have a country can you start forging unity.

Today, I wonder how many histories were lost the moment the Italian nation-state was born, how many languages spoken in what was not yet called Germany have long since been forgotten, how many cultures have been banished to the margins of what we now call the Netherlands. Far from suffering from a lack of unity, the Kurds have always kept their cultural, religious and linguistic diversity exactly because they never had a state of their own. With the emergence of a Kurdish state, this wealth would irrevocably be lost.

As the United Nations made very clear in two important treaties over half a century ago, all peoples have a right to self-determination. But it isn't written anywhere that self-determination must include having 'a nation-state of your own'. It can actually come in many guises, of which the nation-state may well be the least practical, or the least humane. It is the most effective way of ensuring that the right to self-determination of one people becomes the oppression of another.

A STREET CORNER

'But having a nation-state is the only way of being heard internationally,' I'm often told, on social media for instance. 'Without one, you don't have a seat at the UN or any other international intergovernmental organization.' It's the same outrage – often bordering on rage – I get from people who fling in my face that we might as well abolish the Netherlands while we're at it, along with every other European nation. No more nation-states for anyone!

The PKK fighters hold a fundamentally different view. They aren't interested in having a say in cooperations of nation-states that mutually reinforce each other. They aren't interested in the Netherlands or any other country, or in Europe, or even in Kurdistan. That is to say, they are of course interested in Kurdistan, but as a geographic area and as a people, not as a piece of land with a border around it. They are interested in a vision of the future in which there is no place for expressions of nationalism or mechanisms of exclusion and oppression.

'But do you really believe we will ever live in a world without nation-states or capitalism?' I asked Comrade Botan during our talk in that cold, bare room at the Kirkuk base. He shot me a piercing look. 'No, I don't believe it, I know it,' he answered. 'And do you know how I know? Because the current system is not sustainable. The essence of humanity is incompatible with capitalism and the nation-state. Like any other living organism, a society is subject to evolution. If it doesn't adapt optimally to its surroundings, it doesn't survive. Do you believe the capitalist nation-state is capable of developing in a way that will harmonize with humanity, with nature, instead of destroying it like it is doing now? I don't. Sooner or later, it will collapse, that much is certain. That is why we must build up a system now that does do justice to the roots of human civilization. Founding a Kurdish nation-state would be counterproductive. We need to really become one, not as a people, but as many people.' Did he think it would happen in his lifetime? 'Not in my lifetime, or in yours,' Botan said. 'Perhaps the PKK won't even exist anymore by the time the capitalist system collapses. But the foundations of what comes after it, that's what we should be working on now.'

Yet thinking about it more deeply and talking to other fighters, something keeps bothering me about the PKK's relationship with the people of Kurdistan. The word that was constantly on the lips of all the hundreds of people I spoke to in Kurdistan, whether they lived in towns or villages, was 'peace'. I've never heard the guerrillas talk about peace. All that matters to them is the struggle against the capitalist, patriarchal nation-state.

When I ask Comrade Hêlîn about this in the language camp, she says, 'Peace is a concept that was developed by dominant forces to mislead societies and prevent rebellion. I can say this to you, but not to a mother in Bakur. She wants a quiet life without violence. How could I say to her that the word peace is meaningless? I don't strive for peace, I strive for freedom. The HDP in Turkey strives for native language education, for acknowledgement of Kurdish culture, for a constitution that recognizes all identities. A worthy goal of course, but in essence it is all about the ideology, the history, the conditions that have led to our current lack of freedom and equality. The core of this lies in the capitalist system, and that's what I'm fighting.'

The average Kurdish PKK supporter in Cizre, in Roboskî, in Diyarbakır, has learned not to find the nation-state a desirable system. That Kurd will rave about all ethnic groups and religions in Turkey living together. And the wish is genuine. At the same time, countless other people have told me about their dream of a country of their own. They are as patient as the guerrillas, knowing they will never live in an independent Kurdistan. But in the dream shared by these men and women, their grandchildren's grandchildren might just live in this ideal world someday. In all my travels, I've hardly ever heard the locals mention the crumbling foundations of the capitalist nation-state.

It raises the question: to what extent is the PKK still in touch with the people? Of course the fighters themselves come from the people. There are hardly any families in Kurdistan – at least, in the part of it that lies in Turkey – who don't have any members that have joined the PKK or been killed fighting. In that sense, the slogan I've heard so often at demonstrations, funerals and political gatherings, '*PKK halktır halk burada*' ['The PKK is the people and the people are here'], is true. But when a young man or woman takes the decision to go to the mountains and become a fighter, the ties with their people are severed to some extent. For example, one guerrilla told me about her bond with her family, 'My family is important to me because it is where I come from. But once you join the PKK, you leave them behind at a street corner, as it were. You move on.'

The physical separation is the beginning of a life in a completely new system in which education comes first, second and last. In the early years especially, even the first decade, a fighter has very little contact with the people. I was struck by how many young fighters I met in the army bases – men and women in their twenties, even teenagers. The age at which you get an education and you're physically fit and strong enough for the armed struggle. The age at which you are eased away from the system you came out of.

Your comrades become your new family. You die for them without hesitation. It is the other side of the coin of severing ties with 'the people': Öcalan's fighters want to lay down their lives for each other, they want to go to the front to help, and to continue the fight of the many who have fallen. Herein lies much of the strength of the fighters who let Öcalan's ideology lead them in their struggle. I found out just how deep that desire runs in a convalescence home for the wounded in Heseke, northern Syria, where fighters injured at the front north of Raqqa received treatment. Comrade Harun's face was covered in small wounds, his arm was bandaged and his foot was half in bits, but he couldn't wait to get back to the front. Fighter Agit (20) was in the building next door, the home for the disabled. A commander was trying to persuade him to accept the organization's offer of doing the internal PKK medical training. 'You can't go back to the front,' she told him, not for the first time. Losing two fingers in the battle of Kobani was no obstacle to a life at the front. Losing his lower right leg to a landmine at the Raqqa front, however, was. But Agit flatly refused to train as a doctor. He wanted to go back to the front, back to his comrades.

The older guerrillas, the experienced fighters, are the ones who usually take on the non-military tasks. Since the PKK started focusing on creating a system of 'democratic confederalism' instead of an independent Kurdistan, the range of these duties has widened considerably. Committees have been set up for all kinds of issues that are important for laying a new foundation. Economic committees develop and set up the theoretical and practical framework of a cooperative economy, and educational committees establish and innovate an education system in the north Syrian cantons. There are ecological committees, women's committees, diplomatic groups which spread all over the globe, as well as cultural committees with sub-committees for language and literature, music, and so on. Those experienced guerrillas are so well versed in the theory and so far removed from the system the rest of the world lives in, they are not easily fazed. I met some on several occasions, and without exception, they were unbending, unflappable, disciplined, determined, patient, friendly, smiling men and women who would never raise their voices and who don't develop deep friendships with ordinary mortals.

These older fighters were also the ones who acknowledged that there is in fact a rift between the people and the PKK. Most young fighters denied it, claiming that such a rift was impossible – because, 'Comrade Avaşîn, we are the people'. But during a long conversation on a foothill of Mount Şengal, a thirty-year-old I was talking to pondered the question before saying, 'Perhaps you're right. But isn't this the way it should be? We are the people, but at the same time we're trailblazers, the ones who have developed a vision of the future.' He also stated that the fact that the people are not properly instructed in PKK ideology was, in his view, a 'shortcoming' that left a lot of room for improvement on an educational level.

I can't get the urban wars out of my mind. The dozens of young fighters who died; the cities, so dear to me, that were destroyed. Co-leader Cemil Bayık told me in an interview that the PKK's only mistake had been not sending more guerrillas to the cities to help the young fighters. Other fighters point out similar 'shortcomings': the PKK should have supplied more weapons and trained the people properly. According to the PKK, the urban wars themselves and the fact they got so disastrously out of hand were not the organization's responsibility.

But the people's support of the PKK is neither absolute nor unconditional. Rıza Altun, member of the executive committee of the KCK (the Kurdish umbrella organization that covers the PKK, with Öcalan as its honorary chairman), told me this in an interview in the early spring of 2014. At the time, just before the local elections, the peace process was still on track. It was obvious that the state was not making a serious effort to find a solution, but giving up on the peace process was not an option for the PKK. I didn't see the point. Why carry on a peace process that is so obviously futile? 'You might think like that as a human being, as an individual,' Altun said, 'but not in politics and not in a mass movement, because then you are an actor in a society. If the peace process is ever broken off, it has to be perfectly clear to everyone whose fault that was and why the ceasefire did not last. Society might blame us, and that is why we must always be aware of its sensitivities.'

And that, I think, is where things went so horribly wrong in the urban wars.

Portrait

Comrade Bêrîtan is Immortal

'Feel the wind,' Comrade Bêrîtan says. She's standing on the tip of a rock, arms spread wide and eyes shut. 'I've loved doing this ever since I was a child. It feels like flying.' Her younger comrade doesn't have the courage. Holding on to her, Bêrîtan takes her to the edge. 'Close your eyes.' She does. Bêrîtan takes her by the wrists and slowly spreads her arms. A smile gradually appears on the face of the young fighter. Kurdistan stretches out around the two women.

Did this scene ever really take place in Bêrîtan's life? It's very possible. At any rate, it is perfect material for Bêrîtan, the film that Halil Dağ made on Bêrîtan's years as a guerrilla. On the tip of the rock with Kurdistan at her feet, she was free.

I've never met Comrade Bêrîtan. She joined the PKK in 1990, when she was nineteen. She was born in Bingöl Province but is known in the PKK as a woman from Dersim, where her parents came from. It means she was an Alevi Kurd. To Kurds, Dersim is inextricably linked with the large-scale slaughter the Turkish government perpetrated there in 1937 and 1938, killing tens of thousands of civilians. The state justified these acts by declaring that Dersim was 'rebellious', and that this rebellion needed to be crushed. In reality, all the Dersim Kurds did was refuse to become Turkish, and Sunni. The Turkish Father of the Nation Atatürk decided the province needed to be 'civilized'. He visited the province in 1937, a year before his death, to inspect the progress of the 'civilization offensive'. The resistance leader Seid Riza had been hanged shortly before Atatürk's arrival.

Today, Dersim is a symbol of resistance and a freer way of life than that in other parts of Kurdistan, where traditional Sunni Islam had – and still has – a greater influence. It is no coincidence that the first female PKK member Sakine Cansız came from Dersim. Comrade Bêrîtan was a rebel, even within the PKK. While the liberation of women is at the heart of the movement today, that wasn't the case yet in the early 1990s.

Bêrîtan took a stand against the patriarchal mentality of some of her male comrades. Her life forms the most important storyline of the film, though a second one depicts the struggle between dedication and betrayal. At least, that was my interpretation after watching Bêrîtan in the semi-subterranean living room of the language camp in the Qandil Mountains.

The story is set against the backdrop of the political situation in Iraqi Kurdistan in the early 1990s. The dictator Saddam Hussein was still in power in Baghdad. The Kurds had achieved de facto autonomy in 1991, under the protection of the Americans. The two most important leaders of the Kurdistan Region, Jalal Talabani of the Patriotic Union of Kurdistan (PUK) and Masoud Barzani of the Kurdistan Democratic Party (KDP), flew to Istanbul in the same year to forge alliances with the Turkish state. They spoke with the head of the Turkish security service MIT, among other people. Talabani and Barzani wanted sovereignty in 'their' territory, which was prevented by the presence of the PKK in the mountains on the Turkish border. Their wish dovetailed conveniently with the Turkish aim to remove the PKK from the mountains, and a collaboration was forged.

In early October 1992, a couple of days after the PKK had

carried out a large-scale attack in Hakkâri Province in which twenty Turkish soldiers had been killed, they struck. About 5,000 peshmerga launched an attack on the PKK camps, after which the Turkish army started bombing the area. The PKK defended itself, but as the film also shows, some of the commanders wanted to surrender to the KDP. One of them was Abdullah Öcalan's younger brother Osman. He and a delegation went to talk with the KDP to discuss a ceasefire and surrender. Other PKK fighters rejected the agreement. They would fight to the bitter end.

And that is just what Comrade Bêrîtan decides to do. Not that it is a given. At first, the male commanders won't even allow her unit to join the fighting at the front. But she steps out of the back row – today, the women always stand in the first rows – to go to the front and speak. She convinces her male comrades that in fact the women were the ones who needed to take the lead in the struggle for freedom.

Earlier in the film, we watch Bêrîtan's struggle to pry her sisters free from the patriarchal traditions they adhered to. In one highly symbolic scene, the women cover their heads when male fighters approach. Bêrîtan tells them this isn't necessary in the PKK and gently pulls the headscarves from her fellow fighters' heads. All except one allow it.

The filmmaker Halil Dağ, a Kurd from Germany, was a guerrilla himself. In the early 1990s, he was working as a photographer for the first Kurdish TV station that started broadcasting from Europe, MedTV. He was sent to work as a cameraman and reporter from Damascus, where Öcalan lived. Eventually, he decided to join the PKK, where he continued to develop as a photographer and cameraman and started shooting his own films. *Bêrîtan* was released in 2006. It was to be his last film – he was killed in a battle between the PKK and the Turkish army in April 2008.

As a guerrilla, Dağ was able to film inside PKK camps and PKK territory, using his comrades as actors – watching the film a second time later, I suddenly recognize Comrade Nuhayla, whom I met in Kirkuk, as one of the fighters in Bêrîtan's unit. The scenes of the war and of daily life in the camps are true to life.

The peshmerga, supported by Turkish fighter planes, eventually prove too powerful. We see Bêrîtan losing comrades as they are slowly surrounded. Bêrîtan is forced to leave her position. She climbs higher into the mountains to be able to defend herself to the last. Then she discovers that the magazine of her Kalashnikov is empty and she doesn't have a spare one – she's unarmed. In a fit of frustration, she smashes the weapon to pieces against the rocks. She climbs higher, until she can't go on. She seems to waver – what next?

Then she hears a voice. A voice that is speaking to her softly. She turns around. A peshmerga soldier is approaching her slowly. He tells her not to be afraid, that he won't do her any harm and that the peshmerga won't torture her. The battle is over, she will have to surrender. But surrender is not an option for Bêrîtan. She doesn't hesitate for a second. At the top of the rock with all of Kurdistan at her feet, she feels strong. She leaps, jumping to her death. Her loud 'Tee-lee-lee-lee-lee!', the Kurdish battle cry that symbolizes feminine power, echoes around the mountains.

Many of the guerrillas fighting today were not even born at the time that Bêrîtan made herself immortal. But all of them, the women especially, feel indebted to her. Öcalan wrote about her, emphasizing that her courageous act symbolized everything the

PKK stands for. He wrote, 'She did not commit suicide, she set a benchmark for freedom.' Bêrîtan's principles are still essential to the fighters led by Öcalan's ideology. You fight to the bitter end. Surrender is not an option.

Knowing this helps in understanding some of the decisions the movement makes in the war. Take Afrin, the Kurdish enclave in north-west Syria that was attacked by Turkey in January 2018, and was eventually conquered in March. Some analysts said the YPG and YPJ didn't stand a chance against such dominant opponents, and that they would do better to surrender so as to limit their losses and possibly prevent Turkey from advancing further. These analysts have either never heard of Bêrîtan, or not understood her properly. To the Öcalan fighters, Bêrîtan is alive. She only dies if they stop following in her footsteps.

CHAPTER 4

Out of the War

In the field between our two tents, Comrade Rojda and I sit beneath the walnut trees on a piece of cardboard that used to be a box for bags of washing powder. She is showing me photographs she carries with her at all times. Among the group of fighters in the pictures, I recognize a much younger version of her in uniform, mostly smiling and looking proud. She points to each of her comrades in turn, almost all of them. '*Şehit ket, şehit ket, şehit ket, şehit ket.*' Martyred, martyred, martyred, martyred. Hang on, she has more photos to show me, and she grabs her diary. Martyred, martyred, martyred. She has drawn brightly-coloured flowers and hearts around some of the photos, and written short poems beside them. 'Oh, Comrade Avaşîn,' she sighs. 'My heart aches.'

She is eighteen now, and we've just met in the language camp where both of us are spending the summer of 2016. We are in Qandil, and the photographs, about three or four years old, were taken in the north Syrian Serekaniye region, just on the Turkish border. A minor, she went into combat because her own life and that of her family depended on it. The area surrounding Serekaniye has been stable for some years now, but at the time, between late 2012 and the spring of 2013, the Kurds were fighting against the Free Syrian Army, the government army of Assad and Al Nusra (Al Qaida's Syrian branch). The fighting got so close that Comrade Rojda was literally defending her home against the various hostile forces.

After the battle of Serekaniye, her commander sent her back home. Her parents almost died of happiness when their daughter returned unharmed. But Rojda could not re-adapt to her former life – her heart was with her fallen comrades. She wanted to get to know the Kurdish movement better, on and off the battlefield. We leaf through her photo album. There's a picture of her standing next to her father, who is draped in a long, sandy brown tunic and is wearing a checked red and white scarf around his head. She's looking up at him. 'Do you know what I was thinking at that moment, Comrade Avaşîn?' she asks. 'How am I going to tell my father I'm not staying? That I'm leaving to join the PKK and not coming back?'

She told him that same day. The news broke her father's heart, but he supported her decision. Her mother cried, Rojda didn't. She spent one last night at home before being picked up by an open-backed van that headed towards the Iraq border. 'I only started to cry once I was in the van. I didn't want to make things any more difficult for my parents, you know? I cried all day.' She was sixteen.

Until the first year of the Syrian civil war in 2011, Rojda had felt more Arab than Kurdish. For all she knew, the Syrian President Assad was her leader, just as she'd been taught. Neither her teachers at school nor her parents ever told her she was Kurdish. 'We spoke Arabic at home. Assimilation, Comrade Avaşîn,' she says. Even before the war came so close to her village, she'd met fighters who followed Öcalan's ideology. She had sometimes gone to meetings in Serekaniye, where she first learned Kurdish and which awakened her to her Kurdish identity. With the battle fast approaching, she had also undergone her first basic military training there. It was there she had met the people she was to lose again so soon.

On arriving in Qandil, she completed the '*servanên nû*' training for 'new fighters'. She had of course been in combat before, but the first training covers not just army skills but also PKK ideology, and there had been very little time for ideology during the fighting in Syria. In various base camps in the mountains, she took her first lessons in Kurdish history and the history of women before eventually enrolling in a language course. There, she is learning to read and write her own language. An avid learner, she makes lists of words in her diary. She asks me for Turkish and English words, laughing as she jots down Dutch words phonetically in Arabic writing. *Bloem*, *hart*, *water*, *zon* – flower, heart, water, sun.

Where will she go after the language course? 'Bakur,' she says without a moment's hesitation. To Turkey, in other words, to fight the Turkish army. 'My heart is of course in Rojava,' she says. 'But I want to explore the other parts of Kurdistan now.' She knows there's practically no chance that the organization will select her for armed combat at this stage. She probably has several more years of education to go, which will help her process her experiences and give them meaning. 'Life is hard, Comrade Avaşîn,' she says. 'But let me tell you, joining the PKK was the best decision I ever made.'

Finding fighters who joined the PKK, YPG or YPJ as minors is easy. There were five of them among the fourteen participants of the language camp alone. Rojda took up arms at fourteen. Mizgîn, the teacher of my language class who's now in her late twenties, was twelve. Comrade Hêlîn, also pushing thirty, was thirteen; Arjîn, who's just come of age, joined a couple of years ago and Comrade Hesen, in his mid-thirties, was sixteen. I met several underage fighters while camping out in a cave in the Qandil Mountains for a week. Many of the adult fighters waging battle at the Raqqa front had joined as minors, and there were minors at the military bases surrounding the Maxmur refugee camp.

'Child soldiers!' predominantly Turkish Twitter users snap back at me whenever I tweet anything about minors in the PKK. I never use the term 'child soldier', which they see as a classic example of denial. They like using it, as it evokes exactly the associations they want to link to the PKK: abduction and coercion, drugs and brainwashed children, estranged from their families, mercilessly wielding machine guns and spreading death and destruction.

But this association is not the only reason I find the term problematic. The murderous adolescent, abducted and drugged by unscrupulous commanders, is not the only true image of child soldiers – in fact, the definition of a child soldier is neither more nor less than an underage fighter. Rojda was undeniably a child soldier in the YPJ, and by no means the only one fighting in the YPJ and the YPG during the Syrian civil war. Since then, the Kurdish forces in Syria have set things right, and no more children have been sighted at the front. Inside the PKK, child soldiers have been practically non-existent for much longer.

There are children, yes. In fact, from the dozens of interviews, short conversations and countless encounters I've had with refugees during my year spent with Öcalan's armed followers, I would even go so far as to conclude that a life as a guerrilla fighter is far from an unusual choice for a minor to make. Fighters who were over twenty when they joined often declare with a sigh, 'I joined late. Such a shame.'

What would have become of Comrade Rojda if she hadn't taken up arms? There is no telling now, of course, but the outlook for women in the Syrian civil war was pretty bleak. She might have fled, like hundreds of thousands of others. She might have survived her flight and ended up in Turkey, where she would now be trying to make ends meet by working in a sweatshop, or she may have been married off and become someone's second or third wife. Not much chance of her having made it to Europe. She would more likely have drowned in the Mediterranean on her way there. Perhaps she would not even have got as far as Turkey through the violent battle, or past the bullets of Turkish border patrols.

Rojda isn't the only one who makes me wonder what alternative lives she might have had if she hadn't joined the fighting forces in Syria and later the PKK. I've wondered the same about every fighter I met who was either underage or had joined up as a minor.

The boy visiting the language camp, for instance, who could not be more than fifteen or sixteen years old. He was accompanied by an older fighter who was introducing him to life in the mountains by taking him to various camps. He was wearing a brand new guerrilla uniform with a Kalashnikov slung over his shoulder. His movements seemed uncertain at times and there was down on his upper lip. I didn't get the chance to interview him – before I knew it, I saw the pair of them climb up the path, out of the camp, and disappear among the trees – but someone from the camp told me he was from Yüksekova, where he'd been a member of the YPS youth group. I have no way of finding out whether that's true, but he wouldn't be the first YPS fighter who decided to leave the city. Who chose life as a fighter over an almost inevitable 'martyrdom' in the YPS.

I met Evîndar in a base in Kirkuk, Iraq. On the verge of adulthood, she had been a fighter for several years. In Kirkuk she had not been at the front but at headquarters, many miles behind it. She told me she had first decided to join the PKK when a cousin of hers died as a guerrilla. Her story left no doubt about what her life would have been like had she stayed in Şırnak, the city she grew up in: she would have been married by now, possibly with children.

'My parents,' Evîndar confides in me, 'had often told me I would marry my cousin, who was five years older than me. I used to think they were joking, until they suddenly started to plan my wedding in earnest. The marriage had been decided at my birth. It was not what I wanted at all, but I had no say in the matter. Neither did my mother. My father laid down the law.'

Evîndar's cropped black hair is almost completely hidden under a round, dark blue cap. She's short, around 1.60 metres, and slender. Her small head is perfectly round. There's a hole in her skull. 'Feel it,' she says, guiding my hand to a spot above her right ear. I touch it gingerly. The hole is a couple of square centimetres in diameter, and besides tissue, skin and hair, there's nothing there. 'I have to keep my head warm to protect the spot. If I don't, I risk becoming paralysed, the doctor said.'

She was injured in Bakur. She had joined up during the peace process and wanted to stay when war broke out again, but because she was a minor, her commander insisted she go to a base camp just over the border in Iraq. Before she could leave, however, she was hit in the head by a piece of shrapnel in an attack by the army.

And I will never forget Comrade Hira, the young fighter sitting across from me in the car (a fortified van past its prime with seats placed with their backs to the walls so the passengers faced each other, tinted windows, plastic ceiling ornaments and teddies dangling from hooks with 'I love you' written on their bellies) on the drive from an army base near Heseke to a base at the Iraqi border. From there, I was to travel on to Şengal the next day. She asked me to guess her age. Before answering, I wanted to know how many years ago she'd become a fighter. 'Eleven years ago,' she answered. 'In that case, I'd say you were about twenty-seven or twenty-eight, but you look younger,' I mused. 'I'm twenty-two,' she said with an almost triumphant laugh.

So Hira had been eleven. Eleven years old, when she, the youngest of her family, left her home in Rojhilat (Iraqi Kurdistan) with her father, mother and five siblings and set out for the Qandil Mountains. Her father and one of her brothers had had a run-in with the law because of their political activities. They'd been accused of terrorism, which in Iran constitutes the offence of 'enmity against God'. The penalty it carries is merciless: death. 'During our first weeks in the PKK, we stayed together as a family,' Hira told me. 'Then we were placed in different camps for training and education, according to our ages.' Her mother and father became commanders in Qandil and Serekaniye respectively, and her siblings dispersed to camps all over Kurdistan doing a range of different tasks. 'One of my brothers became a martyr in the battle of Kobani. The rest of us are all still alive.'

My view on minors joining the PKK has been coloured by the years I reported from Turkey and Bakur, where I spoke with families whose sons, daughters, aunts and uncles had joined the PKK. What I witnessed there was mainly pain and grief. Old grief, about young men and women who had joined up in the 1980s and had never been seen or heard of since. They are probably lying buried somewhere under a tree or near a river, and no living soul remembers the exact location. Sometimes, the grief I saw was raw and desperate, for young sons and daughters who had disappeared one day and about whose whereabouts the PKK would say nothing more than to confirm soon after that they had become guerrilla fighters. Some of these adolescents represented broken promises. A young medical student in his final year, almost a doctor, about to earn back what his drudging parents had invested in him. Suddenly, he was gone.

I remember a conversation I had in the summer of 2013 in Roboskî, the village where no fewer than thirty-four boys and men were killed in an air raid by the Turkish army on 28 December 2011 (I wrote about it in my previous book, *The Boys Are Dead*). Nineteen of the victims were underage. Among those minors were the fifteen-year-olds Savaş, Bilal, Muhammed and Orhan. They were bombed on the border between Iraq and Turkey while smuggling cigarettes, tea and petrol – one of the few ways the villagers could make a living.

The four boys had been Bedel Encü's best friends. I visited his family in the summer of 2013. On the evening of the bombing, the family had been at home. Suddenly they heard and felt an almighty bang. Bedel started shaking like a leaf, as if he'd instantly grasped what had happened – while gunshots weren't that unusual in the area near the Iraqi border, such booming explosions were. Thirty-four casualties, including his best friends. His oldest brother Kadri (twenty-three) told me, 'The five boys did everything together. They went on picnics, or to the internet café. They had plans for the next day, too.'

According to Bedel's mother Beydin, Bedel increasingly stayed indoors after the bombing and his friends' death. He went quiet. Then one day, over a year after the tragedy, he disappeared. The family were at a site close to the border, fetching sand to build a house when he took to his heels. Some time later, they got a PKK message through the grapevine that he had joined the organization.

'Had he mentioned wanting to go to the mountains?' I asked his family. 'No,' Kadri answered, 'it's not something you talk about. You just go.' 'That morning, he was even quieter than usual,' Bedel's mother added. They didn't seem too worried about the baby of the family becoming a fighter. Kadri: 'We know who he's with. He gets psychological support. It's provided for everyone who joins the PKK, as everyone has to leave their family behind. No one finds that easy.' But shortly afterwards, his mother Beydin tells me about her sense of loss. 'I often cry when I'm at home,' she said. 'Being there makes me think of him, and I sometimes think I can hear his voice.' Kadri talked to his youngest bother in a dream. 'I asked him, 'Bedel, are you coming back home?' He answered, 'No, I'm not leaving this path.'

Bedel's story stayed with me. When I prepared to immerse myself in the PKK for a year, I resolved to keep an eye out for him. Unfortunately, I had no idea what his nom de guerre was, and the fighters don't know each other's real names. I had a hunch that his surname might be Roboskî, however, as many guerrillas call themselves by their native town or region. And ever since the bombing, the name Roboskî has been highly charged. I was also curious to find out about the psychological support that his family said Bedel would receive in the PKK. In my Western wisdom, I thought I could understand Bedel's choice of becoming a guerrilla, but also believed you can't run from your trauma, as you take it with you wherever you go.

The thought often struck me during conversations with Comrade Rojda, too. Whenever she walked past my tent, sighing, 'Oh, Comrade Avaşîn, life is painful.' Whenever she played music and skipped the cheerful tunes while singing along from the bottom of her heart to the slow songs with lyrics about lost comrades, the imprisonment of the leader and the blood-soaked Kurdish soil.

How could Rojda come to terms with her horrific experiences, her loss, her pain?

It slowly dawned on me. This, exactly this, is how Rojda comes to terms with her past. By no longer suppressing her own identity but claiming it, learning its history, and expressing it by learning the Kurdish language. By not resigning herself to watching groups like ISIS, Al Nusra and the Syrian and Turkish armies trampling her people underfoot, but by defending herself, her family, her village and her people. Not just by taking up arms, but by educating herself. Investing in the future is her way of fighting against the denial and destruction. I don't think anything could make her stronger than this. In the PKK, you don't need therapy. Being in the PKK is the therapy.

From my first weeks at the PKK until my final weeks at the YPG and YPJ in Syria, fighters were always keen to teach me how to use a Kalashnikov. I refused categorically, even during arms trainings for guerrillas I attended and despite their repeated insistence that there were all kinds of dangers lying in wait in the mountains that I would have to defend myself against, including wild boar attacks. I reasoned that since I'd never be on my own here, I'd be fine.

Incidentally, watching the arms training was fascinating. In September 2016, I attended a session in the middle of nowhere high up in the Qandil Mountains, a car journey over roads built by the PKK and a steep climb up a mountain where civilians never came. The view of our surroundings was crystal clear – in the distance, beside Lake Dukan, which lay glittering in the sunshine, we could see the town of Ranyê and the PKK-controlled mountain range it bordered on.

After a breakfast of tea, homemade bread, olives and a substance that the labels on the small round tins claimed was chicken, all kinds of weapons were taken apart and reassembled underneath the trees. One of the fighters was squatting next to a rug, a blue scarf with a garish floral print tied around his eyes, calmly taking apart a *doshka*, a heavy machine gun. He laid the parts in an orderly row and then proceeded to put the weapon back together in reverse order. Blindfolded – as of course you need to be able to use weapons not just during the daytime, but at night as well.

In the evening there was target practice. The loud bangs of the guns thundered through the mountains. There was a large fire, which surprised me because of the risk it posed, but the guerrillas said they weren't expecting any air raids or even drones that night. There was dancing. I was sitting on a tree trunk with a fighter, a second one brought us tea made in a blackened kettle on a small side fire.

The further west I went with the PKK and later the YPG and YPJ, the more often fighters urged me to learn how to use a Kalashnikov. In Şengal, I was taken to my next base near Skinî, south of Mount Şengal, by two men. At the time, this was the last village before ISIS territory began. 'Imagine we have an accident here,' one of them said. 'I die, my comrade is seriously injured and you're standing here on the side of the road. Just then, fighting erupts, and soon a group of ISIS fighters are coming towards you. There are two Kalashnikovs on the ground, but you can't defend yourself because you haven't learned how. What good will that pen of yours be to you then?' He was referring to the ballpoint pen I'd jokingly brandished when he'd asked me where my weapon was. None, of course, I had to admit.

But even so, I said, it is not my place as a journalist to carry a weapon. My self-defence consists of my estimating the risks before starting on a story or report, making note of the local circumstances, working with dependable people and wearing my helmet and flak vest. Admittedly, I didn't always manage to stick to that last point during that year. In Iraq, I had both garments with me all the time, but I had to leave the flak vest behind when I went to Syria as it was far too heavy to lug with me on the hike across the border. I had doubts about the helmet, too, but ended up stuffing it to the bottom of my rucksack.

In Syria, near Ain Issa north of Raqqa, I finally relented. One female fighter after another voiced her amazement at my lack of Kalashnikov skills, with ISIS so close by. 'It's not about getting you to fight, Comrade Avaşîn,' one of them said. 'It's about self-defence. In Kurdistan, in the Middle East, you just can't go without. This is a dangerous place.' That's when I asked myself: what was my real reason for objecting? Why would a journalist not have the right to defend herself if necessary, like any other human being? Of course I didn't need to be armed in the Netherlands, or while working as a journalist in south-east Turkey. But here, where ISIS was sometimes literally little more than a stone's throw away?

Commander Delîla instructs a young fighter to teach me how to take the gun apart and reassemble it. She gives me an expert demonstration. The various parts clicking, snapping and locking into place make a satisfying noise. After three tries, I've mastered the correct order. Target practice will have to wait a few days longer. The village we're in has been declared a military area and there are no civilians here, but the place is too cluttered to practise safely. Once we're in the next village, where the houses are further apart, there's hardly anyone in the streets and there aren't any lines of refugees coming from Raqqa, Delîla motions me to follow her. This village is a military area too. ISIS have only just been flushed out.

Delîla is excited. 'Take your camera along so I can take a

picture of you shooting!' she urges. I tell her that sounds like an extremely bad idea to me. If you want to avoid a photograph being unexpectedly taken out of context and going viral on Twitter or Facebook, or appearing on the front page of Turkish newspapers, there's really just one strategy: make sure that photo doesn't exist.

We select a half-crumbled, low wall surrounding a house. Delîla goes up to it and scratches a target on it with a stone. We're standing about 200 metres away from it. She shows me how to position myself, takes aim and fires. I stuff earplugs into my ears, take the weapon from her and do the same. Keeping the crosshairs of the sights on the target is difficult, especially if you wait too long – I hesitate because I'm afraid of the recoil. Once I do pull the trigger, it isn't actually too bad. And I hit the mark. My second shot hits the target too, closer to the middle this time.

Delîla wants to explain something to me, so I let the gun dangle at my side. She reacts immediately. 'Not like that! Always secure the safety catch first, always, never forget,' she says calmly. She wants to make it more challenging. Taking the gun from me, she shows me a stable squatting position. I take the weapon back, squat, push down the safety catch and shoot – it fires three times. Delîla grins. 'You've turned on automatic fire, that way it shoots several times.' The holes in the wall surrounding the target are clearly visible. I push the catch down into semi-automatic position. I take my position for the last round: flat on my stomach. All things considered, hitting the target is dead easy – if you're shooting at a wall 200 metres away in a deserted, relatively safe village accompanied by an experienced fighter, I'd like to add.

I haven't needed to defend myself a single time for real, and have never so much as touched a Kalashnikov after my single shooting lesson. But when it comes to self-defence, I have noticed a distinct parallel between individuals and the people. Just like the young Rojda's human self-defence mechanism kicking in when her native village was attacked and her family threatened, society itself – which is, after all, a living organism too – has a self-defence mechanism of its own. In fact, self-defence is central to PKK ideology, as a legitimate reason for using violence. Fighters do not launch unprovoked attacks, and expecting them to give up their right to defend themselves is equally unthinkable.

I'm reminded of some Yazidi women I saw in a mourning tent in the Şengal refugee camp. They urged the PKK, YBŞ and YJŞ to go on the attack instead of always warding off attacks by others, and if they were killed in the process, then so be it. The fighters explained to them that that went against PKK ideology. There are two wars. One that needs to be fought with weapons, like the battle against ISIS, and another that is waged with education, organization, raising awareness and mental power. The latter war is the one the PKK mainly focuses on. Weapons, though crucial for self-defence, are always a last resort.

This ideology was new to the people of Şengal. Until 2014, they hardly knew the PKK. And just as a people needs to be taught the right way of fighting for civilian rights, adolescents joining the PKK need to be educated before they understand what the struggle is about and how it should be conducted. That is true of all young people, whether or not they've reached the age of eighteen. And just like oppressed peoples, the oppressed adolescents have come a long way. After living in places where there has always been war, where the people have been oppressed for generations and where violence can flare up at any moment, they often want just one thing: revenge. They want to fight against the state, destroy army posts and all the soldiers inside, blow up army convoys. They want death or glory – just like those uneducated Yazidi women.

In the autumn of 2016, the PKK-friendly television station MedNûce starts airing the series *The Sur Uprising Diaries*. Based on the diaries of YPS fighters, the armed youth groups in the Kurdish towns, a six-part series has been filmed on the 'uprising' in Sur, the historic centre of Diyarbakır – or rather the urban war that raged in the city between January and the middle of March 2016. The title song is a catchy tune, '*Diren Diyarbekir*', which means, 'Fight back, Diyarbakır'. The song climaxes in the line, 'Trust in the love of the mountains'.

The series sketches a heroic picture of the urban war. It contains real footage made by YPS reporters, not just of the battle itself but of the preparations preceding it. Young people and adults, even mothers, are building barricades and digging trenches together to keep out the army. Some of the images have been edited. Portraits of the 'martyrs' are projected on the blackened old walls of Sur, others show projections of squatting adolescents holding machine guns in alleyways and on street corners. A female voice-over tells the story of the war as it emerges from the diaries. Passages of text appear against the backdrop of the old city wall of Sur beneath a brightly coloured sunset. Battle noises alternate with heroic music.

The young Kurds were defeated. All except a handful of them died. But, as the thirty-year-old Comrade Çiyager said before leaving Qandil for Sur to lead the uprising, where he was killed in the last days of battle, 'Whatever the outcome, it will be glorious.' A glorious dedication to the uprising, a gloriously fierce defence, a glorious collaboration of the people, the glorious memory of the – now immortal – martyrs.

It makes for glorious recruitment material too, I think to myself watching the first episode of the series during my stay at and around Maxmur camp in the autumn of 2016. Waging a heroic battle against the occupying Turkish army, contributing to the struggle for freedom and then enjoying eternal life as a martyr; surely that's what every Kurdish adolescent wants? Actually, lots of Kurdish adolescents don't want it, but in order to recruit new people for your struggle, you need to address the ones who are potentially prepared to fight and give their lives for the cause.

The PKK-friendly media push the picture of the PKK fighter as a person who launches attacks on the Turkish army, hikes through the mountains with their comrades, a Kalashnikov over their shoulder, dances the *govend* (group dance), fights the many enemies of the Kurds, defends their people and their country in armed combat and is never afraid of death because death does not exist – there is only martyrdom.

In her first months with the PKK, Comrade Zinarîn didn't get it. She is seventeen years old when we meet somewhere in Qandil, in a huge cave housing about fifteen women where female fighters often spent the night passing through. Zinarîn joined the PKK at the end of December 2014 during the battle of Kobani, which is where she wanted to go to fight ISIS. 'I saw the fighters on TV,' she tells me, 'either going to war or dancing and singing. The reality turned out to be very different.'

Like all new fighters, she had to complete the basic training first. Which was tough in the winter – she remembers the snow, the rain, sleeping underneath damp or even wet blankets, the cold, the mud. 'I was lying underneath a blanket, teeth chattering from the cold, and thought, so now I'm a real guerrilla fighter. But I wanted to go to Kobani, that's what I had joined up for. My commander asked me how I'd be able to fight if I couldn't use a weapon. "Can't I learn that there?" I asked. "But what would you be fighting for?" she asked in return. I couldn't think of an answer. She gave me books to read, but I didn't see the point of them.'

Zinarîn tells me about the day she joined. She was living in the city of Siirt and went to school as usual that morning. 'I'd known for a long time I wanted to be a guerrilla. Until that moment, my friends had prevented me, they didn't want me to leave. But on that day I had an appointment at ten o'clock, with a PKK fighter waiting for me in a house somewhere. I sneaked off into the prayer room in the break and quickly changed out of my school uniform into normal clothes. I remember that I kept checking my watch on my way to the house. My sister's lesson ends . . . now. Will she notice I'm not there anymore? Have my parents been told yet? Are they angry, worried? Will they know at once why I've disappeared? Will I get out of town unseen? The year before, my cousin had tried to run away to the PKK, but his family found out and fetched him back home.'

She stayed in the house for one night before she and some others travelled to Cizre with the PKK fighter, then crossed the border to Derik in northern Syria, from where they reached Qandil in several stages, on foot and by car. After the 'new fighters' training she stayed in a camp in Qandil for a while. Then came the 'operations' training, in which she learned, among other things, to launch an attack, assemble roadside bombs and use heavier weapons. 'That was useful training,' she says, looking back. 'We learned to take apart weapons and put them back together again, and we did a lot of physical training, mainly obstacle courses where they made us climb, crawl, cross suspension bridges and run up and down hills. I was nowhere near being able to finish all of them, but I kept improving.'

In the first months, she often thought about her warm bed in her parents' house as she lay under a clammy blanket or traipsed through the snow, or simply missed her family. And she was often angry. 'Especially when I saw martyrs on TV. Then I wanted to fight too, and wondered what I was doing in a camp in the mountains with my nose stuck in a book.' She laughs about it as she shares the story. 'You know, I was often angry at home, too. Then I'd smash things. Drinking glasses, plates. When I get angry here, I talk about it, or try to work out whether I could be the one at fault. In discussion groups where comrades criticize each other, I've been told I should try to control my temper. We treat each other with respect here. You never hold grudges because companionship is important, possibly the most important thing of all. We are adults here.'

Zinarîn thought she would be fighting for a Kurdish state in the PKK, but found out the PKK not only didn't want their own nation-state but actively opposed the idea. She kept asking her fellow fighters why that was. 'It was another thing that made me angry,' she says. 'Why don't we want that?! They explained to me that in a nation-state, the will of the people is irrelevant, and that a state only revolves around increasing the power of the people already in power. This is why women are not respected, while in the PKK, the opposite is true. I understand that now.'

We talk for half the morning, and she herself seems unaware of how endless the list of things seems to be that she has learned in barely two years. 'Did you know I can now cook for forty people on a log fire? They'd never believe that at home,' she laughs. She has even learned to walk, which doesn't surprise me in the least, as I myself am still in the middle of the process of learning to walk in the mountains. It is similar to riding a bike: if you go too slow you wobble and fall over, so you need to keep up your pace, but insecurity tends to slow you down and make you wobble, resulting in bruises and painful ankles. Zinarîn: 'I often felt so feeble, especially during the "*servanên nû*" training! I couldn't even walk properly, isn't that weird? But my commanders told me it was normal for someone who had always lived in the city.'

She doesn't lose her temper as much, but is still as impatient as ever. 'I still want to go to Kobani,' she states. 'That is the goal I left everything behind for. The battle of Kobani is over, but want to see the town with my own eyes. Or else, I want to fight in Botan, attack an army post.'

It's a transformation every young Kurd joining the PKK needs to go through, whether they are underage or not. Many older fighters shared similar memories with me about their first years in the PKK. Like Comrade Ronahî, in her mid-thirties now, who was twenty-one when she went 'to the mountains' and couldn't wait to start fighting. Her commander told her that her dreams about fighting and martyrdom were 'much too narrow'. 'I needed to be educated,' Ronahî told me. 'It's how I learned to dream about life instead of martyrdom.'

Or take Comrade Mizgîn, who was born in Turkey but grew up mainly in Lebanon. She told me, 'I didn't want to attend school there anymore because they made me learn Arabic. My parents raised us to be politically aware. My mother used to say, "You need some kind of education, so why don't you join the PKK?" At fifteen, I did. I didn't know anything, except that there was an enemy I wanted to fight. I expected to be dead within six months. But then they taught me I'd come here to live, not to die.' Mizgîn is forty now.

But it's difficult to attract new recruits with this reality. A television series showing the three-month 'History of the PKK' course given somewhere in a tent in Qandil or a language class sitting under trees, or even one on the evils of the patriarchy and the necessity for men to gain control over their masculine side, won't attract many angry, traumatized, rebellious young men and women. You lure them with the prospect of payback, of giving the enemy a taste of their own medicine, of valiantly defending yourself against the Turkish army and ISIS; with a series on young people leading the resistance against the Turkish state in historic Kurdish towns, who will live forever as martyrs.

This is what attracts young people, over and under the age of eighteen. And why should you refuse to accept anyone under eighteen, knowing you're sending them back to face repression, violence and death, or to be married off too young and against their will? Why should you not accept them, if you as an organization have something to offer that they won't find anywhere else in Kurdistan? In the PKK, YPG and YPJ, they are taught their own language, culture and history, and are given the chance to grow as a men and women, to escape from a system that forces them – using violence, if necessary – into a role. They begin a new existence that is no longer dominated by the daily struggle for survival but focuses on building a democratic Kurdistan and a Middle East that is based on equality instead of sectarianism.

Incidentally, not every aspiring young PKK fighter is automatically 'admitted'. When I meet him at Maxmur Camp, Comrade Fuat tells me that to go to the mountains, you need a 'note'. He is a member of the PKK, but as he only performs civil duties, he's not in uniform. Born in a village in Muş Province, he moved to Istanbul with his family as a boy and was involved in the Kurdish movement from a young age. He spent years recruiting young people for the PKK in the Turkish metropolis. Anyone who came to him was screened first. Fuat: 'We'd look into what family you come from, for instance, and what you do in daily life. Then we'd talk to you about why you want to join the PKK. If you have quarrelled with your family or broken up with your sweetheart, you're better off staying at home. You need to have ideological motives.'

Fuat has always taken great care when encountering young people he suspects are heavily traumatized. 'Everyone in this area lives with some trauma,' he says. 'But if someone is in a bad way, suffering from addictions for example, I talk to them first. We give someone like that books to read, we talk about society, about the history of the PKK and its moral values. In the PKK, you are not to cause harm to yourself or others, which means you have to overcome your addiction before joining. We ask him or her to pick a hero from the movement, such as Agit, Bêrîtan or Arîn, and to study the life and life choices of that hero.'

Agit is one of the PKK's most celebrated heroes: as the very first PKK commander he led the first attacks against the Turkish state in 1984. Bêrîtan hurled herself from a rock rather than being taken prisoner of war (see page 120 for her portrait), and Arîn Mirxan blew himself up beneath an ISIS tank in Kobani, dealing ISIS a hard blow.

'Sometimes,' Comrade Fuat says, 'the young man or woman is unable to go forward, for instance if they can't shake their addiction. Sometimes, the will to become a fighter disappears after a couple of months. This is how we separate the wheat from the chaff.' Sometimes, Fuat sends potential fighters to Diyarbakır or a different town or village in the south-east to do political work first. That way, the recruit and the organization can get to know each other better. Fuat: 'Some of the young members end up doing political work without ever taking up arms after all. Others still want to go to the mountains. The ones that convince me get a note and can go.'

Does everyone who goes to the mountains really have such a 'note'? Remembering young Bedel Encü from Roboskî, I doubt it. Anyway, I can't imagine there aren't plenty of young people who just show up, especially those who are familiar with Kurdistan and know where to find the units. 'Of course,' Fuat says, 'there are those who don't want to do the political work first and leave without a note. And yes, you can get there by yourself if you can locate a unit. But even then you can only stay if you manage to convince the local commander and if he or she writes a note for you. Without it, you can't start your education and training.'

Fuat is thirty-six now. As a boy in Muş, he used to come across PKK members in remote areas occasionally, for instance at his family's grazing sites. He recalls, 'I could tell the difference. To me, the town people were bad and the people in the mountains were *temtemiz*, spotless.' He has been trained to use arms but has never actually been in combat. The PKK had other plans for him, he says. 'They have always given me tasks in the city. We need lots of people there, too.'

Comrade Hira, the fighter from Iranian Kurdistan who went to Qandil with her parents and siblings to take up arms when she was just eleven, drew admiring glances from her comrades. Just eleven, how lucky! – I could read in the fiery looks in their eyes. People believe that the sooner you leave the system of oppression, the better. After all, the longer you live in it, the more the system will live in you, making it harder for you to leave and to get the system to leave you.

The term 'system of oppression' must be viewed from a broad

perspective. It does not just refer to the regimes in Iran, Syria, Iraq and Turkey that don't give the Kurds the right to be themselves. It refers to the systems we inhabit too, namely the nation-state and capitalism, and which we take for granted without fundamentally questioning them. While we may criticize their extreme forms such as nationalism and neo-liberalism, very few people would seriously consider throwing the foundations of these two systems overboard by dismantling the nation-state and getting rid of capitalism. In fact, this option never even occurs to most citizens. We have become so much part of the systems and the systems have become so much part of us that we no longer see them.

In fact, they haven't even been around that long. The nation-state is probably a couple of hundred years old, and capitalism, depending on how you define it, only slightly older. Hadn't humankind lived for centuries beforehand without either of them?

The younger you are when you start cleansing yourself of that system with a PKK education, the easier it is. I know what people will be thinking now: 'There, you see? Brainwashing!' I'd like to throw that ball back into their court. Isn't the fact that we don't have fundamental doubts about the system the way it is now down to brainwashing that has been going on so effectively since our earliest youth that we aren't even aware of it? Isn't our education system geared to groom children for a life in business, for the carrot and stick, for the capitalist elimination race? And doesn't the latter start in school, where performance, performance, performance is becoming ever more important and where we are failing to see that a devastating phenomenon like bullying, as an inherent part of that system, can never be resolved within it? Are we aware of our constant obsession with economic growth ruining our planet while hardly anyone questions the necessity of such economic growth and of capitalism itself? Of how a small and decreasing number of us may oppose nationalism but nevertheless fail to draw the conclusion that the devastation wrought by nationalism is inextricably linked to the existence of pieces of land we have hemmed in with borders and called countries, with peoples whose national identity exists only by the grace of those borders? How that system is exacerbating individualization, keeping us as a community from caring for each other except within isolated family units living in terraced houses separated by partitions and losing touch with each other because we have to work, work, work so we can consume?

A bigger house, a posher car, the latest phone, more and more things. How our focus on satisfaction of our material needs and our isolation reinforce each other, leaving us no time or even the presence of mind to organize ourselves and start a rebellion! That we think we are free and happy because we can dance, drink, date, consume, go on vacations and travel the world, without seeing that this all-consuming emptiness has actually trapped us. That the people doing the most important work in our society, such as cleaners, dustmen, teachers, nurses and carers get paid the least and enjoy the lowest status. That the people whose jobs wouldn't even exist without capitalism, from bankers to stockbrokers and from CEOs to Hollywood stars, are filthy rich, and that we all consider this normal. Just as we take for granted that many jobs which society couldn't do without are done by voluntary workers because apparently we can't spare a penny for their salaries. Don't people see that? Yet they do believe, very astutely, that they have spotted 'brainwashing' going on in the PKK?

As a people, you don't need the capitalist, patriarchal nation-state to stay alive. You can exist just as well, or even better, without an oppressive system, no matter whether you are the oppressor or the oppressed. And the same is true for each individual. You have to get out of the system in order to thrive. During my time inside the PKK, I learned that it is not so much an organization as a society in itself. A society in which personal development takes a completely different direction than in the current system. What could be wrong with beginning this development as a minor?

At the Kirkuk base, I had a brief encounter with a young woman. I don't know whether or not she was a minor, and there, behind the front, that didn't matter. We chatted in the hall for a bit. The sleeves of her uniform were rolled up, and my eye fell on scars on her left forearm. Scratches. Many scratches. 'Did you do that to yourself?' I asked cautiously. 'Yes,' she answered. 'I used to do that before I joined.' 'Not anymore?' I wanted to know. 'No, not anymore,' she laughed. 'I don't need to when I'm here, you know? It's not . . . necessary. Here, I am stronger.'

This answers the question whether the system inside the PKK isn't just as coercive and undermining as the system of the capitalist nation-state. It is not. In the year I spent there, I didn't encounter a single insecure, bad-tempered, weepy, unbearable, spiteful, resentful, worked-up or otherwise disturbed guerrilla. On the contrary, I met strong, open-minded, helpful and well-balanced men and women. Which is all the more remarkable considering that almost all fighters have been traumatized during their childhoods in Turkey, Syria, Iraq or Iran.

To my mind, it would be too simplistic to describe these traumas in terms of a collection of personal experiences the fighters have shared with me. The fact that fighter B. spent a period of time in prison as a boy, where he was raped by adult inmates while the guards watched, is not the point. Neither is it relevant that fighter W. grew up without her father because he was locked up for political reasons. Or that N. believed his head teacher when he told him he'd know if the boy ever spoke Kurdish outside the school, and as a result was mainly silent at home. That N. was beaten up at school after, unsuspecting and bursting with pride, he read out a poem in Turkish written by his brother – the little mite had no idea that it was common knowledge at school that his brother was a PKK fighter, making the reading of the poem impermissible; he hadn't recognized the call to revolution in the obliquely worded stanzas. It is not about how Comrade D. realized at a young age that the will of the male members of her family was not to be trifled with, and that she would be married before her eighteenth birthday if she didn't make her getaway. She had to wait until an evening came when her father fell asleep before he could lock the front door of the house to prevent her from escaping, and once she was outside, she had to run, run, run.

Or rather, it is not only about such stories. They are certainly important. But at the same time, reducing the trauma of the Kurds to such fragments of individual life stories would be simplistic. Precisely because the pain has deeper, systemic causes and has been leaving its mark on generations, relief from it can't be found within the system. Let alone a solution.

This raises the question why we, Western men and women in particular, so often struggle in life. Why we seem unable to resolve our personal dramas, are often deeply insecure and let these insecurities hold us back while searching for the strength to somehow transcend our experiences and become strong enough to choose our own path, free from conventions – if we even dare to want that. Why we think we can find this strength by going along with a system that is in fact undermining our strength and that of others, strength we could also use to connect with each other and to fight the system. We can't, because the system has become part of us.

In the middle of the afternoon of 26 November 2016, I suddenly hear the bleating of a sheep in the PKK base near Kirkuk. The guerrillas quickly pack their bags. I follow their example and we rush to the parking area, where a couple of cars and two pickup trucks are parked. On the back of one of them stands a sheep. It is covered with a net that is secured to the sides of the truck so it can't leap out. We toss our things into the open back of the other truck, split up into the vehicles and speed away from the base. On our way to the front, where there will be a party tomorrow.

The dog that helps guard the camp reacts with aggression to any two-legged creature not wearing a uniform. Luckily, it stays at the entrance of the base most of the time and hardly restricts my freedom of movement. A sand track runs from the barrier and around an earthen rampart to the central area where there's a volleyball pitch and a shelter to park the cars. To the left are the men's barracks, to the right the women's, and in between is a courtyard with two kitchens surrounded by pantries. 'Kitchens' is actually a bit of an overstatement. They are in fact not much more than two large gas rings with two or three cupboards underneath, a couple of large, basic pots, a table that doubles as worktop, a fridge and an open metal storage rack containing basic kitchen utensils like soup spoons, containers and a few pots.

The kitchen is crowded because it's nice and warm and there is cooking to do. In the courtyard, the sheep has been slaughtered. A couple of fighters are skewering some chunks of muscle meat, kidney and liver. The rest of the meat is kept for tomorrow.

A female fighter crouching on the raw concrete floor is preparing a biscuit-chocolate-banana cake, alternating layers of biscuits with layers of banana split lengthwise and chocolate bars melted in a bain-marie. The construction grows taller with each layer. She is experienced, the cake as solid as a rock. A comrade and novice cake builder is making a smaller version that looks much less stable. She is given hints on how to improve it. The words '*Salvegera 39 PKK pîroz*' are written on the larger cake with grated coconut, 'Hurray for the PKK's thirty-ninth birthday'. (I feel it should be thirty-eighth, as it is 2016 now and the PKK was founded in 1978, but they count differently here: the PKK is entering its thirty-ninth year, just as a baby is one in its first year of life.)

The skewers of meat are taken outside. On the edge of the base is a fire surrounded with bricks for the ends of the skewers to rest on while they are roasted. We chew on the rather tough meat. I am only to stay a short while as the fighters here do guard duties, making it an unsuitable place for non-fighters. The dog agrees with this. A fighter walks me back to the barracks.

Later that evening, a few men and women have assembled in one of the common rooms. As an outsider, I am allowed in. To the other fighters, the goings-on here are top secret – they are rehearsing a short play to perform the following day. They wrote the script together, chose the accompanying music and the traditional Kurdish attire that serves as costumes. There is laughter but the work is taken seriously, too. The performance has to be perfect.

The next day is icy cold and clear. It is 27 November, the day the PKK was founded in 1978. Some fighters put a bright red piece of cloth up on the volleyball net. On it, they pin flags of the various PKK branches. Besides the PKK flag, which is red with a green-rimmed yellow circle in the middle and inside it a red star, there are the flags of YJA-Star – an upside-down pyramid, the right side red and the left side yellow and in the middle a yellow sun with a red star inside – and HPG – another upside-down pyramid, the left side green and the right side red with a yellow star in the middle – and finally a yellow flag with a portrait of Öcalan. Next to them is a huge plastic poster showing portraits of eighteen fighters who lost their lives near Kirkuk.

Then the *moral*, that is to say, a performance by and for the fighters that is meant to add lustre to PKK holidays as well as to boost the troops' morale, takes off. Fighters are singing – some boisterously, like the group of seven fighters singing a battle song, some more subtly, like the two shy boys, one of whom is playing the *saz* and the other singing softly. Accompanied by music, Comrade Nuhayla recites a poem in her clear voice. I don't understand it but her intonation is so intense that I can feel it.

Then comes the grand finale of the moral: the play. It's about an ancient people farming the land. Clothed in traditional Kurdish costumes, the guerrillas act out the rhythmical work of operating scythes cut from firm cardboard. Gradually, capitalism makes its entrance. There's a hilarious TV broadcast in which an uncritical female presenter interviews a professor who gives a facetious and fairly macho explanation of the state of the country. The people are free, he says smugly, and the economy's fine too because the oil price is rising. When the presenter asks about the situation of the Kurds, he starts to stammer and turns away from her in his chair, refusing further comment. The guerrillas playing television viewers sitting on the ground watching this criticize the interview and finally walk away. Then they return one by one, put their arms in the air and make a proclamation about the problems that capitalism has brought to society. They represent the founders of the PKK. In the last scene, they are announcing the establishment of the PKK to the people, dressed in guerrilla outfits.

Again, I notice a parallel between the people and the Kurdish youth. For generations, the Kurds hardly did anything to turn the tide of their oppression. Granted, there were Kurdish uprisings such as that of Sheikh Said in 1925, but they were all short-lived and unsuccessful.

Many guerrillas have told me about the failed uprisings. The way they saw it, the rebels and heroes of the resistance didn't offer a real alternative and hadn't analysed the problem properly. The experienced Comrade Mizgîn added, 'Those uprisings depended on their leaders. Once they were killed, the uprising ended. In the PKK, this is different. Our resistance continues, independent of whether or not the leader lives.'

There hasn't been an uprising since the 1930s. The Kurdish resistance seemed crushed for good. The generations that followed opted for a quiet life. They tried thinking of themselves as Turkish, some even succeeding. They lived in the system, became one with the system. Until the PKK appeared. Can we, outsiders, condemn this? Can we point an accusatory finger at the PKK for offering the new generation, who are the future of the people, an alternative, a goal to fight for? Should we caution the young not to go to the mountains and improve as Kurds and as individuals, but to choose an existence inside the system that kept their ancestors under its thumb, because we believe that is safer?

INTERNATIONAL HUMANITARIAN LAW

The PKK committed itself to a treaty with the international organization Geneva Call. Its aim is to move non-state armed groups to stick to the rules of international humanitarian law, especially when it comes to protecting civilians in armed conflict. Not deploying child soldiers is part of this. Geneva Call opened talks with the PKK on this subject in 2008, and an agreement was signed in 2013. In the summer of 2014, the YPG and YPJ followed.

The agreement covers more than just minors in direct combat situations. Especially in northern Syria, where the YPG and YPJ are in charge, it also prohibits such tasks as manning checkpoints, gathering information as a spy or bringing supplies to the front line. Children under sixteen who apply are sent home again. If they no longer have a home or keep coming back, they are put up in special bases where life centres on education and sports.

Meanwhile, the Turkish government is doing everything it can to depict the PKK as an organization which not only deploys child soldiers, but also abducts minors from their families against their will. In the spring of 2015, parents who claimed this had happened to them demonstrated against such 'abductions'. The demonstration took place in Diyarbakır, in front of the town hall. The parents thought that the DBP, the ruling party of the municipality at the time, would be able to wield its influence with the PKK to help them get their children back from the mountains.

By sheer chance, I happen to meet one of the allegedly abducted women in a cave in the Qandil Mountains. She says she hasn't forgiven her family for the lie they have spread about her joining the PKK. There was, she adds, never any kind of pressure. She believes the protest was organized by the AKP, and that the protesters had been paid. There is no way of knowing whether that is true. What is abundantly clear, however, is that the protest, which lasted a couple of days, was widely reported on by all pro-AKP media.

I see no reason whatsoever not to believe this comrade when she says she joined of her own free will. The PKK doesn't need to abduct anyone – plenty of young people join up of their own volition. Besides, coercion is completely incompatible with PKK ideology. In all the months I spent at the PKK, YPG and YPJ, I hardly ever even heard orders being given. Of course orders are important during a combat situation, but in the daily life behind the front line or in the camps in the mountains, I could go for days without being sure who the commanders were. Commander Nuhayla told me, 'It is my job to make sure the comrades achieve the best personal development and learn to take responsibility for themselves. This responsibility makes it hard to be a commander. No one has ever learned anything from giving and following orders.'

Looking at online pictures of the Diyarbakır protests later, I suddenly spotted the mother of the comrade I had spoken to who had supposedly been abducted, holding a photo of her daughter in her hand. It was a very young version of her daughter, wearing a blue and white school uniform. So that's how it works. By using an old photograph, she not only implied that her daughter had been abducted, but also that she had been a mere schoolgirl at the time – when in fact the fighter was nineteen when I met her and had joined up at sixteen.

The PKK asked the supposedly abducted comrade to make a statement for a Kurdish TV station in which she made clear that she had become a guerrilla of her own free will. The video was filmed and broadcast, though the average Turk watching the news on Turkish, government-approved media will never actually see it, let alone believe it. To many Turks, the possibility that young people go to the mountains voluntarily and without any kind of coercion is unthinkable. And those who can imagine it have been left with such an infernal view of the PKK from years of government propaganda that child abduction fits into it seamlessly.

Their imagination fails them; or perhaps the Turks have been robbed of the will to put themselves in someone else's shoes. Of course, the system that has been oppressing, massacring and denying the Kurds for almost a century, has had another effect: the Turks never got to know their Kurdish compatriots. They know nothing of their culture, their language and traditions, their history, struggle and pain. Most Turks never read a Kurdish newspaper and never watch TV stations run by Kurds, not even those published and broadcast in Turkish. Fear or aversion keeps them from visiting the south-east of the country. They never get to know the Kurdish perspective.

Hardly surprising then that the government finds it so easy to pull the wool over its citizens' eyes, making them believe the PKK fighters are nothing but terrorists. That the PKK abducts children and forces them to fight at the front. That PKK camps are a living hell for young Kurds and that those who join want nothing more than to get out again.

The Western imagination is not up to the task, either. From a Western perspective, the existence of underage fighters is condemned as a matter of course. We do it thinking of our own children, who play in the street, spend time with friends the same age, take up sports, play computer games, go to school and are prepared for a life in which education and work are central. We imagine little kids carrying Kalashnikovs over their shoulders, we conjure up mental images of them getting injured in combat or worse, we feel the grief of the parents who have lost their offspring.

Ours is a comfortable position. Most of the Western world is spared armed combat. Which is not to say, however, that our armies are idly playing cards in their barracks and that our F-16 fighter planes are rusting away in hangars – our troops are helping to fight the Third World War in the Middle East. The Kurds are taking part as well. Their land was divided over four countries by Western powers after the First World War, where for decades they have been oppressed with the consent and support of the Western world – whose major interest lies in power and the sale of weapons. The effects this has on local populations is of far less interest, as long as they don't come knocking on Europe's door in the form of refugees.

It doesn't occur to us that joining an armed group can be beneficial to the development of a young person, whether they are of age or not. It is unthinkable to us that it can be more empowering to them than any of the choices they might have in a system that has traumatized generations – more empowering than studying, getting a job, getting married or anything else that will help bolster that system. The thought that the PKK doesn't lead children into war but pulls them out of it, is too disturbing to recognize.

At a base near Kirkuk, I mentioned I was looking for Bedel Encü, the boy from Roboskî who had joined the PKK after four of his best friends had been killed in the Roboskî bombing. I was referred to Faraşîn Cudî. He grew up in Roboskî but had joined the PKK several years before the bombing. 'Yes,' Comrade Faraşîn said, 'I know Bedel. He's not alive anymore. He was one of the martyrs in the Silopi urban wars. His nom de guerre was Tirej Roboskî.' Tirej means ray of sunshine.

I track down Tirej's name on a list of people who died at Silopi. I don't know how he ended up in Silopi, and there's no way of finding out now. Maybe he urged his commander to send him to the city to fight. Maybe he gave his permission because he could tell there was no holding him back. Maybe he didn't give permission but he went anyway. Maybe his grief, his anger, his trauma were so great it was inevitable they would claim his life at a young age.

Background

Şengal, Afrin and Raqqa

On 1 April 2018, the last PKK fighters left the Şengal region in the north-west of Iraq. They had announced their departure a week before. The fighters consisted of about 500 men and women.

The PKK retreat was the last act of a dramatic period for the region which is the home country of the Yazidis, a religious minority living mainly in Iraq. That period started in August 2014 with the advance of ISIS in Iraq and Syria. Officially, the Şengal region was under the authority of the central Iraqi government in Baghdad at the time, but effectively the KDP – the party of Masoud Barzani, the most powerful man in Iraqi Kurdistan and former president of the region – had been in charge for years. The KDP peshmerga were responsible for security in the region.

In August 2014, ISIS charged on Şengal. The Yazidis didn't want to flee at first, assuming the peshmerga would protect them. But the peshmerga took to their heels, back to the Kurdistan Region, leaving the Yazidis to their fate. In a panic, they fled up Mount Şengal. Many weren't able to get away in time, and ISIS murdered thousands of men and abducted thousands of women, boys and girls. It soon became apparent that the girls and women were forced to become 'wives' to ISIS fighters, who swapped them with each other and sold them on markets.

The PKK rushed to the Yazidis' aid from the mountains in the Qandil region. They opened a corridor for the refugees to flee from the mountain into a region in Syria that was under YPG and YPJ control. It wasn't far – Şengal lies close to the Iraqi-Syrian border – but it was a gruelling hike all the same, as it was sweltering hot and they didn't have enough food or water.

In the meantime, the PKK had seized a (small) part of the Şengal region. In late 2015, the peshmerga and PKK drove most of ISIS out of the Şengal region in a joint offensive. It didn't put an end to the crisis, however. Soon afterwards, the KDP demanded that the PKK leave the region again. The PKK had no intention of doing so, however. They had already begun setting up and training the YBŞ and YJŞ, the Yazidis' own defence units. Barzani, the leader of the KDP and still the president of the Kurdistan Region in Iraq at the time, wanted to place these units under KDP authority. Various YBŞ and YJŞ fighters I spoke to in the Şengal region in the winter and spring of 2017 declared they would never agree to that; the YBŞ and YJŞ are the first defence forces the Yazidis have ever had. They also felt betrayed by the KDP, who had left them to their fate in 2014.

The KDP's effort to drive the PKK from Şengal was supported by President Erdoğan. He denounced the idea of ever allowing Şengal to become 'a second Qandil'. But the PKK had no intention of settling in Şengal with camps and training centres. Except for that one mountain, the area is flat as a pancake and very barren – nothing like the expansive, mountainous and verdant Qandil where they can hide effectively. The same circumstances also make Şengal unsuitable as an operating base from which to launch attacks in Turkey. For that purpose it is located too far from the border anyway.

On several occasions, the KDP threatened to take military action against the PKK in Şengal, and things came to a head on 3

March 2017, while I was in the region. It happened near Xanasor, a small town that had been under YBŞ and PKK control since early 2015. A group with ties to the KDP peshmerga tried to force a passage to the Syrian border – just to carry out regulation border controls, the official story went. But a look at the map revealed the truth. If the KDP had succeeded in gaining control over the territory between Xanasor and the Syrian border, it would have completely cut off Öcalan's troops, who depended on supplies from an area in Syria that was under the control of their brothers and sisters in the YPG and YPJ. There was no other way for the Öcalan fighters to reach Şengal from Iraq, as the KDP had hermetically sealed all routes.

In the skirmishes that followed, five YBŞ fighters and two PKK members were killed. A journalist, Nujiyan Erkan, died of her injuries three weeks later.

So what exactly were Turkey and Barzani's KDP so afraid of, if the PKK constituted a negligible military threat in Şengal? For Barzani, it is all about territory and influence. Şengal lies outside of the Kurdistan Region's official borders. It had been in his military and administrative control for years, however, because the central government in Baghdad showed little interest in it. And although he had left the area in 2014, he wanted it back now.

The KDP did not manage to regain control over Şengal. In mid-October 2017, yet another armed group, Hashd al-Shaabi (also known as the PMU, Popular Mobilization Units), moved into the area to drive ISIS out of the last villages. Hashd al-Shaabi is supported by Iran and was under the command of the Iraqi army. The KDP had no choice but to leave Şengal – the PKK, YBŞ and YJŞ stayed.

And Turkey? Turkey is not so much afraid of the Kurds in general

– Erdoğan is able to keep clan leaders like Barzani in line – but of Kurds who organize and defend themselves as a people. If the PKK succeeds in building up a grassroots democratic system (in other words, democratic confederalism) in more and more places inside and outside of Kurdistan, this will pose a real threat to Erdoğan's power.

It follows that the Kurdish cantons Cizire, Kobani and Afrin (captured by Turkey in March 2018) in the north of Syria are also a threat. It is no coincidence that the battle of Kobani (September 2014 to January 2015) was such a decisive factor in the failure of the peace process in Turkey. Erdoğan expected Kobani to fall into ISIS hands, an expectation – or, as many put it, a hope – he gave voice to, but the Kurds managed to turn the tide and drive ISIS further and further back. The Kurds in Turkey showed enormous solidarity with Kobani. Erdoğan couldn't allow such a powerful movement for Kurdish autonomy to exist.

But the Turkish president's real nightmare begins when even regions without a predominantly Kurdish population, such as Syrian Manbij and Raqqa, opt for self-governance according to the principles of democratic confederalism. The Syrian war has not yet been decided, but the more self-governance establishes itself, the more likely it is that Syria will become a federally ruled country after the war. Which will certainly be an inspiration to the Kurds in Turkey. In other words: genuine and acknowledged democratic self-governance that respects everyone's identity and religion undermines the centralized and increasingly authoritarian Turkish government.

It would be a disaster for the AKP and the Turkish state as we know them today. And not least for Erdoğan himself. If he loses power, he faces prosecutions for the blood on his hands and wide-scale corruption.

As a result, Erdoğan would do anything to undermine Kurdish self-governance in northern Syria. It is the reason why Turkey invaded Afrin in January 2018 and brought the canton under its control within barely two months, with the help of an armed group that called itself the Free Syrian Army but which actually consisted of jihadis. Throughout the Syrian war, Afrin had been a quiet area which had offered shelter to tens of thousands of refugees from other parts of the country, including Aleppo. The YPG and YPJ in Afrin did not pose a military threat to Turkey either. The Kurds concentrated on keeping their own population safe and setting up governing bodies and schools among other things.

The YPG and YPJ offered fierce resistance to the Turkish invasion and occupation, but decided to retreat when the attackers reached the town of Afrin. In doing this they prevented an urban war which could potentially have cost the lives of thousands of citizens. Immediately afterwards, vowing to become Turkey's worst nightmare in Afrin, they launched guerrilla attacks on the Turkish army and their auxiliary forces.

Meanwhile, Erdoğan was still issuing menacing statements on the situation in Şengal. He swore to take over the region. Not that the Turkish army would have been able to reach Şengal as easily as Afrin, as it doesn't border on Turkey the way Afrin does; but who knows, it could come quite close to Şengal if it advanced through KDP territory in Iraq. Then, however, it would have come up against the Iraqi army, which had bolstered its presence in the region in the preceding months, and which was already represented in Şengal itself by Hashd al-Shaabi.

The PKK decided not to wait for a potential military confrontation and announced its retreat from Şengal. They did not in fact have a choice. The Iraqi army, out of fear of potential aggression from Turkey but also on a mission to regain territory lost earlier in the war, was keen to take over Şengal. Fighting the Iraqi army would have been an impossible task for the PKK and would have cost the lives of many civilians to boot. What was more, the Yazidi self-defence troops YBŞ and YJŞ, set up and trained by the PKK, already received a (small) salary from Baghdad.

In their own media, the PKK depicted its retreat as a victory. The message was that the YBŞ and YJŞ had become strong enough to defend themselves and didn't need any more PKK support. The videos that circulated of the retreat show the Yazidis bidding a warm and grateful goodbye to the PKK fighters. Without the PKK, the tragedy inflicted on the Yazidis in 2014 would have been even worse. The YBŞ and YJŞ stayed in the region and are still intact, though they are under Iraqi control now.

What the PKK doesn't say is that it has not reached its political goal in Şengal. While I was there in the spring of 2017, the fighters swore to me that they would only leave Şengal once Yazidi self-governance was acknowledged, either by the international community or the Iraqi government. To what extent Baghdad and the PKK have discussed the right of self-determination is unclear. In any case, no commitments have been made. For the foreseeable future, the situation in Iraq won't be favourable to that happening, either. But as I've said, retreat was the PKK's only option. Whether the Yazidis will get any form of self-governance in future Iraq and whether the YBŞ and YJŞ will continue to operate as self-defence troops, remains to be seen.

CHAPTER 5

The PKK is a Woman

Tee-lee-lee-lee-lee-lee! Tee-lee-lee-lee-lee-lee! Tee-lee-lee-lee-lee-lee! Female fighters at the front like to let male ISIS fighters know they are near, about to break through the men's defensive lines and take them prisoner – or kill them. Word has it that the shrill cry, with which women in the Middle East typically express anger or pain, but which in the war has become an assertion of feminine Kurdish strength and vitality, sends shivers down the jihadis' spines. Not surprising perhaps, since any jihadi who gets himself killed by a woman is no longer guaranteed entrance into paradise and can wave goodbye to his seventy-two heavenly virgins. Whether or not that is really part of ISIS doctrine hardly matters. The piercing tee-lee-lee-lee-lee announces the arrival of armed Kurdish women. You'd better hide.

I watch them leave for the front from a small, deserted town north of Raqqa. It's the spring of 2017, Raqqa is still the 'capital' of ISIS. I have spent the last ten days with the female troops at one of the most important front lines of the Syrian civil war. For the past few days, there has been a lull in the fighting. Time for regrouping, drawing up a strategy for the coming weeks and moving the headquarters to a location just behind the new front lines. The SDF, a taskforce consisting mainly of the Kurdish YPG and YPJ with the collaboration of Arab militias, is gradually surrounding ISIS from the east, the north and the north-west.

We're staying in a house in a village from which ISIS was driven out about a fortnight ago. As the entire village has been declared a military zone, civilians can't return to their homes yet. We sleep outdoors. Between 8 PM and half past, we climb up the concrete external stairs onto the flat roof. Up there, we wage a constant battle against the sand. The wind is buffeting the bare village and the desert plains surrounding it. After getting up in the morning, we fold our mattresses so the sand sticks only to the underside and we'll have a relatively sand-free bed to slip into in the evening. The nights are cold and crystal clear, our blankets thick. Sometimes, we move our mattresses next to each other and sleep close together in a row, side by side like sisters. I am half woken from my sleep every hour, when the fighter on guard duty rouses her comrade with a shouted whisper, 'Wake up, Comrade, it's your turn to keep watch!' In the early morning light I see two comrades scan our surroundings, Kalashnikovs slung over their shoulders. One of them is stationed on the corner of our roof, the other on the corner of the adjoining men's roof.

The occasional fighter planes roar through the sky above us. It's impossible to tell from their sound alone which flag they fly under, but I assume they are American bombers. They're not out to get us. Turkish planes haven't been sighted here, as this isn't part of the north Syrian territory controlled by the Kurds, but south of it. And however strongly Turkey might oppose the collaboration of the Americans with the SDF, I assume they wouldn't go so far as to bomb SDF targets. I'm no more afraid here than I was in Qandil. The fighters know what safety measures to take. Experienced and confident, they don't let the powers that be, who would like nothing more than to wipe them from the face of the earth, dictate their frame of mind. And this attitude turns out to be contagious.

In the morning of 9 May, it suddenly happens. Now! Today! The next minute, all the fighters have squeezed into the cars and off-road vehicles to gather at the headquarters. The mood has swung from slightly down and bored to elated and expectant. The front with ISIS is the place to be for every SDF fighter. A day without fighting the 'gangs', as the ISIS jihadis are called, is a day wasted. Of course, this is not the official line. Officially, learning how to read GPS coordinates, cleaning the base, reading Öcalan and manning checkpoints are all just as important. But the fighters' faces are a dead giveaway: their eyes light up at the mere thought of the front.

They are sitting next to each other on rugs under a concrete awning in front of a building, the men on one side and the women on the other. Their shoes are lined up beside the rugs. I am struck by the sight of the women's socks beneath the khaki camouflage uniforms: pink ones with hearts, pale yellow ones with pumpkins and red and white ones that have whiskers woven into the fabric at the toes and eyes and upright ears on the insteps. Next to the building are a number of off-road vehicles as well as improvised tanks – some equipped with automatic weapons – and pickup trucks. After some general instructions and a final pep talk, it's time for the fighters to go.

I want to join them. But, as area commander Comrade Zilan has informed me several times, I'm not allowed to. She's a short, stocky woman with shoulder-length, tightly curled hair that's so red it's almost orange. In the past few days, I've made several attempts to strike up a conversation with her. They left me feeling awkward. While she was briskly and efficiently making preparations for the next phase of the battle for Raqqa, I'd turn up, a journalist, asking which unit I could accompany when the fighting flared up again. 'You're at the front already, Comrade Avaşîn,' she'd say. If I told her I wanted to go closer to the front line, she'd only look at me in silence, eyebrows raised. 'How about a field hospital, would that be possible?' I suggested at another opportunity. She referred me to a small hospital situated a considerable distance behind the future front line. Not exactly what I'd envisaged.

Some of the fighters feel sorry for me as they watch my struggle trying to get through to Zîlan. They advise me to discuss the matter with a different commander, which is pointless, as they all refer me back to Zîlan. As the fighters are getting into their various cars, off-road and armoured vehicles and makeshift tanks, one of the women waves me over. She's sitting in the back of a pickup. Beaming, she calls, 'Come with us, Comrade Avaşîn!' My feet want to rush over and leap on. Good sense prevents me. Comrade Zîlan has explicitly forbidden it, and I don't want to cause any problems here – not alive, not injured, not dead. Someone else shows me to a car I am allowed to get into. They are going back to the base behind the front. I decline the offer, preferring to stay where I am, at this large command centre. I'll just have to do my best to follow developments from here.

Strolling over the grounds, I come across two fellow journalists with cameras who tell me they're planning on going to the front later on. They don't mind taking me along and promise to let me know what time they're leaving and who's taking them. They'll also help me to wheedle permission.

Later, I spot stretchers outside a building further on. I go up to the building, which turns out to be a field hospital. There are American soldiers walking around and I ask one of them some questions. He's friendly enough, but immediately calls his commander, then points at me and says, 'Journalist.' Acting casual, I smile and am about to introduce myself but don't get the chance.

What am I doing here? Who has given me permission? I explain that I'm not a war correspondent but an author writing a book about the Kurdish fighters, and that I'm embedded with them. All well and good, they say, but I've no business snooping around the American section, so scram.

Before I know it, I'm called on the carpet by Comrade Zîlan. She tells me in measured tones that the local troops and American soldiers operate under separate chains of command, that she has no say about their grounds and that I can't just go wandering into their section. I protest that I ended up there by accident, and ask if she has time for a quick word. I want to explain to her, as I've been trying to do these past few days, that I would like to witness some actual fighting to put in my book. She does not have time. She asks a couple of female fighters to take me to the YPJ barracks.

I get into the car and we drive off, leaving the place where all military life is and heading for a house some distance away, the base of the YPJ women. Anger wells up in me. Not another YPJ base. I've seen plenty of those. It's where the women who have not been assigned a role at the front spend their time reading, talking, sewing small beads to their brightly coloured shawls, washing their clothes, cleaning and cooking. For the record, those aren't exclusively women's chores – in other buildings, the men who have stayed behind are doing exactly the same.

At the YPJ base, I refuse to leave the car. I feel like I'm about to explode, but since exploding is not acceptable here, I contain myself. I can't even manage a smile anymore. In a choked voice, I tell the women I won't leave the car and that I want to speak to Zîlan. Shrugging, they drive me back.

Comrade Zîlan can't believe her eyes when she sees me get out of the car in front of her. Luckily, exploding is as unacceptable for her as it is for me. She asks me calmly whether I don't think refusing to get out of the car was a bit childish. Is this mature behaviour? I'm a foot taller than she is, but feel anything but big and strong at that moment. I repeat that I think it's time we had a talk.

Comrade Zîlan, another commander and I go into a room. We sit down on cushions on the floor. 'Thank you,' I say, 'for taking the time for me now. I would like to explain to you what I'm doing here. I'm writing a book about you and since you are an armed organization, it's important for me to see those arms in action. Now that I've finally arrived at the front at Raqqa, isn't it strange I haven't heard a single shot being fired?'

The other commander, who looks at me with a slightly milder gaze, says I'm making things difficult for them. I answer, without snapping at her, that they are making things difficult for me, too. 'But we are waging a war!' Comrade Zîlan says. 'And I am writing a book!' I retort. 'For weeks, I've watched female fighters cook, clean, read and sew, their Kalashnikovs leaning against the wall in a neat row. I need more than that.' Zîlan has misunderstood me, or perhaps I haven't managed to make myself clear. She answers, furious but still without raising her voice, 'How dare you say the women do nothing but cook and clean! We participate fully in the fighting.' 'I know that,' I say, 'but I'm a journalist, I want to see it. That's what I'm trying to make you understand. I can only write a report on the war if I actually get to see the war. Just like the other two journalists I met earlier. They're going to the front, aren't they? Can't I go with them?'

I realize I'm pushing Zîlan to the limit, but I want to be sure I've tried everything. 'Those two journalists have front line experience. They know how to defend themselves, you don't,' she says. 'You can choose: either you're going to the YPJ barracks, or back to the base in Kobani.' 'Kobani,' I say without a moment's hesitation. Within five minutes, a car with a driver has been arranged, complete with another commander to accompany me. I sling my bag over my shoulder and shake Zîlan by the hand. '*Serkeftin*,' I say, which is the usual way of saying goodbye here. It means, 'Be successful'. She curtly wishes me the same before turning to walk away.

All my attempts to strike a balance between my journalistic wishes and the YPG/J's priority to keep me alive and unhurt have so far been frustrated. At the front north of Raqqa as much as in the mountains in northern Iraq, where I'd hoped to get closer to the Turkish border, to regions like Zap, Zagros, Avaşîn, Haftanîn and Hakurk. It's where PKK units cross the border into Turkey to carry out attacks, and where most of the Turkish air strikes take place. How do the guerrillas there cope with this daily threat? How do they prepare for their missions in Turkey? Of course I realize that no matter how frustrating the fighters' wish to keep me safe has been for the journalist in me, it has been advantageous to me as a human being. Unyielding fighters like Zîlan are probably the reason I'm still alive.

But keeping me out of the places with the most violence is also in the PKK, YPG and YPJ's interests. If I kicked the bucket at the Raqqa front or after getting bombed in the Zagros Mountains, the Turkish authorities would lose no time starting up the propaganda machine. Erdoğan's media would make up stories about me being executed by the guerrillas for uncovering abuse in the PKK, or say that the YPG/J arranged for me to be killed at the front because I had accidentally witnessed them committing war crimes. Only those who know the guerrillas fighting in Öcalan's name would know this to be nonsense. Everyone else would either swallow the Turkish lies whole, or at the very least wonder if there mightn't be a grain of truth in them.

I understand it raises questions, too. Newspapers, magazines and websites are full of stories by journalists and photographers at the front. Don't they run the same risk as me of being injured, if nothing more? Of course they do. According to the Committee to Protect Journalists (CPJ), 118 journalists have been killed in the Syrian civil war since it began in 2011, sixteen of whom were foreigners. In Iraq in the same period, forty more were killed, including three foreigners.* The difference between most foreign journalists and me, however, is that I was embedded with Öcalan's troops. From the moment I arrived and started my project, those troops were responsible for my safety. Most other (foreign) journalists are not in that position. They go there at their own risk, or under the responsibility of the news organization that employs them.

So why didn't I go on my own initiative? Because I want to practise a different kind of journalism with this book. My aim is to paint a broader portrait of the troops fighting for Öcalan's ideology. In my field, there is less and less room for stepping back to take the long view. Articles and deadlines are both getting shorter all the time so that the pieces can go online immediately – and the shorter an article is, the more you have to skimp on background information and context. As a result, and to keep with the subject of this book, this perpetuates the image of the PKK and the YPG/J as primarily military organizations who focus mainly on armed conflict.

Such an image is not necessarily bad for the YPG/J, who have, after all, established themselves as the best boots on the ground against ISIS jihadis in recent years. But whether or not a certain image is good or bad for the fighters is irrelevant from a journalistic point of view. My point is this: in my years living in

* On 9 April 2018.

Turkey, I familiarized myself with the Kurdish movement, to which the PKK belongs and whose driving force it has been, but I never managed to get through to the PKK fighters themselves. I did meet some of them in Turkey. Once in the Lice district in Diyarbakır Province, and once a couple of days before I was deported, in a valley in the district of Yüksekova. Those were short encounters, however, and besides, Yüksekova was at war at that moment, and we were surrounded by the noise of battle from the mountains and drones in the air. There was no room for quiet observation and conversation.

I admit that I did get a bit of a jolt when Comrade Zagros contacted me in late 2015 to let me know that the PKK had agreed to my proposal to stay with them for a year. Their permission meant that it was now up to me to decide whether I really wanted to take on this project or not. A tricky decision. To me, only one question mattered: would I be able to do the job in a journalistic manner? I discussed it with several experienced colleagues whose views I respect. I also submitted a project proposal to the Dutch Fund for Special Journalism Projects. The fund assesses subsidy applications on their journalistic value first and foremost, and I decided that if they granted me a subsidy, I would go. As it turned out, I hit the bull's eye with my proposal. The subsidy was granted.

Various people have asked me whether this book had been my idea or the PKK's. Let me put it this way: if the PKK had suggested it to me, I would never have gone. I'm not writing this book for the PKK but for my readers, in the hope of giving them a clearer view of the war and struggle that are going on in Kurdistan. A view that a non-embedded journalist would never be able to depict. Just as it turned out to be impossible for me to get as close to the front as my colleagues who were travelling on their own.

So how come ISIS don't stand a chance against the YPG/J and SDF fighters? Do female fighters really have such incredible powers, or is this propaganda, produced by the troops themselves and targeted at the columns of Western media, from the *New York Times* to *Marie Claire*, in the hope of swaying public opinion in favour of the Kurds? Where do those women get such power? Or are the men actually the ones doing all the hard work in war?

In no other military force on earth do women play a crucial role. Where women such as the troops fighting in the name of Öcalan's ideology are active at the front line, we tend to hold them to the standards of the reality we're used to, concluding that they are doing men's work. Since women are physically weaker than men, we can't accept that these female guerrillas and soldiers play an essential role. This is only a small, sexist step away from reducing women fighters to the attractive propaganda material of the Kurdish movement. In fact, Western media often portray them this way, routinely printing large photographs of beautiful female armed guerrillas in their editorial pages.

This interpretation, however, reveals more about the roles attributed to men and women in the West than about feminism in the Kurdish movement. They take a diametrically opposite view. Women are not doing men's work in a masculine war, it's the other way round. A man strengthens the woman in him in order to play a full part in a feminine struggle, although the male guerrillas put this slightly differently: they 'murder the man in themselves' so as to help create the society they envisage.

On one of my first days in the PKK, I meet Besê Erzincan, a guerrilla whose track record of service in the PKK spans several decades. It was also the first time I was admitted to an accommodation for fighters stationed in the Qandil Mountains. I remember my surprise on arriving at the camp, next to a river, in the gathering dusk of late afternoon. I didn't see a camp. All I saw was a table made of untreated wood that was covered with brown plastic and surrounded by pale brown plastic chairs, and, looking more closely, some tea-making equipment beneath a tree. From the path that led to the table I'd spotted a curtain made of a piece of jute, probably hiding a toilet. Nothing else.

We drank tea and chatted, and when darkness started falling, Besê and two other female fighters suggested we go 'inside'. We followed a track until I suddenly noticed another piece of jute. We drew it to one side. Behind it was a thick blanket, and behind that, a tiny hall where we left our shoes before squeezing past two more blankets. My jaw must have dropped. In the middle of a room, whose floors were covered with colourful rugs, was a large wooden table at which three female guerrillas were busy cutting round shapes out of a flat piece of dough with glass jars by the light of a single energy-saving bulb. 'Welcome! We're baking biscuits. Have a seat. Would you like some tea?' A couple more fighters were watching television, on a set standing in a bookcase that was otherwise packed with books.

On the walls, built with bags of stones and sand, hung flags belonging to the PKK and YJA-Star, the women's armed branch of the PKK, as well as Abdullah Öcalan flags. At the back of the room was a low wall, behind which a gas stove and a small electric oven stood on a worktop. I could tell by the smell that the first batch of biscuits was almost ready.

It was around 7 PM. We watched and discussed the news, drank tea and ate biscuits. An hour later it was time for bed.

Led by the hand of one of the women, I found my way through the darkness to the sleeping quarters – which turned out to be concealed behind the jute cloth I'd seen hanging there earlier. Just in front of it, following directions by feel, I found a bottle of water, delved in my bag for my toothbrush and toothpaste and brushed my teeth. There was no separate toilet, but if I followed the path step by step upwards and to the right, no one would be bothered by my peeing there.

The bedroom, roughly fifteen square metres in area, was pink due to the cloths lining the 'walls', with a bright yellow Öcalan flag as the only decoration. There were two little mats laid out along the sides of the room. A third mat was brought out from a storage space behind a curtain. I was given three blankets, one of which I moved from on top to underneath me halfway through the night, to give my hips and shoulders a bit more padding. Spotless rugs on the floor, and in the corner a white bookcase, which made me burst out laughing. 'Why are you laughing?' asked Besê. 'Living half underground,' I replied, 'and with no toilet but a neat little bookcase, it just strikes me as funny.' 'Do you know where we got that from?' asked Besê. 'From villagers who work in the fields here. They know that PKK members always have books. They had an unused bookcase so they brought it round.'

We talked about the women's battle. She told me that the women's movement within the PKK is working on setting up a TV channel for women. She asked me what I thought about that. As a right-minded Western woman who had just arrived amongst the PKK, it struck me as a controversial plan. As if women were incapable of following the news on general channels. As if themes of particular importance to women should not simply receive attention in any medium.

I said it a little hesitantly, as I instinctively felt that Comrade Besê had a fundamentally different and probably more profound feminist view. 'I know,' she said, 'that Western feminists are particularly focused on acquiring positions within the patriarchy. We think that that actually strengthens the patriarchy. Feminism shouldn't be about conforming to masculine values such as competition, power and individualism. We should stand up for feminine values like community spirit and equality. Women who attain positions in the capitalist patriarchy can only do so by throwing femininity overboard.'

So the Kurdish women's movement is not organized in the same way as the women's movement in the patriarchy is, either. The aim is not to gain access to power, but to set up a complete and independent organization. The armed women's groups come from this idea. They rely on themselves and have a complete command structure in which men play no role. A female Öcalan fighter can never have a male commander – although women can in fact command men.

The women's army units, in other words, are not part of the men's forces but fight on an equal level and with equal decision-making power. It is therefore important that these groups are explicitly mentioned. The PKK, for instance, consists of male fighters from the HPG – People's Defence Forces – and YJA-Star – Free Women's Units. The YPG – People's Protection Units – and YPJ – Women's Protection Units – fight in northern Syria. In Şengal you have the YBŞ – Şengal Resistance Units – and the YJŞ – Şengal Women's Units. You can pick out the women's groups by the 'J' in the name, the 'J' of *jin*, 'woman'.

Like the separate, independent forces, independent media fall under the PKK's feminist ideology. Although the term 'feminist' is actually never used. In the view of the Kurdish political movement the organization of women follows from *jinolojî*, 'womanology', or the study of women in the broadest sense of the word. Jinolojî is one of the foundations of the ideology, and therefore also of education. Womanological committees immerse themselves in the history of womankind in areas such as politics and society, and publish on the subject. The publications are used in education and discussed in a continually extending process.

Comrade Hebûn squats down to wash her face by the hose that brings water from a little mountain stream further up. The early sunlight falls on her face, she's in no hurry. A little while later she walks back to the entrance of the cave, ducks under the thick branch of the large tree which hides the opening from drones. Comrades sit on large stones or drink tea in a squat position. One of the women starts brushing Hebûn's hair and plaits it again. At the same time Hebûn herself carefully takes another woman's hair in hand.

I noticed Hebûn's calm aura and quiet but confident manner as soon as she arrived at this camp high in the mountains of northern Iraq two days ago. She's the commander of a group of around twenty fighters, in spite of the fact that she's only been a PKK member for a year and a half. Now that I know her story, having interviewed her yesterday, I can't take my eyes off her. How has she managed this?

'You should talk to Comrade Hebûn,' the commander of the cave where I was staying had said. She didn't say why. Hebûn agreed, so a day later we sat in one of the rooms deep inside the cave. It's wonderful how quickly you become accustomed to living inside the mountains – within just a couple of days, it felt more or less normal. I walk and climb around the cave as if I've never known any different (okay, I'm exaggerating slightly). What a difference from my first hesitant steps inside.

At the entrance I had to bend down a little. After a high-ceilinged chamber of at most three square metres there was a left turn into a narrow corridor where I was most comfortably able to move on my backside. That tallied pretty well with the idea I had of caves: pitch black, narrow, low-ceilinged, damp, a tad oppressive. In the next room, the kitchen, there were pools of water on the ground. Along the walls were black plastic crates of tin plates and bowls, cutlery, glasses and everyday food such as bread, salt, sugar and rice. Next to them a gas cylinder with a single ring burner. A grey metal door gave access to the rest of the cave. '*Şehit Mazda Sikeft*', was written on it in smudged blue-painted letters, 'Martyr Mazda cave'.

Another narrow corridor, this time with a little more headr-oom, although I still had to bend down. Right turn into a room with a higher ceiling, a wooden table and two long benches hewn from the walls of the cave. Around fifteen people fitted around the table. Two small kittens darted back and forth. On a 'shelf', also hewn from the wall, stood a little electric oven and a water tank with a tap. The corridor ceiling ran higher, I was able to walk upright. Around ten metres further in, I was suddenly flabbergasted: I had emerged into a chamber of a good 100 square metres, at least ten metres high in the centre.

Beside me in the corner to my right I saw a wall of piled up sandbags, like the walls of the half-underground living room at the language camp in the Qandil Mountains. Here, too, a blanket served as a door. Here, too, I removed my shoes before entering. Inside, the sandbags were covered with bright pink fabric. On them hung the YJA-Star and PKK flags and portraits of fighters who had died. The portrait of Sakine Cansız, one of the founders of the PKK, was on show amongst them. Cansız is the woman who was murdered along with two other Kurdish women in Paris in January 2013 by the Turkish secret service, MIT. At least, no one doubts that that was the case. Even the French judiciary explicitly stated it in their report on the investigation into the triple murder.

A TV hung on the wall, hidden from view by a throw draped over it. A small lightbulb hung from the ceiling, around two metres up; in the corner stood a bookcase. The wood boards on the floor were covered with red and blue floral-patterned plastic mats. In the evenings, when we watched the news in this room, the fighters kept on urging me to sit on a cloth mat. The softest seat was for the guest, and that was me.

In another corner of the enormous cave there was a similar construction. I slept there, along with a couple of other women. My place was right under the flag of Öcalan. The wall hangings were placed so as to leave space behind for baggage and weapons. A small lightbulb hung from the ceiling, there was a power strip with a torch charging from it, flags, a bookcase. Further back still in the cave, having climbed a short staircase and descended a longer one, there was another such room, offering space for twenty women to sleep. In the caverns and under overhanging rocks lay the food stores and weapons and munition depot.

It's comfortable in the cave. Outside it's baking, inside it's lovely and cool and so spacious that you never feel claustrophobic. The only awkward thing, for me, is the toilet. It's a little way from the cave and now, in September, it gets dark around 7 PM. The toilet in itself is not the problem. It's robustly constructed from close-packed mud and stones to place your feet on, with jute stretched around it for privacy and always a couple of bottles of water to wash with. On the way back to the cave is a handwashing station with a bar of soap. But stumbling over there in the dark on the hand of a guerrilla has been less successful, although it's always been something to laugh about the next morning.

Comrade Hebûn and I chat in the light of a torch. 'What did

you do before you joined the PKK?' I ask. 'I was married and the mother of three children,' she tells me.

Hebûn grew up in Yüksekova. The influence of what they call *aşirets*, Kurdish clans, is still big there. She talks about it in general terms. Women have few rights, literally no right of speech even, living as the men want them to. The men meet and decide about marriage, their lives, punishment and death. 'That's changed since the PKK gained more power,' she says, 'but it's still difficult to disentangle yourself from it as a woman.'

It explains her chosen nom de guerre, Hebûn. It means 'existence'. That's how she feels: only since she became a guerrilla fighter two years ago has she truly existed.

She has two sons and one daughter. The girl is eight, the boys eleven and six. Hebûn was fifteen when she married a young man of nineteen against her will. In answer to the question of what kind of marriage it was, she replies, 'That's not relevant. From day one I refused to accept the marriage.'

When she had been married a year, she went back, as tradition prescribes, to live in her parents' house for three months. After that she refused to return to the man who was her husband, but her family forced her. 'They said, "If you don't go back, we'll kill you." I considered doing it myself. But I wanted to live.'

Through a friend she came into contact with the local department of a women's group in the Kurdish political movement. There she became acquainted with Öcalan's books. She could hardly believe what she was reading. 'Öcalan knows women better than we know ourselves,' she says. 'He knows better than we do how the mentality of men oppresses women. He says we should live freely. Not in the shadow of a man but truly free.'

The book *My Whole Life Was a Struggle* also strengthened her. It was written by Sakine Cansız, nom de guerre Sara. Sara's strong will, her courage and freedom inspired Hebûn. One day she turned her back on her old life. She was twenty-three.

Hebûn was angry with her parents. Enraged even. Now she sees the bigger picture. 'They made me marry against my will when I was just fifteen, but it wasn't them who started that tradition. They too grew up within the aşiret. They don't know any better. It's so ancient, so deeply rooted. I want to fight that tradition and mentality. How would that have been possible as the mother of three children?'

Fighting against the mentality which dominates the aşirets is important, but that ideal has also expanded far beyond its origins. For Hebûn the position of all women living in capitalist society is at stake. 'Truly living freely is impossible in capitalism. That system uses women for itself, for instance by putting them to work so that the powerful within the system can further enrich themselves. Women must be beautiful. Decisions are made without consulting them. Women live as slaves of men, men live as slaves of the system. The man who was my husband was nineteen when we married. He couldn't get out of it any more than I could. The fact that any woman is not free says everything about that system. If there is one woman who is not free, that defines how free women are in that society.'

She disputes the idea that she has abandoned her children, and especially her daughter. The truth is the opposite, in fact. 'Will my children understand my choice? I don't know. I also don't know if we will ever see one another again. I write everything down in my diary. I write about my life here, about the choices I have made, the philosophy of the leader. I write that my family did not know me and the aşirets do not know women. I can't explain everything yet because I don't yet have all the answers myself. I'm gaining answers as time goes by. The more I learn, the better I can deal with the loss of my children.

'My children will probably get to read my diary when I have become a martyr. But it's not crucially important whether they understand me or not. I didn't join the PKK just for them, but for all women, all children. I can be a better mother here. Here I know what I'm living for. I didn't know that before. What I'm doing now is my greatest duty as a mother.'

Nevertheless she does not say that she fled the life she had or that the PKK is her refuge. 'I only went to school for two years,' she says. 'If my family had allowed me to attend for longer and I had been able to go to university, I would have found out about the organization earlier and might have joined sooner. The PKK is not an escape. The PKK is where I belong.'

I listen carefully to the sound of her voice. I watch how her lips move and look into her eyes. But Hebûn's voice is steady. Her lips do not tremble, her eyes remain clear. I mention this. Hebûn says, 'A woman crying achieves nothing.'

ALLIANCE WITH CONSTANTINOPLE

Kurdish clans and the PKK have been at war with one another since the early existence of the PKK. One of the first PKK attacks, in 1979, was on a Kurdish clan leader, Celal Bucak. He was an MP for a centre-right party that participated in government and was known as a brutal ruler over the villagers under his authority. The attack on Bucak's life (which in fact failed) was a way of acquiring fame for the PKK, which had officially been founded less than a year previously. With this act they showed that they were fighting against patriarchal systems, from the Turkish state to Kurdish feudalism.

As early as the Ottoman Empire, Kurdish clan leaders were closely connected with the central authority in Constantinople, present-day Istanbul. The Kurdish rulers enjoyed autonomy, but that had almost nothing to do with democracy, as the Kurdish people had nothing to say. For the clan leaders the alliance with Constantinople was a way of maintaining their own power and wealth. In the years around the First World War it became apparent how tragic the consequences of that collaboration could be: the Armenian genocide was largely carried out by Kurdish militias, known as the Hamidiye Cavalry, founded at the end of the nineteenth century by Sultan Abdülhamid II to strengthen the relationship between Kurdish clans and Constantinople.

Nothing has essentially changed since then. In the 1980s the state breathed new life into the existing system of 'village guards', in which villagers were armed and paid by the state to help fight against the PKK. Many men were recruited against their will. Some were compelled by the state, which would otherwise burn the entire village to the ground. Others were forced by clan leaders, who took the state's weapons and money, distributing the weapons among their serfs and pocketing most of the money. The system still exists and the state is constantly increasing the number of village guards.

The clans' power has declined substantially in recent decades, and the PKK has been important in this process. Urbanization has also played a role: the system does not do so well outside the original rural clan habitat. But the clans have been far from eradicated. In some Kurdish regions they still have a great deal of influence, if not politically then in the personal lives of clan members. Women traditionally come off badly and are married young, generally to men who are also underage or barely adults. In the judgment of the PKK, clans are really a kind of small state. Families can also be mini-states, with an autocratic father at the head who does not allow his wife any freedom, and the children as the weakest members at the bottom of the ladder. This is the mentality that the PKK seeks to challenge.

I once drew this parallel in an interview with Cemil Bayık. I had thought that the PKK rather resembled an abused wife. After all, the Turkish state simply continues to oppress and murder the Kurds, while the PKK keeps on insisting that it is striving for a democratic Turkey in which Turks, Kurds and all other groups in the population live together on an equal footing. 'Turkey doesn't want you,' I say to Bayık. 'You resemble an abused wife who keeps on returning to her husband because she believes he can change and a day will come when he'll really love her, without violence. Isn't it time to face reality and give up that dream? Why do you want to set up your democratic system within Turkey? Why wouldn't you fight for an independent Kurdistan and build democracy there, without having to wait for the Turks?'

'What should an abused wife do?' Bayık asked in response. 'Leave,' I replied. 'No, she should fight,' he said. 'She can leave to save herself physically, but that doesn't solve the problem. She needs to fight the system that makes the abuse possible. Otherwise it will continue and she will never be free. Just as a woman must fight against abuse, so we fight against the patriarchal system that is the cause of the Kurds' problems. Only when women are free, only when the patriarchal system no longer exists, can society be free and can the Kurds and all other peoples be free. You know our slogan "*Jin-Jiyan-Azadî*" – "Woman, Life, Freedom" – don't you? There's a good reason it's seen as one of our most important slogans. Fighting for a state of our own would work directly against our most important goal.'

SEEING EACH OTHER'S SOCKS ON THE WASHING LINE

That radical feminism comes with a morality we would call conservative in the West. The women's quarters are strictly separated from the men's. Male and female fighters only ever see one another in full uniform. The women never wear their hair down when the men are around. The men are generally smooth shaven. There are rules for how far the zip of your uniform jacket should be done up: at least to the top of the breast pockets, and no lower.

As a woman you don't talk about personal hygiene in front of men, and vice versa. During a *tekmil* – the mini-meeting about the daily business of the camp – I was once criticized by another woman in the camp because I had wished her '*xwesi be*' as was customary after she returned from the shower. You say it to someone who has just showered and it means something like 'May it have refreshed you'. Kurdish is full of such expressions for everyday things. My 'xwesi be' made it clear that she had showered, and in the presence of men that was overly intimate information.

In the days before the Raqqa offensive started up again, there was intensive toing and froing between the men's and women's barracks at the main military base. When men and women visit one another's quarters they announce themselves by saying, 'Would now be a good time?' That gives the fighters the chance to quickly tidy up the base to receive a visit. Generally it amounts to running round at lightning speed, whipping laundry off the line and out of sight. There was great consternation among the women when they thought they'd put everything away but realized they had left underwear in sight just as tea was served to male visitors. The drying rack was moved at top speed. Internally I was in fits of laughter about the panic. After the visitors had left, the female fighters explained the rules to me once again.

Not that I don't get the principle, of course, after all my years in Kurdistan. In Diyarbakır I never hung underwear out to dry in view on my balcony, always behind something else like a towel or T-shirt. The Öcalan fighters come from that society and follow the customs common to that people. At the same time it is an oversimplification to label this behaviour as 'conservative' purely on the basis of our Western perspective. I challenged the women on the subject a little. 'Surely the men know that you wear underwear? It's not a secret, is it? You do realize they wear underwear too, don't you?' 'Of course, Comrade Avaşîn,' was the response of the expressive Comrade Mizgîn (a popular name in the PKK, meaning 'good news'). 'But we don't want to be attractive for superficial reasons. We don't want to arouse such thoughts in our comrades. It's about what we think, our brains, that's what we want to be appreciated for, not for anything else.'

So for those who think that in the PKK and YPG the women do the laundry, including the men's clothes: they don't even see each other's socks hanging on the line.

For Westerners it's hard to imagine that sexuality plays no role in the life of the guerrillas, that young men and women can live a sexless life without problems. It's so unimportant that even starting a conversation about it seemed silly. My potential questions about it said more about the Western vision of sex and romantic relations, which in a nutshell comes down to life without sex being unnatural and a romantic relationship always worth striving for.

That view of life is so ingrained in our society and popular culture that we don't even doubt those 'ideals'.

The only person I dared raise the subject with was a German I met in northern Syria, who had directly experienced the Western perspective. 'Lots of people in Germany, the Netherlands and other Western countries cannot imagine living without sex,' I said. 'It's actually easy,' she replied. 'I've been doing it now for more than twenty years. It's perfectly possible to have meaningful relationships with people and feel a real connection without sex.'

I spoke with other guerrillas about man-woman relationships in general. They come from a society in which marrying (young) and having a family is the norm. What's it like to say goodbye to those expectations in life? 'Kurds have no safe place to start a family and raise their children in freedom,' a man in the foothills of the Şengal Mountains told me. 'Birds don't lay eggs until they've built a safe nest. Where should I build that safe nest?' In one of the most explicit references to sex that a fighter made to me, he added, 'Capitalist societies have this idea that people should pair off for an entire lifetime. Animals don't do that, do they? Surely it's bound up with seasons, for instance, or phases of life? Why should that be different for the human species?'

That's not to say that love is unimportant. Love is everything. The outspoken, slightly macho fighter Botan said heatedly, 'Love: is that having a relationship and then drawing a line under it a couple of years later, and then starting another, then another? That's got nothing whatsoever to do with love. It's an insult to love.'

The fighters aim for a different sort of love. Love for the motherland, but also for their fellow fighters. *Hevaltî*, or comradeship, is placed above all else. A Dutch-Kurdish woman once came to the base in Kirkuk, bringing items donated in the Netherlands for the PKK (toothpaste, thick jumpers, socks). She asked me if I felt like part of the group. No, I didn't. As an outsider I can never be part of their comradeship. They will give their lives for one another. The code is, if a fellow fighter's life is in danger, you throw yourself in front of him or her to receive the potentially deadly blow.

For fighters, love is not an individual matter but is focused on the community. It is the seed I spoke of previously with Comrade Batufa, which lives in everyone and has been more or less suffocated by the patriarchal, capitalist reality. The better you learn to live the ideology, the more that seed is nourished. What counts then is love for the motherland and mankind, which causes the differences between ethnic groups and religions to fade, while respect, love for everyone's individuality, culture and religion grow.

POINTING AT A WOMAN

The PKK is safe for women. Of course the question is to what extent female fighters would confide in me if they were sexually harassed by their male colleagues, but not one woman I asked mentioned a negative experience with men within the movement. I myself never felt unsafe for a second in my year among the Öcalan fighters. And no, that's not because I was often in the company of women. Even in their absence, I was treated as a human being. I never heard a sexist remark, there was no flirting or staring, let alone harassment.

I asked Besê Erzincan, probably the most experienced female fighter I spoke to, what the consequences would be for a man if he were to overstep the mark. She said that at the very least he would be stripped of his responsibilities. Depending on the seriousness of the offence, additional measures might follow, ranging from writing a report reflecting on his lapse and outlining his plans for improvement, to a period in a prison within the organization. Supplementary education is generally also part of the package of measures. The punishment seen as the most drastic is living in isolation within the group for a number of days or a week. You take part in everyday life, but no one talks to you.

'How is that possible?' I ask Besê. 'All over the world, women are bothered by sexual harassment, but here it hardly happens at all?' 'Education, education, education,' was her answer. 'Such problems have everything to do with power and patriarchal structures. We dispense with both here. Men are not even allowed to point at a woman.' She means that literally. Men do not point at women, for instance during a discussion – nor women at men, for that matter. Raising your voice is completely unacceptable. Even during the pep talk the fighters received before advancing on Raqqa, the commander did not raise his voice. In fact he almost whispered. Crossing one leg over the other is seen as masculine behaviour, so you'll never see it in the PKK, YPG or YPJ. I actually found that awkward. Try not crossing your legs for an entire year. Sometimes I did it secretly when I happened to have a moment alone. If someone came in, I quickly placed both feet on the ground.

Various female fighters said that their male colleagues were afraid of them. At the base in Qamişlo I once asked a male fighter about it. 'The women say you men are afraid of them. Is that true?' I asked. 'Yes, definitely!' he replied. 'Women are the source of life. That gives them a power we men can't touch. Of course we're afraid of that.' He was deadly serious.

If a man – or woman – commits an offence, whatever its nature, education is always the most important measure to prevent repetition. 'And if a man sexually harasses a woman and more education doesn't help and things go wrong again, what then?' I ask Besê. She laughs loudly. 'Then we send you away. Off you go, back to your father's house, get out! But in all my decades in the PKK I've never seen that happen.'

All the education in the PKK, YPG and YPJ is mixed, except for the 'fundamental education', lessons which centre on male and female roles. Separate education, especially if it takes place in the Middle East, raises eyebrows in the West. However, it is not about prohibiting men and women from spending time together. This education focuses on freeing PKK members from the thought patterns of traditional, strongly patriarchal society. Men and women have different routes to take in that respect. Men must recognize their position of power, built up over the centuries, and break down the associated masculinity in themselves, while women must recognize their femininity as a source of power and of a new, equal society.

It would be comparable with education to combat institutional racism – if that existed anywhere. Black and white people would have different ground to cover. One group has institutional power and is influenced by it, whereas the other lacks that power. Patterns that spring from those differences would inevitably arise in mixed education and undermine the target of the education, combating racism. Only when you accept the core as a fact – racism exists and is institutional, or, in the PKK, the patriarchy exists and is institutional – can you get to work abolishing it.

TO MY LEADER!

My Leader! Writing a letter to you is actually the most difficult thing of all. Because everything you have invested, the fact that you have succeeded in bringing the revolution, for Kurdistan, for women and even for the Middle East, to this point, fills a person with the most elevated emotions and the greatest happiness, but at the same time we are weighed down with the fact that we fall short when compared with your efforts. There have been all kinds of harbingers of the revolution, symbols of life as a comrade who does not fall short. And the examples of Heval Zinar and Heval Doğa have revealed to us how to be a comrade without falling short. Their lives are virtually manuals for what we need to do when faced with any given situation. I therefore believe, worthy leader, that being a true comrade in this period means that I must follow in the footsteps of Heval Zinar. I want to make that manifest in all honesty. I have in no way made that decision from an obsession with death. On the contrary, however much pain I experience at never having seen you in person, I know that I am with you in spirit, that you are a universal leader for us all, that loyalty to you is of far greater significance than seeing you in person. I cannot completely put my feelings on this point into words, but I want to make it clear that you are not just an individual for us but an institution, the institution of truth.

I therefore know, now that I am on my way to action, that only with my success in this act and my entire emotional world can I be an answer to you. In that understanding I devote myself to the act. I have always been convinced that I would see you on a Newroz morning at the city walls of Amed, saluting the rising sun, and today I am more convinced of that than ever. I am convinced that you as the leader and the Kurdish community as a people have the greatest possible right to that. I feel that that day is not far off. With the promise of a meaningful life and similarly meaningful action I want to embrace you with feelings of affection, longing and respect. I also beg your forgiveness.

[...]

TO THE WOMEN IN OUR BATTLE!

The reality which most fills me with pride in the ranks of freedom and which arouses my emotions, is the progress that has been made in the women's movement and the women's struggle. Whatever we do to be worthy of our Chairman on this point, we will always fall short. Our Chairman has enabled the existence of an identity as a free woman, an identity involving struggle and resistance in order to obtain that freedom. He has enabled us to be more than ordinary everyday women, he has made us a community of women to act as a model to the entire world. All that is a great achievement, for which we have our Chairman to thank. I think that as women, we owe our Chairman even more.

We therefore have an important reason to fight, the most elevated reason, even. On that basis, we as a community of women all over the world will do whatever is necessary, of that I am convinced. I want to make it clear that being worthy of our Chairman, of the line of women's freedom, of his identity as a party leader, will be my personal goal.

Finally, I have also read the note that my female friends sent me. I was very pleased with it. I want to make it clear that I will try to be an answer on that basis, that I will take their expectations into account in my approach. Affectionate greetings to all women in our struggle.

At a base in Kirkuk, twelve women sit outside on stones and

pieces of cardboard under a bare tree. It's November; the sun is shining and warms the company. Comrade Commander Nuhayla is reading out the 'report' by Comrade Güven Amara Roj, who has blown herself up along with another comrade, Harun, on their way to Ankara to launch an attack. They were discovered ahead of time by the Turkish security services. There are videos online, showing the two being ordered to give themselves up and their car exploding into thousands of pieces.

A 'report' is a personal statement, in this case a parting report in which Güven explains her motives for a suicide attack. She briefly outlines her childhood in a 'patriotic family' in Eruh, the village in the province of Siirt where the PKK first attacked the state in 1984. In 2005 – when she was twenty – she joined the 'Freedom Movement'. Five years later she resolved to carry out a suicide attack. The guerrillas do not actually use this term. They call it *fedai eylem*, which translates as 'an act of conviction'.

Comrade Güven is a special case. She is not a PKK fighter. She was on her way to carry out an attack in the name of the TAK, the Teyrêbazên Azadiya Kurdistan, the Kurdistan Freedom Hawks. The TAK is a breakaway faction of the PKK, reputed to have been founded by guerrillas who were dissatisfied with what they saw as the overly humanist course of the PKK. They carry out attacks on military targets in cities, causing deaths not only among the military and the police, but generally also among civilians. How the system precisely works within the TAK is unclear, but Comrades Güven and Harun had clearly received permission from their commanders to carry out an attack in Ankara. Before they set off they wrote another report. Güven's, which covers five A4 pages, addresses several groups: the people, her comrades, her female comrades, her leader (Öcalan) and her family.

The PKK says it has no authority over the TAK and even that they have nothing to do with one another. Why then do they read out a 'report' by a fallen TAK member in class? Commander Nuhayla doesn't see the problem. She says they often use texts by fighters from other groups in training, including Che Guevara, for instance. Clearly Güven's words are precisely what was needed for this training.

But the training is not about committing a fedai eylem. It is about how you can fully develop as a woman by freeing yourself from the patriarchal mores with which you have grown up. The aim is from now on to be led by your will and to strive for freedom. A fedai eylem such as that of Güven inspires: committing such an attack is quite something, but blowing yourself up before you're caught in advance is really the pinnacle. Every woman in the PKK strives for this kind of iron will. Although far from everyone will strive to put that will to work for a fedai eylem.

For women, fedai eylems have a special significance. As a nom de guerre, many female fighters choose the name of a famous woman who they feel is an example of someone so strong-willed that she gave her life for the cause. For instance I have come across a number of comrades with the name Elefteriya. Elefteriya was a Greek woman, mother of a toddler and a baby, who set herself on fire in February 2006 in Athens. She was protesting against the arrest of Öcalan, which had taken place in the same month seven years earlier. Comrades called Zîlan have named themselves after one who blew herself up in 1996 in civilian clothing in the middle of a military ceremony in Dersim, killing eight Turkish soldiers as well as herself.

Öcalan explicitly spoke out against suicide attacks after a real wave was set in motion following his arrest in February 1999. After his rejection, the number of protest self-immolations dropped sharply. The fighters nevertheless speak with respect for those who dare to do it. One of them tells me, 'It's in part thanks to the fedai eylems after he was kidnapped and brought to Turkey that Öcalan is still alive. They made it clear how much he means to the Kurdish people, both in Europe and in Turkey. Fedai eylems are like a ring of fire laid around the leader to protect him. Certainly as women we are indebted to him because his ideology set us free. This is how we protect one another. This is how we enable one another to live.'

Fedai eylems are carried out for various reasons. They are a 'ring of fire', but sometimes also simply the result of developments in warfare in Turkey. For instance the army in south-east Turkey increasingly uses armed drones in its conflict with the PKK. They make 'conventional' attacks on police and army posts more and more difficult. While unarmed drones are only useful for detection – by the time a bomber or attack helicopter has arrived, the guerrilla action on the military post has already been carried out – armed drones can detect the guerrillas and immediately take them out. The PKK is adapting by driving cars or even lorries loaded with explosives towards a target and blowing up the lot.

That kind of attack is also always preceded by a 'report', in which the potential attacker explains the intended target, the suitability of the chosen method and their motivation. If they are granted permission – in these kinds of attacks often by their direct commander – the action is carried out. No permission, no action. Those who carry out such an attack always do so voluntarily.

Then there is the fedai eylem of which Comrade Bêrîtan is the original mother (see portrait on page xxx). In 1992 she jumped from an outcrop of rocks to her death. It was either that or fall into the enemy's hands. Faced with that choice, every guerrilla will choose death. And given the chance, they will take down a number of enemies with them.

Arîn Mirxan did that during the attack on Kobani on 5 October 2014. The YPG/J were trapped by ISIS on the strategic mountain of Miştenur. Mirxan loaded herself up with grenades, approached the enemy and blew herself up under an ISIS tank. Two tanks were destroyed, probably more than twenty ISIS men died. Arîn Mirxan was twenty years old.

I was in Kobani in January 2015, soon after the YPG/J had won the battle. The destruction was complete, most of the city lay in ruins. There was rubble all over the street, tattered roofs hung off the buildings, everything was covered with a thick layer of dust and grit. In May 2017 I returned. The main street, which begins at the border crossing with Turkey, had been unrecognizably smartened up. The shops were open, there were people outside drinking tea, children playing on the pavement. Cars travelled unhurriedly across a large square, once a scene of devastation. In the middle stood a white statue of a woman with large wings. Arîn Mirxan.

Every 'martyr' is a saint to PKK, YPG and YPJ fighters. The word is always on the tip of the fighters' tongues when they mention their dead comrades. You're not allowed to say they 'died', and I didn't use the word during my year with the Öcalan fighters. *Şehit namerin*. Martyrs are immortal.

The transformations of men and women in the PKK run parallel to the PKK's own transformation. In the beginning of the conflict, from the foundation of the PKK in 1978 until the first half of the 1990s, there was not only the aim of a nation-state for the Kurds, but also a related image of the role of men and women. An interesting perspective on this is given in the academic article 'From Kawa the Blacksmith to Ishtar the Goddess', by political scientist Handan Çağlayan, who carried out a great deal of research into women in the PKK.

Kawa the blacksmith is a central figure in Kurdish mythology who lived in Mesopotamia, where the people, having lived in prosperity for centuries, were groaning under the reign of an Assyrian king, Dehak. The king did not know that Satan prepared his food each day in the guise of a royal chef. Dehak thanked the cook, who asked to kiss his shoulder. When he did, there was a flash of light and two black snakes appeared on the king's shoulders. Those snakes, said Satan – now in the guise of a doctor – must be fed with the brains of children from the people.

From that moment the people lived in darkness: the sun literally ceased to rise. Crops stopped growing, birds flew elsewhere and people no longer laughed. One child after another was sacrificed to the king.

The turnaround came when Kawa decided to ignore the order to feed the brains of his last remaining child, a daughter, to Dehak's snakes. Instead of his daughter's brains, he brought those of a sheep. The king did not notice the difference. The news spread at lightning speed among the people and everyone followed Kawa's example.

The number of children saved soon ran into hundreds. They set out for the Zagros Mountains, where they learnt to live in the wild. Kawa was with them and taught the boys and girls growing up in freedom to fight. One day it was time. They left the mountains and set course for Dehak's castle. Many villagers along their way joined the young fighters. Kawa, standing on a rock, gave a signal with his smith's hammer, at which thousands of fighters and villagers shattered the gates of the castle and defeated the guards.

Kawa rushed to the king's quarters. He killed the king with his hammer and cut off his head, killing the two snakes. He then climbed the mountain above the castle and lit a fire to let the people of Mesopotamia know that they were freed from Dehak. Soon fires were burning everywhere and the good news spread. The next morning the sun rose again. Flowers began to bloom, melons grew as they had before, eagles, partridges and peacocks returned. The people laughed and danced in groups around the fire to the music of flutes and drums.*

It is the story of Newroz, the beginning of spring, celebrated by various peoples, including Afghans, Kurds and Persians, every year on 21 March. Fires are central to the celebration. Kurds still dance in groups around them to the music of flutes and drums. The myth does not tell us whether people in Kawa's time jumped over the fires as they do now.

The PKK has given Newroz an important place in the 'construction' of the historic story of the Kurds, or alternatively phrased, in the construction of the Kurdish identity. The history of the Kurds may be centuries old, but in the end every national identity is a construction and the Kurdish identity is no exception. The myth of Kawa places that identity in the broader history of Mesopotamia.

One of the PKK's founding members, Mazlum Doğan, linked Kawa with the modern battle of the Kurds. He was arrested in 1979 and incarcerated in Prison No. 5 in Diyarbakır. The prison was notorious for the severe torture that went on inside it, which,

* Abridged, free retelling of 'Kawa and the story of Newroz', written by Mark Campbell, published 21 March 2014 on the site of the Kurdish Institute of Brussels.

particularly after the coup of 12 September 1980, got so out of hand that prisoners died. On 21 March 1982, on Newroz, Mazlum Doğan set himself on fire in his cell to protest against the inhumane treatment. He grew to be a legend, 'the modern Kawa'. Mazlum's portrait can be seen all over the place among the PKK, both in photos and posters and on the little pins often worn by fighters. I also frequently came across his portrait in the organization's cemeteries. His legend added power to the PKK's summons to fighters to sacrifice themselves for the struggle.

Women, too, obeyed the summons, writes Handan Çağlayan. Until the mid-1990s the only victim – don't use that word when talking to PKK members – of such an act was the perpetrator herself. In 1996 that changed with Comrade Zîlan's fedai eylem in Dersim. She took at least eight Turkish soldiers with her in death when blowing herself up during a military ceremony. Although it was late June, she approached the group of soldiers wearing a jacket. The explosives underneath must have made her look pregnant.

Zîlan's story became a new myth, one that did justice to the ever more important position women held, not only within the PKK but in the entire Kurdish movement, from Kurdish politics to human rights organizations. In the ideology, the roots of the Kurds became increasingly connected with the matriarchal Neolithic society in which goddesses symbolized the central role of women. One of the most important goddesses was Ishtar, who has many guises, including that of a fertility goddess, connected with the land and its produce. A creative power, and thus a perfect figure to link today's Kurdish movement with its matriarchal origins. But there was no 'modern Ishtar', in the way that Mazlum Doğan embodied the 'modern Kawa'. After her fedai eylem, Zîlan was cast in that role. At the end of the 1990s, Öcalan wrote about the symbolic 'creative mission' that Zîlan had given to women in her action. The 'modern Ishtar' was born. Öcalan wrote of her, 'The old masculinity died the moment Zîlan's identity was revealed.'

If femininity wins, the nation-state is condemned to death. In other words, the PKK as representative of feminine power will defeat the state, which preserves masculine dominance. Victory is certain. After all, the origin of mankind, and its power, lies in feminine values from the Neolithic era. The PKK therefore no longer gives women the power to break out of traditional roles, to take up arms and become socially active, as in the early years of the PKK in the 1980s and 1990s – or at least, that is still the case, but there has been an important transformation. Now it is the feminine values which give the PKK, YPG and YPJ their power. Without that the fighters lose their strength.

It sounds like a destructive ideal to give your life for the struggle as Zîlan did, but it's not. Political scientist Handan Çağlayan writes, based on Öcalan's books, that the 'creative role' allotted to women, the role in which they create by giving their lives, is strictly connected with the 'successful execution of tasks and the realization of victory'. In practice that is reflected in the report you have to write as a potential candidate for carrying out a fedai eylem, in which you have to convince several people that you have developed yourself sufficiently to carry out such an act. Of course, you might wonder – as do I – whether those reports really say anything about a person's development, or whether they tell us more about their skill in the use of the right jargon to convince commanders. Not everyone attains that level of development.

But still. Anyone who spends long with the fighters sees how they strive every day to develop and to carry out their tasks to the best of their abilities. Not because the commander says they should – as they seldom receive commands – but because it is part of the task to be completed. The young Comrade Evîndar, whom I met at the base in Kirkuk, is the example most clearly imprinted on my retina. What dedication I saw her bring, day after day, to even the dullest of tasks, such as sweeping the hall. After the lesson in which Comrade Güven's report was read out, I asked her if she too hoped someday to carry out a fedai eylem. 'Of course, Comrade Avaşîn,' she replied. 'That is the aim of every one of us. But I still have many shortcomings. I am working every day to overcome them. That is my motivation in everything I do.'

PORTRAIT

COMRADE KIMMIE WANTS TO DIE FOR THE REVOLUTION

YPJ fighter Kimmie did not arrive at the front in Raqqa without a struggle. It took all her powers of persuasion to convince the commanders that that was her place, that only there could she carry out her task and that she was the only one for the job. Her determination helped. So when the offensive to drive ISIS out of Raqqa started up again, she jumped into the pickup truck with the other women fighters and went.

That unique task was given to her, Kimmie tells me during a pause in fighting in a village south of Ain Issa in the north of Syria, by a Yazidi woman. It was in the summer of 2015. She had just come from England, where she had grown up, and arrived in Syria to see the 'revolution' she had heard of close up. A year earlier, ISIS had attacked the Yazidis in Şengal, a bloodbath directed at the men, with thousands of women and girls taken prisoner. 'I visited a Yazidi refugee camp,' Kimmie says. 'Conditions there were so bad, there were shortages of everything. There were women who wanted to give me their babies so that I could take them to Europe. When I said that that was impossible, a woman asked me at least to tell the world about the fate of the Yazidis. I promised to do that.'

In order to tell the story as well as possible, Kimmie reasoned, she had to go to the front. 'I grew up in the West and I know the media there,' she explains. 'If I were really the first British woman to take up arms against ISIS, I would certainly receive media attention.

Then I'd be able to tell people about the Yazidis. That's why I particularly wanted to go to the front.' Initially the commanders didn't understand her reasoning. They gave her supportive tasks on the YPJ's media team. She did what she had to in that position, but it did not get her access to Western media. 'In the end, I convinced them that it was important to grab the chance now. After all, Raqqa is the last large city from which ISIS will be expelled. We're not going to get that chance again.'

HORROR FILM

Kimmie, whose full name is Kimberly Taylor, grew up in Blackburn, north of Manchester. After studying maths at the University of Liverpool she decided to go travelling. Particularly in Africa, she was confronted with problems to which she saw no solution; not in feminism, nor in any of the other ideologies in which she immersed herself, such as communism and anarchism. That's why she wanted to see what precisely was involved in that 'revolution' in the north of Syria. She was immediately sold on it. She decided to remain and join the women's army, the YPJ. Her nom de guerre: Zîlan. She followed a language course and says her Kurdish is still poor, but I'm impressed by how far she has come in a year and a half. She talks, makes mistakes, laughs them away, tries again and makes progress every day.

She's not afraid, she says, when she fights. It's only the nocturnal guard duties in villages where ISIS has just been wiped out that she finds nerve-racking. 'Compare it with a horror film,' she tells me as the two of us keep guard on a base and tuck into a lunch of chicken drumsticks and bread. 'You know that something scary or dangerous can happen any moment, the tension is constantly increasing. ISIS may have been expelled from the village, but they often come back in the night, alone or in small groups, to carry out an attack. But it's dark so you can't see anything, you have no overview. Every sound can mean that the enemy is nearby. In the end you have to shoot. That's the moment that you jump up out of your chair from the release of tension in the climactic moment of a horror film.'

What precisely so attracted her to what she found in the north of Syria? In what way is this a 'revolution'? 'People here are working to rebuild society from the ground up,' Kimmie explains. 'It's not a reform of what there was, but a radically different society, in which the patriarchy no longer has any place. Not just in education, for example, or government, but on all fronts. Militarily, economically, socially and judicially too. People really have the deciding voice on their lives on a local level. Their individuality is respected, no one dominates another. I call that a revolution.'

According to Kimmie that revolution offers a solution to all problems resulting from the political and economic systems which currently blight the world, namely capitalism and liberalism. 'The revolution taking place here could take root everywhere. That gives me hope, for problems I saw in Africa as well. As in the Middle East, Western systems have been introduced there which have destroyed the more communally organized society.'

Her home country, too, with its deeply rooted and constantly growing class differences, Kimmie believes, offers an excellent breeding ground for the anti-capitalist, anti-patriarchal revolution preached by Öcalan. She mentions the revival of fascist ideas in Europe and says, 'If you call yourself a revolutionary, and I do, then you must be prepared to die for your ideals. I see it as my responsibility to take up arms to physically fight fascism. Look at Europe's history with Nazism. The resistance wasn't organized enough. The Jews were put on trains and no one did a damned thing! Here the resistance is organized. I'll do whatever it takes to protect this revolution. Against ISIS's fascism and Erdoğan's Turkey for now, then against any other threat that presents itself.'

NEGOTIATING TABLE

Her hope to gain media access by being the first and only British woman to take up arms against ISIS was thoroughly fulfilled. There were big stories in newspapers such as *The Guardian*, *The Times* and *The Independent*, and she spoke on the BBC. Large photos featured Kimmie at the front in military fatigues, Kalashnikov on her shoulder, floral Kurdish scarf around her head or shoulders, thick blond hair in a ponytail. She collected a multitude of followers on Facebook. Whenever an internet connection becomes available, she posts updates on the progress of the battle, shares photos of the front and provides insight into her motives for fighting. She mentions the Yazidis in every interview. The liberation of Raqqa will, she hopes, lead to the liberation of at least some of the thousands of Yazidi women who are still in ISIS's hands.

'I see the liberation of Raqqa as the last big chance to draw the world's attention to the revolution going on here,' Kimmie says. 'It's important to increase public support for this force, which is Syria's only hope against capitalism and Islamic fascism. Public support puts governments under pressure. That's important, as they determine who will be next to sit at the negotiating table and talk about the future of Syria.'

Meanwhile Kimmie is worried about the first commander she had as a YPJ fighter, Comrade Narlîn. She was stationed on the mountain of Qaraçox, in the north-easternmost part of Syria, when Turkey bombed the area at the end of April 2017. Did Narlîn survive? She has asked around, but no one can say for certain. Not until all fighters are called together for what they call a *talimat*, an official announcement of the latest news about the battle and an explanation of the political and military relationships in the region. A talimat, literally an 'instruction', is generally a good ten pages long and expressed in impassioned language. One or two fighters read them out. Every talimat finishes with instructions for the continuation of the conflict, which basically always boil down to intensifying the revolution.

The name of Commander Narlîn is mentioned. She is one of the 'martyrs'. Kimmie suspected as much, yet she is still shocked. Once the talimat has finished, she walks away crying. A couple of comrades follow to comfort her. Some embrace her for a moment, but not too long. 'Comrade Narlîn was a good commander with a great deal of influence,' Kimmie's direct commander says. 'Don't cry about martyrdom. Take your emotions with you into battle.'

PASSPORT

A couple of months later, after the battle for Raqqa, Kimmie re-emerges on Facebook. She shares her joy about the successful operation and writes enraged posts about the manner in which Erdoğan tries to frustrate the success of the Kurds. Then suddenly her account disappears. The newspaper interviews stop.

Perhaps she's preparing for her return to England. She guesses she'll be arrested as soon as she sets foot on British soil. Anyone who fights in Syria, even against ISIS, among the troops supported by the West, is suspected of terrorism. Based on the experiences of compatriots who have preceded her, all of them men, she does not expect to be detained long. They will take her passport for the duration of a criminal trial, so she will have to spend that time in the UK. She will embrace the situation in order to extend her 'diplomatic work', as she calls it: giving still more interviews, travelling the country for lectures, perhaps writing a book.

Perhaps her fighting experience has brought her to Afrin. Perhaps she wants to keep that secret because fighting against Turkey, a NATO ally, may cause bigger legal problems. If she's fighting there, the announcement of her 'martyrdom' could come any day. Of course she doesn't want to die, Kimmie told me, immediately tacking on an additional question: 'How do you do that, not dying? I have no idea. It's about how you live. Here I'm more alive than ever. I know I'll die for this revolution. It's just a question of when.'

CHAPTER 6

The Revolution is Not Bloodless

Five AKP politicians were murdered while I was with the PKK, between the end of May 2016 and the start of June 2017. In summer 2017, two more politicians followed, and a teacher was abducted and later found murdered. The victims were taken by a PKK roadblock and later found dead, or overpowered close to their homes or work and executed on the spot. The culprit: the PKK.

So in response to the question of whether the PKK kills civilians, the answer is yes. It's not just an issue of recent years. In the forty-year history of the organization, civilians have always died, whether as direct targets or as collateral in actions against military targets. One of the first PKK attacks, in 1979, was even directed at a civilian, namely the Kurdish clan leader Celal Bucak. He survived.

If you ask the guerrillas whether the PKK murders civilians, they say no. All fighters I spoke to were strict on this. Civilians, they say without exception, can never be the target of an attack. Executing civilians is completely unacceptable.

The PKK posts videos of attacks on the Gerilla TV site, where the favourite targets are army bases, police stations and military convoys. The locations are always somewhere high in the mountains, far from the inhabited world, with a negligible chance of civilian victims. Attacks on military convoys are somewhat more risky because civilians also make use of mountain roads. It makes watching roadside bomb video clips a breathtaking affair. You see civilian traffic passing by, knowing a bomb will go off any moment, with background murmuring from those about to detonate the bomb from a distance. A white minibus drives out of view, a blue car disappears around a bend. Then the first military vehicles come into view. A bang, shrapnel flying around. The voices say, '*Bijî serok Apo!*' – Long live leader Apo!

The Turkish media still sometimes use the word 'mine' when writing about such attacks. That's incorrect. The PKK renounced the use of mines in 2006, because they result in random rather than targeted victims. The PKK uses roadside bombs.

In the mountains in the north of Iraq, I speak with a fighter just back from Bakur, or Kurdistan in Turkey. He had been stationed there for years and carried out many such attacks. 'How do you manage to plant those bombs?' I ask him. It seemed impossible to me that it could be done without being seen, even at night. He replies, 'They're called roadside bombs, but they're not in the roadside verge, they're underneath the asphalt. We dig tunnels, so we can place the explosives under the road surface.'

After a successful attack, he tells me, the person responsible receives a small gift. 'You're given a pin, for instance, or a pistol.' Apparently it's just what's available, or what's fitting for the successful perpetrator of an attack. I've received those pins occasionally myself as a gift from a fighter when I said goodbye after spending a while on a base. It is usually adorned with a portrait of Öcalan or an important fighter who has become a 'martyr'. My collection now includes Sakine Cansız, Bêrîtan and the leader himself.

Nevertheless civilians do die. A mayor is a civilian, as is a teacher, the leader of a local AKP youth movement (in practice a club for adults), and the son of a leader of a local village guards association.

But PKK members do not see those they murder as civilians. The public grieves for the teacher, mayor or governor, but by murdering them the PKK has eliminated a spy, a traitor, a collaborator against the people. 'Punished' is the term the organization uses in reports to the press and public. Those reports are sent out by HPG-BIM, or the press and communication centre of the HPG (the armed branch of the PKK). Via HPG-BIM they arrive at Kurdish press offices, the most important of which is Firat, abbreviated to ANF. They state why such civilians have been 'punished'. Turkish media report only briefly on the announcements. At most they state that the PKK has claimed the murder, without informing the public of the underlying reason.

In October 2016 Aydın Muştu was murdered. He worked for the district of Özalp, in Van Province. The HPG declared that Muştu had been 'punished' for providing assistance to the district administrator. The same day saw the end of Deryan Aktert's life. The PKK declared that he had been 'punished' for his 'collaboration' with the state in planning 'massacres and genocide', this time in the district of Dicle, Diyarbakır Province. A year later the PKK murdered Aydın Muştu's successor.

It's no coincidence that such murders began after the AKP government changed the municipal law in August 2016, a month after the failed coup. It was suddenly a piece of cake to replace democratically elected mayors with administrators, which the AKP started doing a month later. According to a report by the Union of Southeastern Anatolia Region Municipalities, mayors were replaced in thirty-seven town halls within the first three months of the new law taking effect. They were all municipalities in which the DBP, the regional little sister of the nationally operating HDP, won the 2014 local elections. At the end of 2017 the number of mayoral posts taken over by the AKP had risen to ninety-four. Around seventy mayors were in prison at that time. Judicial investigations are in progress against the rest of the replaced men and women who had worked as mayors (every DBP municipality has a dual mayoral position). According to the new law, those investigations are necessary to justify the replacement of mayors with administrators.

The Kurdish political movement and the PKK call this 'political genocide'.

And the murdered teacher? He was abducted at a PKK roadblock. At such blockades PKK members check the identities of travellers. Normally people are allowed to proceed after listening to a lecture on PKK ideology, but sometimes someone is picked out and taken away (i.e. abducted, although the PKK calls them arrests). This was what happened to the teacher, whose corpse was later found in a stream. According to a PKK press release, his work as a teacher was a cover for his role as a state spy. Is that true? Who can say? It's no secret that the south-east is riddled with state infiltrators.

At the PKK roadblocks, which for years the organization has placed in various parts of eastern and south-eastern Turkey, it's a matter of obediently doing as those carrying weapons command. Anyone who hastily turns around and drives off, as people sometimes do in an attempt to avoid checks, may pay with their lives.

So it's not a question of whether or not you wear a uniform, but of the extent to which you are complicit in state suppression, that determines whether the PKK sees you as a civilian or not. PKK members are thoroughly familiar with local relationships. Which clans and families are 'patriotic', and therefore pro-PKK? Which of them have been collaborating with the enemy for decades and work for the governor, the police, the army or the secret service? Which family supplies lots of village guards, or recruits young people to take up arms under state payment? They know precisely who is involved. Those who go too far are at risk of 'punishment'.

In the Maxmur refugee camp I have long conversations about it with Yılmaz. He comes from Central Anatolia and joined the Kurdish movement as a left-wing Turk. We meet in the camp guesthouse, where he is staying for a while. I'm there for a couple of days for a stop-off on the way to my next location. Yılmaz is between two 'missions' and is awaiting new orders. He doesn't want to say any more about it. He's not in uniform. The fact that he's wearing jeans and a shirt, however, does not mean he's a civilian. In our conversations I get to know him as a friendly, calm and uncompromising fighter. He smiles at my questions.

What I want to know is whether the murder of 'collaborators' is not counterproductive. The Kurdish movement and the armed forces in particular, I point out, have cultivated so much good will through their tireless and successful battle with ISIS, and then the PKK goes and murders civilians. All that sympathy down the drain. Isn't that stupid? Who benefits from that?

'Whose sympathy?' he wants to know. The sympathy of part of the Turkish population, I reply. In the 2015 parliamentary elections they voted for Kurdish candidates more than ever before. In the 2014 presidential elections, together with the Kurds, they pushed HDP candidate Selahattin Demirtaş up to an unexpected ten percent of the vote. And the sympathy of politicians and the public in many European countries, I add. The Kurds' struggle has already been pigeonholed as terrorism. Why would you contribute to that picture by killing local governors and teachers, however involved they are in collaboration?

To put it coarsely, he doesn't give a toss. The Turks and Europeans can keep their sympathy. In a quiet voice Yılmaz says, 'Thirty-three deaths in Suruç, more than 100 in Ankara, Mehmet Tunç, the applause in the stadium in Konya. Surely you're aware of what's happening? The level of fascism has risen enormously in recent years. What should we do to counteract that?'

Yılmaz is referring to crucial moments in Turkey's most recent history. Suruç is a small town in Şanlıurfa, pretty much bordering on the Kurdish town of Kobani, on the other side of the border between Turkey and Syria. Thirty-three young people were killed in an ISIS attack on 10 July 2015, half a year after the end of the battle for Kobani. They had come to Suruç in order to try to cross to Kobani, where they wanted to help build facilities for children. They had cuddly toys, coloured pencils and colouring-in books with them, as I saw when I was in Suruç the day after the attack and came across mini-altars decorated with the toys.

An attack in Ankara on 10 October 2015 went down as the biggest in the history of the Turkish republic. There were 102 deaths and hundreds of people were wounded. The victims were Turks and Kurds who had come together in the capital to appeal to the government to resume the peace process between the state and the PKK. That evening, when a minute's silence was announced for victims in a stadium in Konya, Central Turkey, before the Turkey–Iceland match, part of the audience started whistling and hissing. They supported the attack.

The attacks in Suruç and Ankara are attributed to ISIS but according to the Kurdish movement the AKP is responsible. It's known that the security services had eyes on one of the two culprits, Yunus Emre Alagöz. His father had alerted the police to the fact that he and his younger brother Şeyh Abdurrahmen Alagöz had probably left for Syria as jihadists. Şeyh Abdurrahmen was the perpetrator of the attack in Suruç. Two days before the June 2015 elections, a friend of the brothers, Orhan Gönder, had carried out an attack on an HDP election meeting in Diyarbakır, in which five people had been killed and around 100 wounded. How is it possible that the security services failed to prevent the attack in Ankara?

Yılmaz also mentioned Mehmet Tunç, co-chair of the People's Assembly in Cizre. During the urban war he had sought refuge along with others in the cellar of a building, which was set on fire by the army in January 2016. He called from there to the conference I was attending in the European Parliament. To many Kurds Tunç is a hero.

'The pain we live with,' says Yılmaz, 'is the background of the murders of those you call civilians. The AKP is no ordinary political party. The AKP and the state have become one. Anyone who works for the AKP by definition collaborates in oppression. Those in Europe who support or respect us because of the war on ISIS but cannot understand us killing so-called civilians prove just one thing: they were born and brought up in the West and have no idea of the reality here. That kind of support, that kind of respect, is of no interest to us whatsoever. We're waging our own war.'

Yılmaz smiled again at my question as to whether the definition of 'civilian' might be narrowed down. 'If the AKP is the state,' I asked, 'and everyone who works for the AKP is a potential target, then in your view, could AKP voters eventually also become legitimate targets? And what about teachers, nurses and doctors who work for the state?' 'Not everyone who works for the government is actively involved in the practices of the state, in coming up with them and carrying them out,' he replied. 'And AKP voters? I don't know. Maybe. If necessary there will be a civil war. There is no such thing as a bloodless revolution.'

PKK fighters do not all feel the same way about this. There is consensus over the idea that local AKP leaders or spies are not civilians. On the question of whether Turkey might need to go through a civil war before a new republic is possible, opinions are divided, but most PKK members I asked did not think much of the theory.

The strange thing is, I wasn't sure whether Yılmaz himself was a '*kadro*', a PKK fighter who had sworn lifelong loyalty to the organization. The PKK harbours many Turks. There were even a couple among the most important men in the very beginning, such as the legendary Kemal Pir (who died on hunger strike in Diyarbakır prison in 1982) and Haki Karer (murdered in Gaziantep in 1977). Currently, however, there are also many Turks fighting in Kurdistan who belong to other groups. The collaboration between the PKK and the left-wing Turkish groups was officially clinched in March 2016, with the founding of the HBDH, the People's United Revolutionary Movement. Besides the PKK, the members include ten Turkish left-wing groups. In Syria a similar collaboration has been set up, known as the BÖG (United Freedom Forces). During my wanderings I came across various fighters from groups belonging to the BÖG.

In Qaraçox, in the furthest tip of north-eastern Syria, for example, I met a fighter who said that he was fighting for the MLSPB, the Marxist-Leninist Armed Propaganda Unit, which is part of the BÖG. I couldn't quite place the name and asked who his commander was. A YPG member? His answer was 'Mahir Çayan'.

Everyone in Turkey knows the name. Çayan, born in 1946, was a communist revolutionary who died in 1972 in a gun fight with the Turkish army and who continues to inspire left-wing Turks today. Perhaps Yılmaz belonged to the same group. Or perhaps he was a member of the MLKP (Marxist-Leninist Communist Party). As was Ayşe Deniz Karacagil, a 25-year-old Turkish woman from Antalya who was arrested during the Gezi protests, which turned Turkey upside down in 2013. Ayşe was released months later and departed post haste for Qandil. She fought against ISIS in the region of Raqqa, where she lost her life in May 2017. The flag on the coffin in which she was carried to the cemetery was not that of the Kurdish fighters or the SDF, but belonged to the MLKP.

Perhaps Yılmaz was also on his way to Syria.

I just want to make it clear: not everyone who fights alongside the PKK, YPG or YPJ feels the same. Yılmaz was more radical than most Öcalan followers I have spoken to. Those who had had years of training in the PKK were much more reserved about the level of violence necessary in Turkey in order to achieve freedom. Where Yılmaz did not in principle reject the idea of seeing AKP voters as future targets if necessary, PKK members looked at me in bewilderment when I steered the conversation in that direction. For them violence is first and foremost a means of self-defence. The revolution may not be bloodless, but it is carried out primarily through living the ideology and where possible putting it into practice in society.

It is a broadly held idea among Öcalan fighters that European sympathy is irrelevant to the Kurdish conflict. The Western world is in part responsible for drawing up the borders of artificial nation-states in the Middle East a century ago, for the colonization that went before and for the Third World War now being fought out in the Middle East. That's what greases the wheels of the arms industry. And that same Western world then condemns a Kurd who takes up arms to stand up to the resulting oppression? The Western citizen who lives in peace, striving for happiness, pleasure, self-realization, sex and romantic love, without being essentially aware of the damage the system in which he lives inflicts elsewhere in the world, and so does not really question that system, loses sympathy for the Kurdish struggle because a fighter eliminates an oppressor whose genocidal intentions are shrouded in civilian clothing? Should the PKK really be worried about losing the sympathy of the governments of that citizen? Come off it.

When I was asked where I came from and I answered 'The Netherlands', I was bound to be met with laughter and told, 'Ah, the Netherlands, cradle of capitalism!' It was an eye-opener for me. The Dutch are proud of having invented the polder model long ago to avoid conflict, so that trade could always continue. We therefore allow conflicts to bubble away beneath the surface. We are proud of the resulting form of peace. Don't be too outspoken, don't put your head over the parapet, don't challenge injustice too militantly, don't rock the boat, don't tinker with the status quo and don't polarize matters, because watch out, you might endanger the money-making. It is the mentality which leads to the Netherlands, and the West in general, only half-heartedly speaking out against large-scale human rights violations in Turkey.

But the PKK is no stranger to hypocrisy either.

On 10 December 2016 two bombs went off right beside the football stadium of Beşiktaş in Istanbul. Forty-four people were killed, the majority police. Almost 170 were wounded, It was a TAK classic: a military target but with the near-certainty of civilian deaths too, in a prominent place in a large west Turkish city with a culprit who blew himself up.

I'm in Maxmur that day, and the next morning (we always go to bed early and the attack was at half past ten in the evening) I meet two fighters walking back and forth in the courtyard. Twenty-five metres one way, twenty-five metres back. They walk quietly, but their eyes gleam with excitement. 'There could have been more deaths,' I hear one of the two fighters say, 'but this is good.'

A little later we sit shivering over morning tea around the petrol stove. The TAK has not yet claimed responsibility for the attack. In theory it could still be the work of the DHKP-C (Revolutionary People's Liberation Party/Front), a left-wing group who carry out attacks in Turkey and often pick military targets. Because of the disproportionate state violence in the south-east, however, the TAK is the more likely perpetrator. One fighter, nodding and almost whispering, informs me, '*Biz yaptık*,' or, 'We did it.'

Well yes, 'we'. The fighters around the stove said that of course the TAK is not the same as the PKK. The PKK would never do this, right in the city centre with such an enormous chance of civilian victims. Not their style. You leave civilians alone. They don't seem very sad about it, however. Not that anyone's cheering either. The atmosphere is indifferent and the few words the fighters exchange about the attack are uttered in soft tones. What is there to say about it anyway? On to the order of the day.

There is cool resentment, however, when I persist in asking about the matter after the TAK has claimed responsibility. Not resentment about the bombings, but about the national and international condemnation which flares up so suddenly. Forty-four deaths in Istanbul, mainly police, compared with hundreds of civilian deaths in the south-east of the country, hundreds of thousands of displaced Kurds and a number of Kurdish cities bombed to smithereens. Where was the national and international indignation then? What prominent figure, political or otherwise, in Turkey spoke out against that? What international leaders or organizations condemned Erdoğan, not to mention undertaking concrete action to stop the state violence? Turkish newspapers will be bulging with the TAK attack; foreign media will all report on it, while the violence in the south-east rarely makes it into the papers.

The TAK press release I read a couple of hours later stated, 'While the imprisonment of Leader Apo continues, while the fascism of the Turkish republic under the AKP tortures mothers every day in Kurdistan, plays with the corpses of young women and murders children, Turkey should not expect to live in peace. It's time for the people of Turkey to say no to this fascism. Because AKP fascism is solely responsible for this chaos.'

The bomb attack in Beşiktaş was not the only one which the TAK carried out in the year I spent with the PKK, nor was it the only one in which civilians lost their lives. A month earlier, in November 2016, twelve people were killed when a car bomb exploded beside a police station in Diyarbakır. Eight of them were civilians. In the same month there were two deaths in the southern city of Adana. Earlier that year, in June, eleven people – seven police and four civilians – died in a TAK attack in Istanbul. In January 2017 a policeman and a court employee were struck dead by the TAK in the western city of Izmir.

Not all TAK bombs killed civilians. In an attack on a minibus in the Central Turkish city of Kayseri in December 2016 fourteen soldiers lost their lives. The unit was the target, the TAK claimed, because it had played an important role in the urban wars in the south-east.

The hypocrisy lies in the fact that no PKK member with whom I spoke about the TAK denounced the group's attacks or civilian deaths, despite emphatically claiming that the PKK and the TAK are not the same. An earlier conversation with Cemil Bayık fits the same picture. We were talking about a TAK attack on a police station in Ankara in February 2016, in which thirty people, including the perpetrator, were killed and around sixty wounded. Among the victims were fifteen civilians, all but one in the service of the Turkish army. The Turkish press states the nature of their work for the army. I see a driver and an employee of a photo and film lab, an employee of a bank branch on military terrain and a defence personnel member with a civilian position.

In response to my criticism of the attack, which took place in the heart of Ankara, Bayık declared that the target of the attack was really the army base anyway. In other words, it's not the TAK's fault that that base is in the centre of the city. The car bomb belonging to the perpetrator, Abdulbaki Sömer, went off at a traffic light beside a military site with residential blocks for high-ranking military officials, where there were also two minibuses of military personnel waiting for a green light. 'When it comes to the fate of civilians,' I said to Bayık, 'clearly the TAK isn't that bothered.' His reply: 'Can we define civilian defence personnel and other employees on an army base as civilians?'

In another conversation about civilian deaths, Bayık had once demonstratively taken hold of his uniform jacket. My question was about the fighting in Diyarbakır Province, in which according to Turkish media civilians had died. In fact that was not a TAK matter, but an act by the HPG. He pulled on his jacket a couple of times and said, 'If I take this off and put on civilian clothing, am I suddenly a civilian? Surely not? Those paid and armed by the state are not civilians, even if they don't wear uniforms.' The dead, the HPG claimed after the incident, had been village guards.

Guerrillas distance themselves from the TAK. But the organization certainly serves a purpose for the PKK. Not just the purpose which the TAK gave in its statement, namely rubbing the Turkish people's noses in the reality of the war. The possibility of carrying out attacks on military targets that are not in the civilian-free zone is also convenient for the PKK.

Of course it's useful, a group that you're not in command of, allowing you to plead innocence before outsiders, while rubbing your hands in glee at their attacks. In my opinion, if you don't care what outsiders think, if you believe so strongly in your own aims and strategy and do not condemn the TAK attacks internally, if your definition of 'civilian' is different from the one generally understood, you should stand up for the attacks in the cities.

I know what the PKK would say in response. They simply are not the TAK. That's all there is to it. The TAK and the PKK share an ideology and a leader, but that's where the connection ends.

I can't come to a definitive judgment on the subject. I have to work with what I saw and heard. The justifications and approvals of TAK attacks. The use of Comrade Güven's 'report' in women's training. The framed portrait of Abdulbaki Sömer that I saw on various bases – thin, short hair on a round head, green polo shirt, faint smile, mouth slightly open. The reports of other TAK members who carried out a fedai eylem and TAK declarations revealing that the attackers all started their careers as fighters in the ranks of the PKK.

Comrade Güven also started out in the PKK. When I asked Cemil Bayık about it, he said, 'Surely we're not responsible for what people do after leaving the PKK? Ex-PKK members can be found everywhere, as far as the peshmerga.'

The difference is that all TAK members come from the PKK, whereas you really have to dig deep to find former PKK members in the peshmerga. Moreover, portraits of ex-PKK members who died while in the peshmerga are nowhere to be seen in any PKK base. They have not only left the organization but also kissed goodbye to its ideology in order to fight on the side of capitalism. In the PKK's eyes they are traitors, and you don't talk about traitors.

NO NOTE

Six or seven pairs of female guerrilla eyes stare at me in indignation. What? I've turned up without a note? A fighter from a neighbouring room sticks her head around the door and asks what the problem is. 'Her,' says one of the women, with a nod in my direction. 'She arrived without a note.' 'Really? How is that possible?'

Well yes, how was it possible? In Şengal I'd unsuspectingly stepped into a PKK car that was going to Syria. I planned to try and reach the front at Raqqa. Comrade Ekîn, whom I'd previously interviewed in detail, was sitting next to me. It had drizzled a little the previous day and little purple flowers were poking their heads up, but the landscape was otherwise desolate and dry as a desert once again. The network of roads through the sand confused me. They kept on splitting at large bends only to merge again later, a waterless delta.

The border crossing was unmarked, I think. There were just

checkpoints. 'Is this the border crossing?' I asked whenever we passed gateposts. Even to my ears it sounded like an irrelevant question every time. Only when we turned onto a tarmacked road was I sure of it: we were past the no man's land and now in Syria.

I travelled straight on to Qamişlo, one of the largest cities in the north-east of Syria. Onward transport to the west would be available on a large base there. A month and a half previously I had spent a night on that base in Qamişlo, on my way to Şengal.

That story is a tad complicated. It begins with the fact that Şengal in north-west Iraq was inaccessible to PKK fighters via Iraq. At the time, Barzani's KDP controlled all roads there and only let KDP members and sympathizers through, so no PKK members or their fellow travellers. To get to a PKK base in Iraq via the PKK-controlled region in Şengal, first you had to enter Syria, on foot, in the middle of the night. From Syrian territory in the hands of the YPG/J you could then go by car to the PKK-controlled region in Şengal.

Those unfamiliar with the local situation sometimes claim that Şengal was an important spot for the PKK to control because it was between the Qandil Mountains and northern Syria, and therefore guaranteed a route to Syria. Nonsense. For PKK members, Şengal was only accessible from Iraq via Syria.

In any case, the commander on the base in Qamişlo still recognized me when I arrived. She gave me a bit of a strange look when I came walking in alone. The driver of the minibus, in which a number of fighters also sat on their way to other destinations, had dropped me off at the base entrance. The guard had made contact with the women's barracks to say that 'Comrade Avaşîn from the Netherlands' was here. I was permitted to proceed. One of the fighters served tea. The commander asked about my destination. 'Raqqa,' I said. 'Note?' she asked, already reaching out her hand to take it. 'Note . . . ?' I responded sheepishly. 'What do you mean? I don't have a note.' The commander and fighters stared at me as if I were some strange new species. Look at her! No note!

Travelling without a note – known as a *not* by the fighters – is illegal. Always. Those who break the rule encounter disciplinary measures. Isolation from the group, for instance, for a day or so. No one talking to you, which is seen as a severe punishment in the communal life of the organization. But I only heard all that later. At that moment, I thought, I'll just explain who I am and what I've come to do, and tomorrow I'll get into a minibus to Kobani, the final stop before the front at Raqqa.

But it doesn't work like that. Commander Rojbîn brings in her colleague from the men's barracks, Commander Botan, to consult him. I'm told there are three options. One: I get a note here. Two: I have to go to the headquarters in Qaraçox, two hours' drive east and therefore in precisely the wrong direction, to explain myself to the commander-in-chief, who, if I'm approved, will then give me a note. Three: the commander-in-chief, Comrade Berçem, comes to Qamişlo to talk with me. Option one is most convenient for me, of course, but secretly that's not what I'm hoping for. I've committed a serious offence and the more difficulty I have getting away with it, the more interesting I think it will be.

It's five days before Commander Berçem sits facing me on the broad gravel path beside the base. She had to be there that day anyway and there's time for a conversation with me too. So I'm the woman who turned up without a note? That's right, I confirm. I explain that I really had no idea about the note system. I've come from Iraq and travelled in the mountains there and to PKK bases in Maxmur, Kirkuk and Şengal, but always without a note. 'I think,'

I say, putting my thoughts of the last few days into words, 'that my contact in Qandil always called the receiving commanders to discuss my visit and that I never needed a note because of that.'

She inquires as to what I have come to do in the north of Syria. A moment later I'm kicking myself for my answer. I say, 'I'm a journalist from the Netherlands and I'm writing a book about the PKK.' 'If you're writing a book about the PKK, what are you doing in Syria?' she asks coolly. 'There's no PKK here.' Shit.

I can't get away with laughing it off: 'Yeah, yeah, I know, I mean about the PKK and the YPG and YPJ, but I said PKK for convenience.' In recent months I've noticed that quite a few guerrillas recognized me from my work in Turkey and Diyarbakır, but Comrade Berçem has clearly never heard of me. In her eyes I'm a uninformed Western journalist bungling noteless into her camp and clearly intending on writing in a book, 'for convenience', that the PKK is in northern Syria. You can't blame her.

She begins to thaw when I explain that I'm taking a whole year for my research, with permission from Cemil Bayık and Besê Hozat. I tell her that I was living and working in Diyarbakır when I was expelled from Turkey for my work about the Kurds. I impress upon her that I really do know the difference between the PKK and the YPG/J. She smiles. We agree on a better way of explaining my purpose on my journey deeper into northern Syria: 'I'm writing a book about those who are led by Öcalan's ideology in their battle.' Because yes, of course I can have a note. I can go with the first car that leaves for Kobani.

The base at Qamişlo turns out to be a fighters' distribution point. Fighters arrive there virtually every day and men and women also travel to and from Qaraçox, Heseke, Kobani and Gire Spî. I'd spent two nights on the base at Qaraçox six weeks earlier. There on the mountain, it was a hive of activity. Besides the military barracks there was a media centre and other facilities. An enormous broadcasting mast stood prominently on the top. Qamişlo is quieter. The base lies some way outside the city. Some fighters stay only a couple of hours, others a couple of days before travelling on.

One morning, a girl – I can't think what else to call her – enters the base. Uniformed, in a colourful floral scarf, Kalashnikov over her shoulder, thick curly hair just too short to tie back in a ponytail. Upturned nose. Freckles. A cheeky look to her. Sozdar is her name. Turns out she's sixteen and her destination, like mine, is Kobani. What's she going to do there? 'Training,' she says, lighting a cigarette. Clearly she has no interest in talking.

Two days later we leave the base together in a minibus with another female fighter and five or six men. I insist on a smoking ban, to the irritation of some. Sozdar looks at me with a sigh and raised eyebrows. Stubbornly announcing no smoking in the car or minibus has proven successful in the past – although not always – and this time I'm in luck. 'Why?' the adolescent asks crossly. 'It makes me ill. And you too,' I reply. She doesn't speak Turkish, my Kurdish is too bad for a real conversation. Fortunately she stops grumbling. She bursts out laughing about the comrades who fall asleep with their mouths open. Soon afterwards her head sinks onto my shoulder.

At the end of the afternoon I'm looking from the hill of Miştenur out over Kobani. I only know Kobani from the other side of the border. In the battle for Kobani you could see from Turkish territory which flag flew on the strategic peak just near the city: the black ISIS flag or the yellow or green of the YPG/J. I spent week after week by that border writing reports and updating Dutch and English radio stations on the progress of the conflict.

In those days many journalists had gathered on a hummock in the landscape that had been declared the 'press hill' by the Turkish governor. They followed every plane, recorded every bomb. I scanned the tiny villages along the border. There, Kurdish youths attempted, largely in vain, to cross the border and join the battle. There, Kurds from all over Turkey gathered to show their solidarity with the Kurds in Kobani. They danced, they made fires, sang songs, formed human chains, wrote long slogans in the earth with stones. If too large a group of people dared approach the border, the army intervened and teargas grenades rained down.

And now here I am at last, on the legendary Miştenur, on the earth wall that encircles the base. The fighters not only built a barracks but also created a garden there. Plants with large, bright yellow flowers climb iron archways. Grass, poppies, a fountain. I see a large run with rabbits, chickens and peacocks, one showing off its magnificent tail. Two dogs on long ropes.

Comrade Serdeşt, a fighter in his twenties from eastern Turkish Van, stands next to me. He fought here. He points out Suruç, the town a couple of kilometres from the border that was then a hub of activism. Back then, I found a place to sleep there every night, often with families of the municipal police. He points to other places I've been to. There: the tiny village where large groups of people stood on the roof of the mosque for a better view. A little further to the right another small village, where at the time dozens of activists found accommodation in a couple of houses and the mosque, and there was dancing. 'We could see and hear all that, yes,' Serdeşt answers the question I've so long wanted to ask a fighter. A bright white stripe cuts through the landscape. It is the wall Turkey started to build at the end of 2016 on the Turkish-Syrian border. It's almost finished.

From the barracks young Sozdar comes walking towards us. She climbs up beside us. With Serdeşt assisting as interpreter she tells me her story. Her childhood remains somewhat vague, but I understand that she lived in Syria until she was three. Her mother died of a disease, her father in a car accident. She ended up in Germany, with her granddad, and also spent a couple of years in the Finnish capital Helsinki. At the start of the Syrian civil war her brother joined the YPG. ISIS caught him. Granddad travelled to northern Syria to look for him, 'But he only found his arm,' Sozdar tells me. A broken granddad returned. 'If you want,' he'd said to his granddaughter, 'join up and fight.' She went, along with a couple of older cousins. Nothing to lose, everything to win. She hasn't yet fought. She's increasingly impatient but still too young.

I see Serdeşt looking at Sozdar. I see pride in his eyes. He turns to me and says, 'Look at her. She's our future commander.'

The discussions regarding the similarities and differences between the PKK, YPG/J, SDF, YPS and KCK often grow intense. To many Turks, and even more so to the Turkish state, they're all the same. The state makes no distinction because of the predicate 'terrorist organization' which the PKK carries in the European Union and the United States. By claiming that other organizations led by Öcalan's ideology are the same as the PKK, Turkey attempts to convince its Western allies not to work with those organizations. There is even intense Turkish lobbying to get all the other organizations, and in particular the umbrella organization the KCK, onto international terrorist lists.

It is crucial for Turkey to portray the conflict with the PKK as a fight against terrorism. Whereas, going by international law, the conflict between the Turkish state and the PKK should be defined as a 'non-international armed conflict', based on its duration and intensity, the level of organization of the non-state party (i.e. in this case the PKK), the type of weapons used and the question of whether civilians are displaced, among other details.

The difference matters. After all, in an armed conflict, violence by both parties is permitted – to a certain degree, as international humanitarian law, which mainly focuses on protecting civilians from violence, applies to both international and non-international armed conflicts. The Turkish state expressly does not protect civilians – see for instance the disproportionate state violence during the urban wars in 2015 and 2016 and the massacre in Roboskî in 2011. It wipes any notion of civilian protection off the table by claiming that it is carrying out a legitimate fight against terrorism. That is not what Turkey is doing.

Drawing a distinction between the various groups fighting for Öcalan's ideology, in short, is not in Turkey's interest. For precisely the opposite reason, the PKK continually insists that it is not the same as the KCK, the YPG or the YPS. The more successful they are in convincing international players of this, the better they can do international business. The clearest example is the situation in Syria. There the YPG/YPJ and the SDF are America's most important allies in the war against ISIS, while the PKK is on the United States's list of terrorist organizations.

The Öcalan fighters acknowledge that their war on the Turkish state is a 'non-international armed conflict' and that international humanitarian law applies. That is why they make commitments via covenants with organizations such as Geneva Call on combating the deployment of child soldiers and the use of landmines. The way in which the Öcalan fighters deal with prisoners of war also conforms to international standards applicable in times of war.

Those with no direct interest in the discussion, beyond the international legal side, simply attempt to unravel the Kurdish acronym tangle. I include myself in this group. How do all those groups relate to one another? Who commands who? How are they linked?

AUTONOMOUS POSITION

The KCK is the easiest. It is the Kurdistan Communities Union, an umbrella organization of political Kurdish groups in Turkey, Syria, Iraq and Iran. The KCK was founded in 2007. Öcalan is its honorary president. The co-chairs of the Executive Council are Cemil Bayık and Besê Hozat. The PKK is one of the groups that falls under the umbrella of the KCK, as is the PYD in Syria, the PJAK in Iran and the PÇDK in Iraq. The PKK is therefore a political group, with the HPG (men) and the YJA-Star (women) forming the armed branch. The HPG and YJA-Star are active in a military capacity in Turkey.

Are the local branches of the youth group YPS in the Kurdish cities in south-eastern Turkey under the command of the KCK, PKK or HPG? Are the women's youth group YPS-Jin controlled by the YJA-Star? No. The youths, like the women, have an autonomous position. As far as I have been able to find out, the YPS has taken on the task of providing military defence to urban regions that declared themselves autonomous in the summer of 2015. They saw that as being in line with Öcalan's ideology, which promotes autonomy and the right to self-defence. PKK fighters came from the mountains to help, the PKK supplied weapons and some youths went to the mountains for basic training, but the defence order did not come from the PKK. The youths only take orders from one man, and that is Öcalan.

Since April 2015 he has been in almost complete isolation on the prison island of Imralı, after a period of intense contact between Ankara, the island and the mountains in the north of Iraq during the 'peace process'. The Turkish government knows that Öcalan can effectively defuse rising tensions with a click of his fingers. There has been recent proof of this. In late 2014 to early 2015 he called on youths in places such as Cizre to dismantle barricades, which happened in the blink of an eye. At the end of 2012 he put an end to a widespread hunger strike among political prisoners. The hunger strike was on the verge of taking lives, which would probably have led to serious riots. After Öcalan's call the prisoners broke their fast and the acute danger dwindled. Had Öcalan not been deprived of the opportunity to speak in spring 2015, the urban wars would not have taken place.

The PKK is part of the organizational structure of the KCK at the same level as the PYD (Democratic Union Party), but the two are not the same. The PYD is an unarmed political group in Syria. The YPG was founded in 2004 as an armed branch of the PYD. The YPG's sister organization the YPJ, the women's army, was created in 2013. Currently the YPG and YPJ are controlled by TEV-DEM (Movement for a Democratic Society), the governing body of the Autonomous Administration of North and East Syria (unofficially called Rojava, or West-Kurdistan). The PYD is one of the parties with a seat in TEV-DEM.

The initiative for the foundation of the SDF (Syrian Democratic Forces) in 2015 came from the US army, which needed a multi-ethnic group as boots on the ground in the war against ISIS, to counter Turkish criticism that they worked with the 'terrorists' of the YPG. When ISIS is kicked out of an area, as it was from Raqqa in 2017, then it is the task of the SDF to provide military defence for that region. Meanwhile political groups work on setting up the system of democratic confederalism, among other things by introducing district and village councils reflecting the local demographic composition.

Officially the SDF is the armed power of the Autonomous Administration of North and East Syria (AANES), including areas in which the majority of residents are Kurds and which have been working on grassroots democracy since 2012. When I was in northern Syria in spring and early summer 2017, I only saw the SDF flag outside the regions mainly inhabited by Kurds, such as to the north of Raqqa, which itself is mainly Arab. In the rest of the AANES the YPG and YPJ are predominant.

It stands to reason that the various armed groups employ different tactics to achieve their goals. The YPG, YPJ and SDF are not guerrilla militias. They are not waging a guerrilla war, but, if necessary, rather a conventional war. They are de facto the groups that have the monopoly on violence in the Autonomous Administration of North and East Syria. They do not interfere with Turkey.

The HPG and YJA-Star, the armed branches of the PKK, have their main bases in the mountains in northern Iraq. Their conflict is primarily focused on Turkish territory. They have the mountains in the north and north-east of Iraq under military control, but in an administrative sense (education, roads, other public facilities) the area falls under the Kurdistan Region of Iraq. In Turkey the HPG and YJA-Star do not control territory but they are involved in a guerrilla war. In Iraq they only take action if it is acutely necessary, as in Şengal in 2014. They do not interfere in the situation in Syria or Iran.

Iran and Iraq, too, have Kurdish political organizations that fall under the KCK: the PJAK (Kurdistan Free Life Party) and the PÇDK (Kurdistan Democratic Solution Party) respectively.

After a year among Öcalan's troops, I wonder more than ever what the PKK really is. The fighters rarely use the acronym, if ever; they refer to themselves more specifically and on their bases they paint HPG or YJA-Star on the outside walls, not PKK. When the PKK sends out press releases and statements, they are never signed PKK: instead the KCK is deemed to have spoken. My conclusion is that, forty years after its foundation, the PKK has become the source from which the entire movement has grown. A symbol, an internationally recognized brand, idolized and hated by millions. In this symbolic sense the PKK is everywhere. The organizational reality is that the PKK has been lost among the branches that have grown from it.

Yes, fighters are exchanged. In Maxmur in Iraq I spoke with Comrade Mizgîn. She was born in the Turkish city of Gaziantep. After the coup of 1980, when she was a young child, her family moved to Kurdistan in Syria. From there they later left for Lebanon for a couple of years. She has Armenian roots, she told me, but grew up with Kurdish culture and considers herself a Kurd. She joined the PKK at the age of fifteen. After that she worked both in Rojhilat (Kurdistan in Iran) and in Turkey, where she did civilian 'community work' in a number of eastern cities, such as organizing and recruiting people. After Maxmur I came across her again in Kirkuk.

Comrade Rojda, who as a minor fought for her birth village in Syria and whom I met at the language camp in Qandil, could easily be sent to Turkey after a few years of training, or to another location that needs her. In a rehabilitation hospital for wounded fighters in Heseke in Syria I met Kurds from Turkey who had previously fought in the PKK ranks and had now been wounded at the front at Raqqa.

At the Syrian front, there are SDF commanders active who joined the PKK years ago and due to their experience were deployed in the war against ISIS. Some ordinary fighters in Syria also have their roots in the PKK, but from the moment when they exchange their customary traditional PKK uniform for the more conventional green-brown camouflage uniform of the YPG, YPJ or SDF, they are no longer PKK. Then they are fighting in Syria and no longer have duties focused against the Turkish security services. Unless those security services cross the Syrian border, of course, as in the summer of 2016 and again recently in the north-western city of Afrin in January 2018.

The common ground between all these groups is Öcalan's ideology and his status as their leader. Concluding from that that the PKK equals the KCK equals the YPG equals the TAK is malicious oversimplification. Occasionally a half-cooked academic sauce is poured over this claim: it's in the nature of terrorism to lead people up the garden path with all kinds of confusing subgroups, so the story goes.

The reality is that the organization which was founded in 1978 by, roughly speaking, a few dozen Kurds and Turks and was named the PKK has grown, forty years on, into an exceptionally well organized and oiled machine which had long extended its activities beyond military territory alone. Besides thousands of women and men who have sworn lifelong loyalty to the movement, many times more people work for Öcalan's ideal. Not as 'members of the PKK', but as men or women who feel part of a mass movement that springs from the same ethnic group and the same resistance to oppression as that from which the PKK once sprang.

They run women's organizations, cover news, plead and defend themselves blue in the face as lawyers. They man administrative positions in municipalities in the north of Syria and (when it was still possible) in Turkey, they organize district and village councils, hold sit-ins Saturday after Saturday to demand clarity over the lot of their family members who 'disappeared' during the dirty war of the 1990s. They give Kurdish language classes. They are active in cultural associations which among other things record Kurdish dance and song on videos which are broadcast by Kurdish TV channels.

They set up crèches where very young children can speak their mother tongue. They demonstrate in villages and towns, act as human shields in the rural areas where there is fighting, they keep the ancient Kurdish storytelling art *dengbêj* alive. They research Kurdish history and record it in writing.

And they sit in parliament in Ankara. They have done so for decades, under the flag of different parties each time. HADEP, DEHAP, DTP, BDP, all forerunners of the current HDP (Peoples' Democratic Party) and its regionally operating sister branch the DBP (Democratic Regions Party). Those forerunners almost all ceased to exist because the Constitutional Court of Turkey banned them. The HDP and DBP are in fact facing the same fate, although officially they still exist. With the thousands of lawsuits against countless members and sympathizers (literally countless: even the parties themselves have not succeeded in keeping accurate records of prosecuted and imprisoned members) and thousands of people locked up, whether convicted or not, it has been made completely impossible for them to operate.

And the TAK? The question is whether the PKK would tolerate another organization alongside it, in its sphere of influence in the conflict in Turkey. My American colleague Aliza Marcus, who has written a book about the origins and growth of the PKK, does not believe so. For that reason she thinks that the PKK has more to do with the TAK than it admits.

In interviews with me, Cemil Bayık has sometimes alluded to the possibility that the Turkish secret service MIT might abuse the TAK to carry out attacks that can be attributed to the PKK. That caused me some confusion. If he really believes that the MIT holds sway over the TAK, why does he explain in detail why civilians who die in TAK attacks cannot always be identified as citizens? Not that it's impossible that 'TAK equals MIT', mind you, because I believe that the Turkish state would try anything, but so far I've seen no convincing evidence.

Not a single fighter whose opinion of the TAK I asked stated that it was an MIT project. Most said that they did not know the details. I asked, 'Imagine you want to become a TAK member; would you have to quietly leave the PKK and find your own way? Or do you write a report to your commanding officer stating that you want to transfer to the TAK?' None of the men or women I asked professed to have any idea.

When I asked a PKK representative about the organization's reaction to a TAK attack, he refused to comment. After all, it was not a PKK issue. He added, 'Let's just say, at last someone is talking to Erdoğan in a language he understands.' No slip of the tongue, as he wrote it in an email.

The attitude to violence among those fighting according to Öcalan's ideology in fact focuses on a single word: self-defence. Every living being has a mechanism to defend itself against attacks from outside. Given that a people is also a living organism, a self-defence mechanism is essential to it too. The armed forces of the political parties that fall under the KCK provide that self-defence. You find it in the 'P' in every one of their acronyms, which stands for the Kurdish word *parastîn*, meaning 'defence' or 'protection'. The HPG: Hezên Parastina Gel, or People's Defence Forces. The YPG and YPJ, or the People's Protection Units and the Women's Protection Units.

The Kurds may not have a state and the Öcalan fighters may not want one, but they will not put up with being left to the whims of the armies of the nation-states in which they live. Whims is a cautious word. State security services (such as the army and police) hold an exclusive right, according to international law, to violence on their territory. But what if they turn that violence against their own population? What if in doing so human rights are violated on a large scale and for decades on end, as is the case throughout Kurdistan? Don't the Kurds have a right to an armed force on their own side?

I read through the Universal Declaration of Human Rights one more time. The preamble states that, '[I]t is essential, if man is not to be compelled to have recourse, as a last resort, to rebellion against tyranny and oppression, that human rights should be protected by the rule of law'.

A SMALL RISK

Commander Aziz, thirty-six years old, still clearly remembers how he and his comrades entered Kirkuk at the start of August 2014. They came from the mountains in the north of Iraq. The villagers on the way to Kirkuk stood along the roadside to welcome them. There was applause, some people threw sweets. Aziz: 'It put me in mind of the martyr Mazlum Doğan, a fighter from the early years of the PKK. He said, "There will come a day when we can openly state that we are PKK members." That day had arrived. We could travel openly to Kirkuk to protect the people. Now that we have reached that point, our responsibility has only grown. As long as there is the slightest risk that the people are not safe, there is a task for us.'

Aziz and I talk at a large base at Kirkuk, where I am staying for two or three weeks at the end of 2016. August 2014 was a crucial period for the deployment of PKK units in Iraq. Within a week the HPG and YJA-Star alighted in Şengal, then Maxmur, then Kirkuk. Each of those cities had been threatened by ISIS. In Şengal the KDP peshmerga ran away, in Maxmur both the peshmerga and the Iraqi army did the same. The city of Mosul was taken over by ISIS in June and Kirkuk was exposed to the same danger. The Iraqi army, which surrendered at lightning speed, decided not to defend Kirkuk either. The peshmerga took the city.

'What was your business in Kirkuk?' I ask Commander Aziz. 'A request came in,' he replied. 'Without that we don't go anywhere. Unless the situation is really acute of course, as in Şengal and Maxmur. A request like that can reach us in all kinds of different ways. I wasn't involved in this case, but I believe there had been a village meeting and the community had decided to ask the PKK to protect them. The representative transmitted the request to us, so we came.'

The PKK considers permission from authorities in control in a region, in this case the peshmerga, unnecessary. That permission came implicitly: the roads to Şengal, Maxmur and Kirkuk, which in August 2014 were in the hands of the KDP (and closer to Kirkuk in the hands of the PUK peshmerga) were open and the PKK met with no obstacles. Neither does the KDP have the power to prevent PKK movements. They are not militarily strong enough. They know that their own Kurdish supporters will not put up with KDP leaders taking up arms against their fellow Kurds from the

PKK. The KDP had also already lost all credibility, after they left the Şengal Yazidis and the refugees in Maxmur Camp to their fate. Failing to grant the PKK passage would have represented absolute moral bankruptcy.

It immediately raises the following question. In and around Kirkuk the PKK has not often had to take action, but in Şengal and Maxmur they effectively made short work of ISIS and really did succeed in protecting the population. What's the difference between the Iraqi army, PUK and KDP peshmerga on the one hand and the PKK on the other? What makes the PKK so strong?

Aziz uses the Turkish word I so often hear in the PKK: *irade*, willpower. 'We have no other motivation than the people,' Aziz explains. 'That's a stronger force than others are fighting for. Soldiers fight for money or because they have been conscripted. The peshmerga are also fighting for an income, even if a month's salary only feeds their families for ten days. Fighting for a weak system makes you weak, however brave many of the peshmerga may be. Part of the weakness is that the peshmerga are uneducated. Our will is strong because we're educated and know precisely what we're fighting for.'

It reminds me of what another fighter, Comrade Bager, said to me, in a cave in the mountains near Şengal. I observed that, just like the PKK, enemies such as ISIS and the Turkish state have strong ideologies, whatever you may think of them. How did the PKK succeed in defeating ISIS, when ISIS had far better weapons? Bager said, 'In us, for the first time, ISIS find an opposing ideology stronger than their own.'

The Öcalan fighters are convinced that it is their irade that makes them virtually unbeatable. This also shows in their vision of the historic battle for Kobani, at the end of 2014. They do not see the American air support as decisive in the final victory. The fighters' narrative is radically different from that of many analysts, who claim that the Kurds were only really successful when the US decided to fly into that small stretch of Syrian airspace with the bombers. The YPG and YPJ say that the Americans chose to support them because they saw their strength.

On the latter point I think they are right. That summer, ISIS had advanced irrepressibly in Iraq and Syria. The US urgently needed a partner to function as boots on the ground. After all, no war can be fought with bombers alone. But whether you could say that the Americans needed the YPG/J more than the other way round remains questionable. Perhaps the needs of both sides kept one another in balance.

Back to Commander Aziz in Kirkuk. He speculates as to what the city where he is stationed could be: 'Kirkuk is a mosaic of peoples and that makes it suitable for democratic confederalism that recognizes diversity.'

The reality, meanwhile, is that various groups claim authority over the city. The main reason Kirkuk is so desirable is its enormous supplies of oil. As you approach Kirkuk you can see how extensively the pump installations and refineries determine the view of the city. Since October 2017 the city has been in the hands of the central government in Baghdad, who decided to reclaim power after Barzani, KDP leader and (then still) president of the Kurdistan Region, held a referendum on Kurdish independence. Despite the fact that there had not yet been any decision as to the question of whether the city belonged in Iraq or the Kurdistan Region, Barzani still allowed the people of Kirkuk to cast their vote. Baghdad interpreted that as a Kurdish attempt to annex the city once and for all.

Many Kurds claim that Baghdad had used the referendum to eradicate the peshmerga from the city. That may be true. The war against ISIS, after all, was going well. Even Mosul, occupied by ISIS in 2014, was jihadi-free again. The then Iraqi prime minister al-Abadi probably simply thought it was time to get back to the way things were pre-ISIS. In any case, since the referendum, the discussion as to who owns Kirkuk has exploded at full intensity again. The Kurds point out – rightly – that Saddam Hussein allowed tens of thousands of Arabs to move to the city and thus changed the demographics. Baghdad invokes the constitution, which states that only a referendum on the status of Kirkuk can settle the conflict as to 'ownership' of the city. That referendum should have been held years ago but of course there were arguments about who would have the right to vote. Would that include the Arabs who had come under Saddam? And so on, ad infinitum.

Commander Aziz shakes his head and says, 'It shouldn't be about territory. The only owners of Kirkuk are the people who live there. For us that's the only thing that counts. That's why we teach the people how to defend and govern themselves. Only when it is certain that they can take care of themselves and that they are safe will we leave.'

What Aziz describes is precisely what the HPG and YJA-Star were doing in Şengal: training the people to govern and defend themselves.

What about the stories of ethnic cleansing by Öcalan fighters, then? How can they be reconciled with the ideal they preach of respect for the diversity of the Middle East?

In October 2015 Amnesty International published a report with the title '"We had nowhere else to go"', revealing that the YPG compelled people to move from Syrian villages where the organization had conquered ISIS. The YPG was also accused of destroying houses and even entire villages. This related to operations around the town of Suluk and further east, south of Qamişlo. Amnesty classified the acts as violations of humanitarian law and therefore as war crimes or crimes against humanity.

The YPG responded in detail to Amnesty's findings. The biggest mistake in the report, the YPG stated, was the failure to take into account the raging war. According to Article 7 of the Rome Statute of the International Criminal Court, forced displacements are a crime if they are 'without grounds permitted under international law'. The same goes for the destruction of houses: this is a crime unless 'justified by military necessity'.

What does that mean? Militant groups can force civilians to leave their villages or destroy their houses if that is the only option for the safety of the people or for compelling military reasons.

The YPG claims that the evacuation and in some cases destruction of houses was entirely necessary. The central command of the YPG portrays the war they were waging against the Free Syrian Army, ISIS and groups allied with Al Qaida as unprecedentedly fierce. Even once ISIS has been driven from a place, the threat may not be gone. Small cells can go underground and carry out car bomb or suicide attacks later on. Houses in villages which have long been occupied by ISIS are often stuffed full of booby traps and explosives. Sometimes, if you want to save lives, there is nothing for it but to raze such a house to the ground. Those are among the exceptions which the Rome Statute provides.

Amnesty say that their witnesses obstinately maintained that there was no threat and that they were nevertheless compelled to leave. The organization offers no other evidence. Are they saying civilians are better placed than fighters to assess where danger lies in wait?

One of the journalistic sources listed by Amnesty is a website allied to a group that is ill-disposed towards the YPG/J. That source speaks of forced displacements of Arabs, while Amnesty in its report states that they were Turkmens. The civilians mentioned in the Amnesty report, moreover, were not always present in person in the situations they describe. For example, a woman fled her village to find, on her return months later, that her house had been destroyed. She says, 'I don't know who did that.' Others say that they were compelled to leave by 'fighters who looked like they belonged to the YPG'. Yet another speaks of 'fleeing' from the violence of war. That is different from being compelled to leave without justification under pressure from fighters.

I still remember the explosion of criticism when the Amnesty report came out. For years I felt a strong bond with Amnesty, even before I reached adulthood. I was an Amnesty member for a good fifteen years. At the beginning of my career, in the first half of the 1990s, I volunteered as a writer for the organization's youth newspaper for a couple of years. As far as I'm concerned it's an honest club which writes well-founded reports. And if the YPG/J really committed war crimes, the culprits deserve to be punished, as Amnesty wrote in its recommendations at the end of the report. Let it be said, my heart lies closer to human rights than to any fighters.

But in this case I'm not convinced. The report is on shaky ground. In no way whatsoever do the assumptions chime with the Öcalan fighters' mentality, which I felt I knew reasonably well by that time. Now that I've spent a year embedded with the fighters, I find it even less credible. North of Raqqa, where I was at the front in spring 2017, I visited a number of cleared villages. I saw evacuations and heard civilians complain about not being permitted to return to their villages. I saw how the fighters dealt with the inhabitants of the region.

I spend two days at a checkpoint where SDF fighters check fleeing civilians and their baggage. The refugees come from villages north of Raqqa which are still in ISIS's hands. Coalition planes had dropped announcements that war could break out again and the residents had to leave to avoid ending up in the firing line.

When I wake up in the morning on the roof I see the endless line of slowly progressing vehicles already on the move. I see from close up how people have bagged up all their earthly possessions and lashed them to whatever means of transport was available. There are some mopeds and cars, but mainly agricultural vehicles with trailers. Women and children sit on piles of mattresses, blankets and clothes, plastic water pitchers and buckets dangle on straps, enormous pots of rice, sugar, tea and olives filling the last available spaces. From the bundles of possessions rise the cackling of chickens and crowing of roosters. At the wheel sits the head of the family or his son, beside them women and children.

Fighters check identity documents and open glove compartments in search of guns and knives. There are not many of those. Many families are then waved on through, to the next checkpoint and eventually a refugee camp further north near the city of Ain Issa. Some families are subject to a stricter baggage check. It's warm but not yet excessively so, although certainly dry and extremely dusty and sandy.

How do you pick out the ISIS fighters here, who must surely try to escape in this endless procession to do who knows what later on? Some men are required to hold their shirts up to show that there is no explosive belt underneath. Some men in their twenties and thirties have their shirts pulled down from the neck. Mazlum, a fighter, explains it to me. 'ISIS fighters wear thin material which does not provide good protection against the weight of weapons. Red marks and welts around the neck are therefore a telltale sign that someone has been carrying weapons. We hand over men with such marks to our intelligence service.'

For hours now an Arab man has been hanging around the checkpoint on his own. That afternoon I speak to him, with the aid of an Arab fighter who speaks enough English to act as an interpreter. I ask the man what he has been doing at the checkpoint for so long. 'I handed over my son to these troops this morning,' he says. 'He was seventeen and a member of ISIS. His younger brother was also a member but he died in an American bombing. This morning we had to leave our village. I ordered my son to get on the moped behind me and told him I was going to report him. He obeyed. He had no choice. The SDF have taken him away for questioning. He'll be imprisoned for a while.'

It strikes me as quite something, a father reporting his own son. I ask him how he feels. He says, 'I've barely slept in years, I've been so worried about my children. They were members of a malevolent group. Now finally I can sleep again, because I know he's in good hands. I feel at peace.'

Although I find the atmosphere at the checkpoint relatively peaceful, I notice that the fighters from the SDF, YPG and YPJ are hyper-alert. For instance when suddenly two young men come running in, hurrying past the procession, with a sick elderly man between them on an improvised stretcher of wood, rope and blankets. I see a minor drama. The fighters see a major risk. They order the men to put down their cargo immediately and check the elderly man thoroughly and at lightning speed for explosives.

Now and then shots are fired, once when a couple of men drive large flocks of sheep across the field towards the checkpoint, once when people want to drive past the queue, blocking the other half of the road. Mazlum: 'That half must be kept clear so that military transport vehicles and the organization's cars can get by. People can't come across the field because we can't check them that way. And there could be mines there. It's just not safe. We're not aiming to hit anyone, of course, they're just warning shots.'

At the end of the afternoon a commander stops at the checkpoint to ask if there are any problems. A woman with two children comes out of the queue of refugees and approaches his car. She complains that the children are hungry. Shrugging, the commander gives her a plastic bag. I recognize the contents: two polystyrene boxes of food, prepared daily by a large team of men and women on a base nearby, for the fighters at the front. Mince with rice, chunks of tomato, potato and a pepper.

There's nothing the fighters can do about the main complaint. The village where the base is located, just past the checkpoint, has only just been liberated but people are already turning up wanting to return home. They do not receive permission, however insistent they are. The village has been declared military terrain.

Nevertheless the following afternoon two women knock on the door of the house that serves as a women's base. It's situated just by the road the refugees are travelling along. YPJ members are preparing for the next offensive and taking turns on checkpoint duty on the road or guard duty on the roof. There's tea, of course. I and a couple of others sew beads onto scarves, chatting as we work. The two women at the door, it transpires, used to live in the house and are in need of baby clothes. Could they please, please just ... ? Commander Zîlan beckons them in, the women get to work. 'How do you know that this house really belongs to these women?' I ask Zîlan. 'And why don't you check whether they're carrying explosives?' She considers this for a moment and decides on a brief answer. 'You know what, Comrade Avaşîn? You have to trust the people you liberate.'

But wait a minute. Those Öcalan fighters, do they never make mistakes? Do they always behave like the virtuous men and women they claim to be, even in wars as horrific as that in Syria? Even the PKK and YPG/J leadership would never be so bold as to make that claim. Of course the rules are sometimes broken.

A famous example is an incident in the canton of Afrin in February 2016. After a big battle against troops from the Free Syrian Army, won by the YPG, dozens of corpses were driven through the streets of Afrin city on a trailer behind a truck. The YPG flag was clearly visible on the truck. Indefensible, proclaimed the TEV-DEM, the civil organization which in principle commands the YPG/J. A representative said, 'This goes against our values. We're not the kind of people who terrorize our enemies in such a shameful manner. These are the methods of ISIS, or the Baʿath regime (the Syrian government) or military dictatorships. These are not the kinds of methods we should be employing.'

We can assume that those responsible for the offensive parade in Afrin were punished. They would at least have lost their positions and been obliged to undergo extra training sessions, because such lapses, the reasoning goes, are always the consequence of too little education. Whether other measures were taken, I do not know.

The PKK and YPG/J have taken responsibility for mistakes on various occasions. Accusations are investigated. The leaders of the organization are accessible to any journalist or human rights organization. Investigators such as Amnesty International, Human Rights Watch or Geneva Call (the organization which combats the deployment of child soldiers among other things) all have access to the area controlled by the YPG/J and SDF. They can carry out their research unhindered, as even Amnesty noted in its accusatory report.

A SHEET OF SQUARED A4

In fact no PKK member is a stranger to criticism. Anyone who wants to can express criticism of the organization or of individual fighters – as long as they do so according to the rules. When writing your criticism, please use an A4 sheet of squared paper, four blocks for the left-hand margin, four for the right, one block between each line. When expressing your criticism verbally, preferably do so during a tekmil, a short meeting held every couple of days, or during the big criticism and self-criticism sessions regularly scheduled. Always formulate your criticism carefully. Never raise your voice. Be constructive.

Expressing criticism of comrades out of the blue is not done. A German at the language camp called out another woman for occupying the shower and washroom for too long. She really laid into this comrade when she turned up freshly showered. The German was later criticized for not having expressed criticism correctly.

The idea of criticism sessions often makes outsiders shudder, raising spectres of dictatorial communist tribunals in which people are humiliated to the bone and even forced to fabricate self-criticism to maintain credibility before their comrades. Tribunals in which the highest ranking officers can make or break lower-placed party members, while remaining emphatically out of the firing line themselves. It would certainly be an abomination if that happened not only in Mao Zedong's China, to take a random example, but also within the PKK.

So it's fortunate that the organized criticism and self-criticism day I observed and the occasions when fighters spontaneously took one another up on their behaviour were nothing like that.

At the end of each PKK course there is a 'criticism day', in the PKK and YPG/J called a 'platform'. After the language course I followed in the Qandil Mountains in summer 2016, students and teachers are also obliged to face one. In the morning I walk with my neighbour Rojda from our class camp through the wood and along the river to the base language camp. She is wearing an old uniform. In a small plastic bag she carries a newer one, freshly washed. 'Are you going to say something about me, Comrade Avaşîn?' she asks. 'You have criticisms of me, don't you? But will you say something nice too?' She is virtually exploding with nerves and excitement.

At the language base camp the large tent is only accessible to women. Inside they swap old uniforms for new ones and blouses for uniform jackets. Three comrades sit one behind another, plaiting each other's hair as beautifully and neatly as possible. One of the women has a shard of mirror in her hand and is trying to look at herself from all sides. No fluff on her trousers? Check. No creases in her sleeves? Check. Jacket zipped up to precisely the right level? Check.

In the small open area of the camp where the tall dining table is normally positioned, a comrade sets out plastic chairs in straight rows. At the front stands a little table covered with a cloth and a vase of flowers in the corner. The commander of the language camp, Hacer, is busy putting up the yellow flag with the portrait of Öcalan and the PKK flag between the trees. The final participants trickle into camp – the men close-shaven, hair combed, uniforms immaculately clean.

Comrade Hacer chairs the session. A second comrade is needed to assist her. The Italian Viyan is unanimously elected. She's not a PKK member but everyone in the camp likes her for her humour, energy and openness. Viyan calls the fighters forward one by one. In modest poses they stand before the Öcalan flag: head slightly bowed, eyes cast down, hands folded before or behind them. Every man and woman reflects on him- or herself, on the progress he or she has made as a person and as a fighter and on their shortcomings. I notice that people speak in hushed tones, as they generally do during class and tekmils. Then it's up to the others to raise positive and negative points. For each fighter two or three comrades stand up to raise an issue.

Viyan also calls me forward. This is not obligatory for me, since I'm not a PKK member, but I'm up for it. My self-criticism consists of an admission that I could have worked harder, that I talked too much Turkish and grasped too few opportunities to just chat with others on the course to practise my Kurdish. I also want to share something about my place in the group. I say that I have felt accepted as an outsider, but that all the same being on the outside was sometimes hard. There were a couple of other foreigners in the group, but they were there as 'revolutionaries', whereas I was there as a journalist. 'As a journalist,' I say, 'you're an outsider by definition. That has sometimes been extra difficult here because I've been here for three months, without being able to step out of it once in a while.'

I also offered criticism. I didn't think the language classes were well structured. I don't go into too much detail, because I've already written about it extensively in the evaluation form everyone had to fill in at the end of the course. I also find it annoying, I say, that I wasn't given certain tasks which everyone else in the camp, including newcomers and non-members, were assigned, such as turns at cooking and night guard duty. Why had no one explained why I was exempted? I suspect, I say, that it was because of my age. Unacceptable. 'You can't allocate tasks based on age,' I state, undoubtedly formulating it clumsily in Kurdish. 'I may be older than everyone else here; it doesn't make me too old to participate.'

Two people stand up to say something about me. Comrade Viyan comments on my place in the group. She says in a friendly tone that I am also to blame for being outside the group. For instance, didn't I myself opt not to have a photo taken for the ID card we would be given at the end of the course? That card proves you've followed the course. Everyone was photographed with the KCK flag behind them. I refused. A semi-official portrait with the KCK flag as background sounded like precisely the kind of photo of me that simply must not be allowed to exist. I supplied an existing passport photo on a USB stick. 'Why couldn't you just have your photo taken with the flag?' asks Viyan. 'It doesn't mean anything more, does it?'

I don't feel like explaining and thank Viyan in a friendly tone for her interesting view. Comrade Mizgîn, my class teacher, stands up. 'Patience, Comrade Avaşîn,' she says. I had lost my patience a few times in class, she points out, more than fairly. 'But if you want to write a good book about us, you're going to need patience. Only if you take the time, will you learn to understand our lives.' 'Thank you Comrade Mizgîn,' I reply. 'You're right. Thank you for your patience with me.'

What I'm not going to do is expose the criticism and self-reflection of other comrades. These sessions are deeply personal and crucially important to the guerrillas. The most difficult war waged by any PKK – or YPG or YPJ – member is not armed warfare but the conflict within themselves. The aim of every man and woman in the organization is to become as good a person as possible, someone worthy of being called an Öcalan fighter. It's worth noting that none of the fighters, not even an old hand like Cemil Bayık, see themselves as fully formed PKK members. True PKK members are people who fully devote themselves to the organization and no one succeeds in that, not while they are alive. Only the martyrs have made the ultimate sacrifice. Only the martyrs deserve to be called PKK members.

How your comrades and the camp commander see you in part determines the next task you are assigned and with it the path you will take within the organization. Whether you are seen as ready to go to Bakur, for example, or whether you first need more training, in which case it determines the nature of that training. Whether you will be sent into armed conflict at all, or whether you receive a place in the women's work, on an economic committee or judicial council passing judgment on mistakes by fellow fighters. Whether you become a teacher somewhere or a cave builder, spend several months in a workshop sewing uniforms or are trained as a journalist, doctor, translator, sniper, commander or deminer. Whether you're ready for command, or not yet but have the potential.

It's enough to say that everyone had a turn. There was no distinction in rank. Everyone was taken equally seriously. It was deadly serious and somewhat solemn, but there was also laughter. Some fighters were clearly nervous, but no one became emotional. Everyone spoke thoughtfully and quietly and chose their words carefully.

There is one person whose story I can share. It is a self-criticism by Comrade Hêlîn. She shared it with the group at a big tekmil. These monthly meetings, in which we discussed the daily routine and minor points of criticism, were also an opportunity to raise bigger issues. Hêlîn made a confession at one such tekmil. Unfortunately due to language problems I didn't completely understand, so I asked her about it in an interview. She said, 'You know, Heval Avaşîn, I'm learning to read and write my mother tongue here at last. That makes me a more complete person, but it also saddens me. A culture can't exist without a language, so can I be a true Kurd if I can express myself better in Turkish than in Kurdish? How can I be complete if I don't know the wealth of my culture and history because I haven't mastered the language? I've never been so confronted with that shortcoming as here.'

The PKK as an organization is as good as every individual fighter, or as a fighter once said to me, 'Everyone is personally responsible for the PKK.' Criticism and discipline are essential to keep everyone on the same page. From relatively minor misdemeanours – a man crossing one leg over the other, a man or woman washing his or her socks in sight of a member of the opposite sex, raising your voice – which are swiftly dealt with, to major offences that are never tolerated. Torture. Sexual harassment or rape. Disrespect for the dead, whoever they are. Mistreatment of prisoners of war. Ethnic cleansing. Killing civilians or choosing civilian targets for attacks.

These are offences which go against everything that every PKK member stands for individually, and thus against the entire organization. That's not to say that things never go wrong. But all fighters know they will never ever get away with it. Discipline is everything. Impunity is inconceivable.

Background

Peshmerga and the PKK

The Kurds are the most important partners of the United States and Europe in the war against ISIS. Is that true? Yes and no. 'The Kurds' consist of different militant groups representing two ideologies. The two are diametrically opposed.

Those who are led by the ideology of Öcalan in their conflict, fight mainly in Syria against ISIS. They are the YPG, YPJ and SDF. In Iraq the PKK has fulfilled an important role in the war against the jihadists in three places: Maxmur, Şengal and Kirkuk.

In Iraq the Kurdish peshmerga have also fought against ISIS. However, that was largely after they fled in 2014 in Şengal and Maxmur. In 2014 the Iraqi army revealed a similar weak side, leading, among other defeats, to the important city of Mosul falling into jihadist hands in the summer of 2014. In 2015 the peshmerga took their revenge. They helped the PKK to drive ISIS out of Şengal and, alongside the Iraqi army and with American support, played a crucial role in the liberation of Mosul in 2017. In 2014 ISIS also advanced on the Kurdish capital of Erbil, but there the peshmerga succeeded in defending themselves.

The YPG/J and the peshmerga in fact also worked together in Syria, during the battle for Kobani. The peshmerga came to the aid of the YPG/J after Erdoğan, under great international pressure, permitted the peshmerga to travel over Turkish territory to Kobani.

Öcalan fighters and the peshmerga do not see one another as enemies. They are all Kurdish fighters who do not want to make one another's lives difficult. When I travelled with the PKK in Iraq, we were never given any trouble at KDP or PUK checkpoints. Not a single guerrilla speaks negatively of their peshmerga colleagues. Several fighters even said that they would never, ever want to use a bullet against a peshmerga fighter. The peshmerga feel the same about the Kurds of the PKK.

The peshmerga are the classic Kurdish fighters who have fought for almost 100 years in Iran and Iraq. In Iraq they are the institutionalized fighters of the Kurdistan Region. They were once a single force in Iraq, forming the Kurdish resistance against the dictator Saddam Hussein. After the Kurdistan Region was given de facto autonomy under American protection in 1991, that unity soon came to an end. The Kurdistan Democratic Party (KDP), founded in 1946 by the legendary Kurdish leader Mullah Mustafa Barzani, acquired a competitor in the form of the Patriotic Union of Kurdistan (PUK). The KDP is still run by the Barzani clan; the PUK is led by the Talabanis.

The KDP and the PUK each have their own peshmerga army. In the 1990s they fought out a civil war. Currently the KDP controls the northern part of the Kurdistan Region in Iraq, around Erbil. The PUK controls the southern part, around Suleymanya. Armed clashes have long ceased but on a political level the KDP and PUK still cannot abide one another. Attempts to merge the peshmerga armies have so far come to nothing.

Masoud Barzani (son of Mullah Mustafa) has long maintained excellent relations with the Turkish President Erdoğan. Barzani is in fact economically completely dependent on Turkey. The economic prosperity of the Kurdistan Region in the first decade of this century would not have been possible without substantial investments from Turkey. The KDP clan is much better off financially as a result. Corruption and clientelism still reign supreme. In combination with mismanagement, this effectively means that the ordinary people live in poverty and the elite become ever richer.

In the eyes of PKK members, clan leaders such as Barzani are traitors to the Kurdish cause, comparable with the leaders of Kurdish clans in Turkey, and in the Ottoman Empire before it. They too 'collaborate' with power for their own gain. This makes them exponents of the patriarchal capitalism against which the PKK fights. Barzani would like to crown his power with a state of his own, Kurdistan. He organized a referendum on the issue in September 2017. The vast majority of the Kurds voted for it.

But Barzani overplayed his hand with the referendum. Baghdad wouldn't stand for it, bringing Kirkuk – under peshmerga control (part KDP, part PUK) between 2014 and 2017 – and Şengal, among others, under its central authority with little difficulty. The Kurdistan Region was politically and economically isolated. Baghdad even closed the two international airports in Kurdistan (Erbil and Suleymanya). They reopened in spring 2018. Erdoğan also threatened to take measures against Barzani's independence plans.

The border between Turkey and Kurdistan, however, remains open. Erdoğan has Barzani precisely where he wants him: in a vice. If Turkey closed the border, the shops in Kurdistan would be empty in no time. Since then, Turkey has substantially increased its military presence in the Kurdistan Region. A year or so ago there were around twenty posts belonging to the Turkish army and intelligence service MIT in the KDP zone of the Kurdistan Region; now everyone has long lost count. There is nothing Barzani can do about it. In fact, from time to time he has to make a show of taking the 'war on terror' seriously. That's why international fighters from the YPG and YPJ, for instance, were still sometimes arrested by the KDP peshmerga when they crossed the border from Syria into the Kurdistan Region to catch a plane home from Erbil or Suleymanya.

On the spring day when Barzani announced the referendum on independence, I was in Qandil for a couple of days. The PKK members I was with shook their heads at the news. The PKK as an organization did not speak out against it. In principle, they are against the nation-state, but they would never deny Kurds the right to express their opinion on it in a referendum.

CHAPTER 7

Silhouettes

It's after midnight when we arrive in a camp in the mountains somewhere in the north-west of Iraq. Artificial light is forbidden, but the moon is shining, so we're not ascending in pitch darkness. It's less than 100 metres to our tent. We take our shoes off before stepping inside and feel our way to our sleeping places and blankets. There are six of us women. We fall asleep immediately.

Yesterday evening, at dusk, we set off by car from a YPG base on the other side of the Syrian border. The group was large, twenty to twenty-five people, some fighters and some outsiders like me. We were travelling as lightly as possible. I'd thrown out some items from my baggage at the last minute, leaving behind batteries, some pens. It was a minor difference, but every gram would count on the walk ahead.

The engines were revving when, with a twinge of regret, I intuitively chucked one more thing out of my bag: a Kalashnikov cartridge I'd been given months before as a keepsake by a PKK member in Maxmur. The journey we were about to begin might end badly. For me the worst case scenario involved getting caught by the peshmerga troops of the KDP in Iraqi Kurdistan, as sometimes happens to people who illegally cross the Syrian-Iraqi border. Everything in my baggage supported my identity as a journalist – laptop, camera, recording equipment, notebooks full of writing, my journalist's ID card – but a cartridge could undermine that, I thought. Certainly if it was found by people who were not kindly disposed towards me.

I was nervous. My legs were trembling. From the YPG base we drove for half an hour, maybe three quarters, got out and received whispered instructions. Walk in a line, don't talk, move briskly, always immediately follow instructions from the lead guerrillas. Go!

Six weeks or so earlier I'd made the same journey, but that time in the other direction, from Iraq to Syria. The group was much smaller then, there were seven of us, including two fighters as guides. By the time we arrived at the large YPG base camp on the mountain of Qaraçox I had an enormous blister under my left foot and my ankles felt as if they were breaking with every step, they hurt so much. I hadn't had a good look at the terrain in the dark but it seemed as if we had walked a long way in wheel tracks, so that I twisted my ankles with virtually every step. Stones underfoot also forced my ankles into almost impossible positions. All this went on for two and a half to three hours, with no opportunity for a break or even to slow down.

Would it be the same this time? At a large goods distribution point I had visited, a fighter had given me thick socks. I wasn't afraid of blisters this time. But my ankles? My endurance and strength? Another worry had been added to the mix. The authorities of Iraqi Kurdistan knew that I had travelled to Syria illegally. A colleague who had worked there for years had let me know that the KDP had their eyes on me. 'Watch out when you return,' he'd told me.

The craziest scenarios ran through my head. I had received my permit from the KDP in Iraqi Kurdistan. Their computer system therefore stated when it would expire – in two days' time. If they were really watching me, they knew from Twitter that I had arrived back in Qaraçox the day before yesterday, having travelled around northern Syria, so it wasn't so hard to conclude that I might come stumbling back over the border at any moment. How much do the KDP want me? I'm just a small fish in the large shoal of journalists in Iraqi Kurdistan. But I'm the only one embedded with the PKK. I'm also hated by one of the best friends of KDP leader and president of the Kurdistan Region, Masoud Barzani, namely Turkish President Erdoğan.

The route is different from the outward journey. The terrain is easier. I succeed in planting my feet firmly. The pace is still fast but manageable. All the same, I curse myself, because my baggage is too heavy. A medium-sized rucksack on my back, a smaller one on my chest. I shouldn't have brought that helmet, and perhaps not the laptop either, and I should have purchased a lighter camera. My hope that no one would notice me toiling away turns out to be in vain: soon one of the guide guerrillas gestures to me to pass him the bag on my chest. I hand it over, feeling pathetic.

We climb, I keep going. We see lights. They're searchlights, sweeping the night landscape. Stop, wait a moment. In the dark seconds between two beams of light we have to quickly cross an open area, unsheltered by bushes, rocks or caves. The guerrilla with my bag on his back grips my hand. Now! He pulls me, drags me, I keep moving, he not only pulls me along but also supports me, simply with the strength of his hand. Some way further on, there is a steep climb. He goes first, offering me his forearm. I take hold. He's like a rock-solid steel cable; I pull myself up.

Another foreigner in the group gives out energy tablets. It's not low blood sugar making my legs tremble, but I take two. We rustle on through scrubland, ascend, descend, are sometimes ordered to duck down and wait so that the guides can check which route is safest. We walk some stretches along the River Tigris, which forms the tiny official border crossing between the Kurdistan Region and Syria a little to the north. I also crossed there in spring 2015. At the time, journalists could gain KDP permission relatively easily to take a peek at the struggle of the Syrian Kurds.

We need to cross that river. We're already in Iraq. We sit down at the water's edge. There is a little boat that can take four or five people at a time. You, you, you too, come on, quick, quietly. On the other side we disembark hastily, my shoe sticks in the mud between the reeds. I feel around in the water and find it, sit down further along in the grass and pull it back on. And onwards, straight through grain fields now, the ears of corn already high. Then a field of ridges, my ankles twisting. The guerrilla in front of me turns, stretches out his arm and says, 'Potatoes.' Tourist information on what we're seeing is always useful. One field on, he whispers, 'Tomatoes!' Interesting. Then a sandy path. Here we are.

Cars approach. We fall flat in the verge. The cars stop. They turn out to be ours. We distribute ourselves between the vehicles based on our next destination, quick, quick. As fast as possible on the untarmacked road, we drive off into the night. The moon rises. The planning is stunningly slick: when the moon is shining it's too dangerous to attempt this trip.

In the morning the fighter responsible for onward transport informs me that a taxi will come for me. It will take me to Suleymanya, my final destination. Do I have money for the taxi, she asks? I do. Is my residence permit sorted? Yes, but I explain I've been warned that the KDP is on the lookout for me so I'm a bit anxious about the KDP checkpoints between here and there. The region around Suleymanya, basically the southern part of the Kurdistan Region, is safe for me. There it's not the KDP but the PUK who hold power and they're rather more kindly disposed towards the PKK.

She asks who my contact person is. I give her the number of a PKK member in Qandil. I go to collect my things from the tent and walk down to the car park under the trees. Suddenly I'm ordered to step into a white minibus. The taxi that was coming for me has been cancelled. I sit on the middle seat between two PKK members. On the back seat are three fighters, another three in front of us. Also the driver and the two others in the very front are guerrillas. They're all in guerrilla uniform, each with a Kalashnikov or M16 beside them. I'm in the middle, dressed in my civilian clothes, with my bag on my lap. The windows are darkened. They turn on some music and we move off. I feel safe.

At the KDP checkpoints the music is switched off and the window half opened. The PKK member greets the KDP member in a friendly tone, receives a dry nod in response, closes the window again, turns the music back up and on we go. Until we approach a checkpoint with an enormous portrait of Jalal Talabani, legendary Kurdish leader and ex-president of Iraq. Talabani is one of the founders of the PUK and his portrait means that I'm in territory that's safe for me. Home and dry.

The moment I stepped out of the car in Suleymanya, I definitively left behind the world of the PKK, the YPG and the YPJ. Of course I can visit the fighters again, and I will. I can interview Cemil Bayık or Besê Hozat again. Perhaps I'll pay another visit to a camp and, who knows, perhaps progress further towards the front line, working alone in the coming years, than I managed to do while embedded. But I'll never again be as close as I've been over these twelve months.

Never again will I sleep, in a row with four female fighters, under a mountain of blankets, in a field in northern Syria. Never again will I participate in a tekmil, or subject myself to criticism at a 'platform'. Never again will I spend afternoons swimming in the ice-cold river at the camp in the Qandil Mountains. Never again will I shower behind a jute curtain in the open air, beside a blackened kettle of boiling water on a wood fire. Never again will I learn Kurdish in a small class under the trees. I will no longer participate in the life in camps and on bases, simply be able to walk around as if I belonged and grab a blanket in the evening, lie down and go to sleep. Dance with the others at a govend near the conflict front. Watch a weapons training and, after the thunderclaps, drink tea around a fire. See the contents of ammunition depots packed into trucks, even receive a brief Kalashnikov lesson and later help to clean the guns.

But neither can I return to my own life. Not the way it was. In my thoughts I compare myself with an astronaut who has seen the earth from space. From a distance you see a different reality. Human boundaries do not exist. The earth is simply a globe in need of protection, where we, as humanity, will have to make it. I imagine that those who have seen it never lose that perspective after returning from space.

So that's what my contact person in Qandil meant when he told me at the start of the year that the PKK is an organization 'outside the established order'. It struck me as rather obvious, but over the months his words have gained significance. Especially when I really realized the contradiction. How do those thousands of men and women create a parallel reality, while also succeeding as the best fighters in the Middle East?

The answer is: there is no contradiction. There is determination, and the unshakeable belief that their ideology offers a solution to the Middle East – and perhaps the rest of the world. That ideology is taught and consistently lived on a daily basis. The Öcalan fighters shrug their shoulders at the military groups in the region that consist of the usual ingredients, such as the drive for territory and struggle for power. They despise methods such as stirring up sectarianism, ethnic cleansing and other large-scale human rights violations. The ideology rests on breaking down institutional power, undermining territorial thinking, and respect for everyone's humanity.

Those who know that are better equipped to understand the daily news about the PKK in Iraq and Turkey and about the YPG/J in Syria and do a better job of evaluating the reporting. They can more accurately pick out the misperceptions and dismiss the lying propaganda.

The misperceptions are far from always intentional, I believe. In order to see the Öcalan fighters for who they are, you need a willingness to think outside the boxes created by our society. For many people, and I'm no exception, that's difficult. We live in a system, the system lives in us. Or to put it better: it holds us in an iron grip, with our families, jobs and positions, our property and mortgages. There is no softer, warmer, more human society with more solidarity to fall back on.

The young man or woman who sets off for the mountains

is uprooted from the system and enters another world. He or she learns to see the essential faults of the patriarchal, capitalist nation-state. Because the PKK and YPG/J function fundamentally differently from it, that new knowledge can immediately be put into practice. Within the organization, after all, there is no capitalism, no patriarchy, no state. That doesn't hold for us. If we're open to it, we receive a different perspective and attempt to understand it, but we are unable to escape the system. No one can. There is nothing else. We grew up inside it. Our children grow up inside it, however terrible we think it is that they must learn from an early age to maintain the status quo in a harsh, rotten society. The society we call ours but which has nothing to offer us as the human race.

I am reminded of Comrade Batufa's seed. The seed from the Neolithic era which still lives in every one of us. Those who feel and acknowledge its existence, who seek nourishment to make it flourish, feel cheated by our society. They notice the friction, and it hurts.

Honest misperceptions among those who help to form our view of the world, such as journalists, columnists, commentators and analysts, are understandable. But, to be honest, I don't think there are many. Playing a part in determining the Western view of the conflicts and relations in the Middle East is a great responsibility. Anyone who does not take that responsibility extremely seriously, whether out of laziness, convenience, cowardice, for personal gain or pure malice, legitimizes abuse of power and helps conceal large-scale human rights violations.

So the next time you read a journalistic article in which the underlying thought is that the YPG/J want their own state in

Syria, or in which the PKK is casually referred to as a 'separatist movement', be on the alert. Of course, Kurds dream of an independent Kurdistan. But the underlying yearning is a longing for what they finally hope to find there: peace, quiet, equality, justice, freedom. The PKK's struggle is based on those yearnings.

Much of the media tend to pigeonhole the front-line movements of the PKK and YPG/J. A couple of years ago, in 2012, the PKK attempted to gain ground against the Turkish army. Until then that had never happened. After all, the guerrilla war is one of sudden attacks and lightning retreats. You see, people said, the PKK wants territory! But it wasn't about that. The PKK see themselves as the legitimate self-defence forces of the Kurdish people in Turkey. Their demand for autonomy for the people cannot be seen separately from that role. The Turkish army cannot take on that task. Due to their large-scale human rights violations over the past 100 years they have lost all legitimacy in the region.

In 2012 they did not actually succeed in gaining control of towns. At least, not for longer than a day, a record achieved in Şemdinli, Hakkâri Province.

After the breakdown of the peace process in 2015 the movement tried the opposite approach: first call for autonomy, then defend it with weapons. That got terribly out of hand in the urban wars. Mistakes were made. I would go even further in my criticism: I believe it showed that the PKK sometimes lost its connection with the people. But what it doesn't show is that the PKK is after territory. It is about disseminating the ideology and putting it into practice.

Just because all other players in Turkey, Iraq and Syria are after territorial control or expansion, from the Barzani and Talabani clans to the Turkish, Iraqi, Iranian and Syrian state, does not mean you can straightforwardly project the same motives onto the Öcalan fighters. The PKK and YPG/J members further complicate the picture; that is undeniable. But is that a reason for simplifying and misrepresenting the story?

A similar thing happens with human rights violations. There only has to be a single suspicion in that respect against the PKK or YPG/J and it will rear its head in stories about the organization for years to come. Every suspicion is a welcome rod to beat them with. Why are those who are led by Öcalan's ideology in their struggle judged so harshly for sporadic mistakes and sketchily substantiated or demonstrably untrue allegations? Often, to make matters worse, the media, commentators or people calling themselves journalists demonstrably deny, diminish or attempt to justify the crimes of Erdoğan and Assad.

The fighters are open to honest criticism but they do not need hypocrisy to keep them on the straight and narrow. They have their own consciences, and those really are very well developed. The fighters themselves would be the last people to accept human rights violations on the part of the PKK or YPG/J.

But look, say the critics, they make deals with the Syrian regime! The YPG/J are friends with Russia, and with the United States too, they remark condescendingly, portraying the fighters as purebred opportunists. That happened again in the early months of 2018. Turkey entered Afrin Canton. The YPG, YPJ and SDF defended themselves. Civilian victims resulted from Turkish bombs and artillery. Turkish soldiers abused civilians. The mercenaries of the organization that calls itself the Free Syrian Army, but who have turned out largely to be jihadists, sang songs about the armed

Islamic conflict, destroyed property, stole cattle and agricultural machines and shot civilians dead, simply because they could. Do not believe Turkey when it says that it tries to avoid civilian casualties – never in its almost 100-year history has Turkey once been caught doing that.

After almost a month of war the Kurds did a deal with the Syrian government in Damascus. The Syrian army would supply a symbolic presence in Afrin to help defend that part of the Syrian territory. Why? Because the Kurds are great friends with Assad? Of course they're not. It is a tactic to protect the civilian population against escalating Turkish violence. That's the first priority. For the YPG/J a real alliance with Assad, or any dictator, is impossible by definition. In the end the arrival of Assad's troops didn't help: in March 2018 Turkey took over control of Afrin.

At the end of 2017 an SDF commander said that the SDF would one day be absorbed into the Syrian army. Indignation rained down. The Syrian army has by far the most deaths in the Syrian war on its conscience – and the SDF wanted to be absorbed by that? For convenience most articles omitted the context. What the commanders had said was that the SDF could be part of a completely restructured Syrian army, that the legitimately armed forces would belong to a Syria that was no longer a dictatorship but a federally governed country in which everyone's ethnic and religious rights would be completely respected. Syria's reality is miles from that dream, but it is the ideal for which the SDF and YPG/J are fighting. The militant groups would not be dissolved but would reform to become part of the legitimately armed forces, which would not protect the interests of the state, as the Syrian army does now, but those of the people.

Something similar applies to the PKK in Turkey. I don't think that the PKK will ever lay down arms. A number of fighters have said as much to me. In 2015 I asked a female guerrilla in Lice,

Diyarbakır Province, when she would relinquish her weapon. 'Never,' she said. 'I will always continue to protect my people, in any circumstances. Yes, even if there is a peace agreement someday. Autonomy will be part of that peace. There will be a legal role for us to play within that autonomy.'

It was not in Suleymanya that I said goodbye to the Öcalan fighters, after that car journey in which I felt protected by them. In my heart I had said goodbye a couple of days earlier. It was early morning, in a hamlet south of Kobani. A small group of female fighters had taken up residence in a simple little house at the end of an olive grove just outside the hamlet. Due to the bombing at Qaraçox, sleeping outside was a necessity. The veranda – a slab of rough concrete – provided space for five women to sleep.

I don't know what woke me. The sun was coming up and the first rays shone straight into my eyes. I squinted slightly to protect them and saw nothing but silhouettes in the absolute silence of the morning. Olive trees, a tractor, a dog scratching around for food. The women beside me breathed slowly. I didn't move, hovering between sleep and wakefulness.

At breakfast I said, 'I'd like to share something with you. This morning in bed I suddenly realized that my time with you is almost up. The sun appeared over the horizon and I felt as if I wasn't quite awake but no longer asleep either. I still feel that way a bit. I'm still here, but the transition to my own life, the confrontation with a different reality, is coming. In a couple of weeks I'll be back in the Netherlands. I think the year I spent with you will feel very unreal then. As if I've been in a different world.'

The youngest women around the breakfast blanket were silent. Perhaps they couldn't imagine it at all. But the slightly older Comrade Roza said, 'I understand. I know the feeling. When

I remember my life before I joined the movement, it feels like a different world too. As if it wasn't really me. The day I went to the mountains, I was born again. I can never go back.'

Acknowledgements

One conversation with the PKK press officer, Comrade Zagros, will always stay with me as a journalist. It was at a camp in Qandil. I wanted to move on to the next location and felt everything was moving too slowly. In order to motivate Zagros to speed up my transport, I said, 'It's also in your interest. I want to write a good book about you, but to do that I need access!' He laughed and said, 'Well, there are so many bad books about the PKK, one more won't hurt.'

It was a joke. Zagros was a fantastic help to me all year. Nevertheless his remark speaks volumes about the mentality of the armed groups led by Öcalan's ideology: they're so confident that they don't bother to try and steer my work or influence it, other than simply to arrange access and talk with me. If I write a rubbish book, that's primarily my problem, not theirs. I also think the organization trusted me to carry out this project in good faith. I feel I can say their trust was well placed.

I was in no way pampered by the PKK, nor have I ever been paid by them. They provided my transport all year (and on routes where no PKK transport was available, I paid for the taxi organized by them), supplied accommodation, food and drink (water and tea, never alcohol as that is not consumed in the PKK). I also accepted the following items: two pairs of socks, sufficient toothpaste and shampoo for the period, a towel, a lovely black vest, two scarves (one dark green, one black with flowers), two haircuts, a notepad, a pencil and rubber. There were also small gifts: I was given a handmade bracelet, a small rope necklace with a stone pendant displaying a Mazlum Doğan sticker, a pale green stone from Botan, three pins (one of Bêrîtan, one of Sakine Cansız, one of Öcalan) and a Kalashnikov cartridge. Various fighters gave me a song as a gift. One of them appears on my Vimeo channel.

I didn't reimburse the PKK for my living costs for the year I was with them. Besides that being an insult to Kurdish hospitality, I have no wish to be charged with 'financing a terrorist organization'.

Warm thanks to Zagros for his help and humour. Thanks to all the fighters, from young Comrade Evîndar to the veteran Comrade Cuma, for the glimpse they gave me of their lives and inner worlds, for the hours we spent together in camps, on bases, at the front, on the road in Kurdistan and outside, and for our conversations. I felt safe, and (almost) always welcome.

A number of colleagues helped me bring order to my thoughts on this project. Dear Amberin Zaman, with whom I became friends in Istanbul and to whom I didn't need to explain what my 'crazy plan' was: thanks for your unwavering honesty. Perhaps I really am rather like a moth drawn to a flame, but you're one of the people who keeps me alert in the process. Colleague X, who asked me not to name her because she still travels to Turkey once in a while: your vision affected me and your immediate enthusiasm for my plan strengthened me – thank you. And Linda Polman in Amsterdam, what you said definitively pulled me over the line: the truly crazy choice would have been not to embark on this journalistic quest.

Writing coach Tanny Dobbelaar helped me structure the enormous mountain of information with which I returned to the Netherlands at the end of the year. It fell to Kinge Siljee, supported by her team of 'Study Masters', to crack the whip: interim deadlines, schedules, her egging me on to 8,000 words in a day and a half, and the occasional well-timed glass of wine – I couldn't have done it without her! Kinge also cast her strict eye over the final product. My second reader was filmmaker and writer Beri Shalmashi. We formed a golden trio. Thank you!

The love and support of my readers cannot go without mention. Without you I wouldn't do what I do, nor would I have been as able to cope with the intensity of it all. You make me less powerless.

The last few years have changed me. I'm finding it difficult to return to the Netherlands. I need time and space to find a new balance. I'm taking that time. I dare to take it because I know that my family and friends support and trust me and won't let me go. There is nothing more valuable.

Fréderike

Amsterdam,
11 April 2018

Timeline

~ 10,000 BC
Neolithic era

Beginning of the 16th century
Kurdish region (apart from the part in the Persian Empire) becomes part of the Ottoman Empire. The Kurds guard the outer borders of the Empire and receive far-reaching autonomy in a number of provinces in return.

Mid-19th century
Under Sultan Abdülmecid I the Kurdish areas are frequently brought under control of the central authority in Istanbul using a great deal of violence. The sultan hopes that this will prevent the Ottoman Empire from crumbling.

1915
Armenian genocide. Under orders from Istanbul between 800,000 and 1.5 million Armenians are murdered by the Ottoman army and the Kurdish Hamidiye Cavalry.

1923
Foundation of the Republic of Turkey.

1925
First Kurdish rebellion in Turkey, under leadership of Sheikh Said, in Diyarbakır.

1937–38
Dersim Massacres.

1946
Foundation of the KDP (Kurdistan Democratic Party) by Mullah Mustafa Barzani, in Rojhilat (Kurdistan in Iran).

1971
Military coup (eleven years after the first coup in Turkey of 1960). Many left-wing groups, including (incognito) Kurdish groups, are banned, left-

wing leaders are imprisoned or hanged.

1975

Foundation of the PUK (Patriotic Union of Kurdistan) in the Kurdish region in Iraq. The PUK is a breakaway faction of the KDP.

1978

Foundation of the PKK in the village of Fiş, Diyarbakır Province.

1980

12 September: Military coup in Turkey, followed by unprecedented oppression. Many PKK members are also arrested and severely tortured, in the infamous Diyarbakır prison among others.

1984

First attacks by the PKK on the Turkish state, in Eruh (Siirt Province) and Şemdinli (Hakkâri Province).

1988

16 March: Poisonous gas attack by Saddam Hussein on the city of Helebce (Halabja) in Kurdistan in Iraq. Between 3,000 and 5,000 people are killed. The attack on Helebce is part of the Anfal campaign, in which at least 100,000 Kurds are killed between 1986 and 1989.

1991

De facto autonomy for the Kurds in Iraq's Kurdistan Region under American protection after the First Gulf War.

1992

In October and November, peshmerga troops, working alongside the Turkish army, attack PKK positions in the mountains in northern Iraq.

1993

Turkish President Turgut Özal dies, bringing an end to a budding peace process with the PKK.

1990s

Years of extreme violence in south-eastern Turkey. At least 3,000 Kurdish villages are razed to the ground by the Turkish state, millions of Kurds flee to the Kurdish cities and to cities in other parts of Turkey (Adana, Ankara, Istanbul, Izmir), and Turkish army death squads carry out hundreds of illegal executions.

1998

October: Öcalan leaves Syria, after Turkey threatens war over his presence in the capital Damascus. He tries unsuccessfully to gain asylum in Greece, Italy, Russia and other countries, and eventually flees to Kenya.

1999

15 February: Abduction of PKK leader Abdullah Öcalan from the Greek Embassy in Kenya by the Turkish secret service, in collaboration with the CIA and other organizations. Since then Öcalan has been imprisoned on the island of Imralı.

2003

End of Saddam Hussein's reign in Iraq.

2005

The autonomy of the Kurdistan Region of Iraq is officially established in the Iraqi constitution.

2011

Beginning of popular uprisings in Syria against the Assad dictatorship, culminating in the Syrian Civil War.

28 December: Roboskî airstrike, in which thirty-four Kurdish citizens are murdered by the Turkish air force.

2012

President Assad's government forces leave the Kurdish areas in the north of Syria and Kurdish autonomy begins.

2013

9 January: Sakine Cansız, co-founder of the PKK, is murdered with her comrades Leyla Şaylemez and Fidan Doğan in Paris. It emerges that the Turkish secret service MIT ordered the murders.

21 March: The day of the Kurdish New Year, Newroz, marks the official beginning of a peace process between the Turkish state and the PKK.

2014

June: ISIS conquers Mosul, Iraq

June: The Iraqi army leaves Kirkuk, which is threatened by the rise of ISIS. The KDP and PUK peshmerga take over the city. In August 2014 the PKK comes to Kirkuk to help defend the city against ISIS.

August: Massacres and mass abductions of Yazidis by ISIS in Şengal, Iraq. The KDP peshmerga leave the area and decline to protect the Yazidis; the YPG and PKK come to the people's aid.

August: ISIS attacks Maxmur Camp in Iraq, the PKK successfully defends it.

September: Beginning of the battle for Kobani, which the YPG and YPJ (with the help of the peshmerga and American airstrikes) finally win against ISIS in January 2015.

2015

April: Öcalan placed in isolation again.

7 June: Parliamentary elections in which the AKP loses its majority for the first time. The HDP achieves a historic thirteen per cent of the votes.

Summer: Peace process definitively collapses; resumption of violence between the PKK and the Turkish army.

20 July: Bomb attack in Suruç causes the deaths of thirty-three Kurdish and Turkish youths on their way to Kobani to help with the construction of the city.

10 October: Bomb attack on a large peace demonstration in the Turkish capital city Ankara, in which 100 people die. It is the largest bomb attack in Turkish history.

2015–16

Urban warfare in various Kurdish cities in Turkey. Hundreds of people, including many civilians, are killed in excessive state violence, at least half a million people are uprooted.

2016

15 July: Attempted coup in Turkey, after which a state of emergency is announced throughout the country. The state of emergency continues.

2017

16 April: Referendum on the introduction of a presidential system instead of the parliamentary system in Turkey. The yes camp wins with fifty-one per cent of the votes.

25 September: Referendum on independence in the Kurdistan Region of Iraq. As much as ninety-three per cent of the Kurds vote for independence.

October: The Iraqi army takes back control of Kirkuk, with little resistance from the KDP or PUK peshmerga. Baghdad wants to take back control of the previously lost territory now that ISIS has largely been beaten. Şengal and other areas are also taken over from the peshmerga with minimal bloodshed.

October: The SDF, in collaboration with the US army, banishes ISIS from its 'capital' Raqqa.

2018

20 January: Turkey attacks the Kurdish canton of Afrin in north-west Syria. In March the YPG and YPJ retreat in order to prevent a battle for the city of Afrin, with many potential civilian deaths. Turkey has occupied the region ever since.

1 April: The PKK leaves Şengal.

List of Names, Concepts and Abbreviations

KURDISTAN GEOGRAPHICAL NAMES

Afrin

Name of the region, mainly populated by Kurds although ethnically diverse, in the north-westernmost tip of Syria, bordering on Turkey. Between 2012 and 2018 Afrin was the westernmost canton of the Democratic Federation of Northern Syria (DFNS, called Autonomous Administration of North and East Syria since 2018). It is now occupied by Turkey, in conjunction with jihadist militias.

Amed

The symbolic Kurdish capital. Amed is the Kurdish name for the city officially known in Turkish as Diyarbakır. The name Amed has political connotations. Many older Kurds call it Diyarbekir, the name of the city before the Republic of Turkey was founded in 1923.

Bakur

Kurdish for 'north'. Used to refer to northern Kurdistan, or the part of Kurdistan located in Turkey.

Başûr

Kurdish for 'south'. Used to refer to southern Kurdistan, or the part of Kurdistan situated in Iraq. Başûr is larger than the area that officially belongs to the Kurdistan Region of Iraq.

Botan

Kurdish name of the region in south-eastern Turkey that approximately encompasses the provinces of Şırnak and (parts of) Hakkâri, Siirt and Van.

Cizire

Name of the easternmost canton in the Autonomous Administration of North and East Syria, bordering on Iraq and Turkey. Most important city: Qamişlo.

Cizre

Kurdish city on the banks of the River Tigris in south-eastern Turkey, near both the Syrian and Iraqi borders.

Dersim

Name of the eastern Turkish province renamed Tunceli in 1936. The name change was part of the prelude to the massacres of Dersim, carried out by the Turkish army in 1937 and 1938, in which tens of thousands of Alevi Kurds lost their lives.

Erbil

Capital city of the Kurdistan Region of Iraq. Under the KDP's political control. Kurdish name: Hewlêr.

Kirkuk

Ethnically and religiously diverse city in Iraq, just outside the Kurdistan Region. Control over oil-rich Kirkuk has long been disputed between the Kurds and the central Iraqi government in Baghdad. The Kurdistan Region held sway here between 2014 and 2017, after the Iraqi army decided not to defend the city against ISIS. After a referendum for independence in the Kurdistan Region in September 2017, to which the Iraqi government was fiercely opposed, Baghdad resumed control of the city.

Kobani

Name of a canton in the Autonomous Administration of North and East Syria, bordering on Turkey. From September 2014 to January 2015 the city of the same name was besieged by ISIS, but the YPG and YPJ succeeded in repelling the attack with the help of American airstrikes and peshmerga material and teams from Iraqi Kurdistan. The battle for Kobani played an important role in the failure of the 'peace process' in Turkey (2013–15).

Rojava

Kurdish for 'west'. Used to refer to western Kurdistan, or the part of Kurdistan located in Syria.

Rojhilat

Kurdish for 'east'. Used to refer to eastern Kurdistan, or the part of Kurdistan located in Iran.

Suleymanya

Second biggest city in the Kurdistan Region in Iraq. Under the political control of the PUK. Kurdish name: Silêmanî.

Sur

The historical city centre of Amed/Diyarbakır. Largely destroyed in the urban war that raged between the end of 2015 and the start of 2016.

Suruç

Town on the Syrian border in south-eastern Turkey, virtually bordering on Kobani. During the battle for Kobani, Kurds gathered here, along with a whole contingent of foreign journalists, to follow and support the conflict. Kurdish name: Pirsûs.

Şengal

The region in north-west Iraq, home to the Yazidis, a Kurdish religious minority. In early 2014, ISIS stormed into the region; the peshmerga did not defend it. The PKK came from Qandil to save whatever was left, and eventually withdrew from Şengal in March 2018. Şengal is the Kurdish name for the region and the most important city, which is called Sinjar in Arabic.

Yüksekova

Kurdish city in the east of Turkey, on the border with Iran. I was deported from Turkey here in September 2015. Kurdish name: Gever.

TURKEY

Abdullah Öcalan

Founder and ideologist of the PKK. Honorary leader of the KCK. Born in 1946 in the village of Amara (Turkish name: Ömerli) in the province of Şanlıurfa, Turkey. Has been serving a life sentence on the prison island of Imralı since 1999.

AKP

Adalet ve Kalkınma Partisi, Justice and Development Party, officially known as the AK Party. Founded in 2001. Has ruled Turkey since 2002.

Apo

Nickname for Abdullah Öcalan.

Besê Hozat

Co-leader with Cemil Bayık of the executive committee of the KCK, the umbrella organization to which the PKK also belongs. Besê Hozat is an Alevi Kurd from Dersim.

Cemil Bayık

Co-leader with Besê Hozat of the executive committee of the KCK, the umbrella organization to which the PKK also belongs. Bayık is one of the founders of the PKK.

DBP

Demokratik Bölgeler Partisi, Democratic Regions Party. The regional branch of the HDP, which gained administrative control over more Kurdish municipalities than ever before in the local elections in 2014. There are now dozens of DBP mayors in Turkish prisons suspected of terrorism.

HDP
Halkların Demokratik Partisi, Peoples' Democratic Party. Often referred to as the 'pro-Kurdish' party in Turkey, but that description is incorrect. The HDP was founded in 2012 as a collaboration between the Kurdish political movement and all kinds of left-wing Turkish parties and action groups. Their supporters are largely Kurdish, but the HDP expressly stands up for all marginalized groups in Turkey, from Kurds and Alevis to the LGBT community and the working class.

HPG
Hêzên Parastina Gel, People's Defence Forces, or the armed branch of the PKK. The HPG is also active in Iraq.

Kemal Pir
One of the Turkish founders of the PKK. Arrested after the military coup in Turkey in 1980 and died, with three others, in 1982 in Diyarbakır prison after fifty-five days' hunger strike.

KCK
Koma Civakên Kurdistan, Kurdistan Communities Union. Umbrella organization for Kurdish organizations in Kurdistan, including the PKK. The aim of the KCK is to implement democratic confederalism, Öcalan's ideology. Founded in 2007.

Mazlum Doğan
Legendary founding member of the PKK. On 21 March 1982, at Newroz, he set himself on fire in his cell in the prison of Diyarbakır to protest against torture and other inhuman conditions in the prison.

MIT
Milli Istihbarat Teşkilatı, National Intelligence Organization, or Turkey's homeland security service.

PKK
Partiya Karkerên Kurdistan, Kurdistan Workers' Party. Political party founded in 1978. The PKK falls under the umbrella of the KCK and is thus a sister party to the PYD in Syria, the PÇDK in Iraq and the PJAK in Iran.

Recep Tayyip Erdoğan
President of Turkey since 2014. One of the founders of the AKP and prime minister of Turkey from 2003 to 2014. Born in Kasımpaşa, Istanbul, in 1954.

Sakine Cansız

Legendary co-founder of the PKK. Nom de guerre: Sara. She had worked for the organization in Europe for several years when she was murdered in Paris on 9 January 2013, along with her comrades Leyla Şaylemez and Fidan Doğan. Her book, *My Whole Life was a Struggle*, is much read within (and outside) the PKK and her portrait can be found all over the place in PKK bases. The French prosecutor found that the Turkish secret service MIT ordered the murder. The case never came to trial: the murderer died of brain tumour in a Parisian cell.

Seid Riza

Leader of the resistance against the Dersim massacres, 1937–38.

Selahattin Demirtaş

Lawyer, member of parliament and former co-leader of the HDP (June 2014 to February 2018). Candidate in the presidential elections in 2014, in which he gained ten per cent of the vote. The charismatic Demirtaş, along with his (Turkish) fellow party leader Figen Yüksekdağ, succeeded in pushing the HDP up to thirteen per cent of the vote in the parliamentary elections in June 2015. Demirtaş, like Yüksekdağ and a number of other HDP members of parliament, was arrested on 4 November 2016. He is still in prison in Edirne. The various cases running against him for crimes relating to terrorism call for a prison sentence totalling more than 100 years.

Sheikh Said

Leader of the first Kurdish uprising (in 1925) after the foundation of the Republic of Turkey (in 1923).

TAK

Teyrêbazên Azadiya Kurdistan, Kurdistan Freedom Hawks. Group that carries out attacks (mainly) in cities in central and western Turkey, generally on military targets but almost always at locations in which civilian victims are inevitable. The TAK is led by Öcalan's ideology but the PKK claims to have nothing to do with the group and not to command them. Founded in 2004.

YJA-Star

Yekîneyên Jinên Azad ên Star, the Free Women's Units, the female armed branch of the PKK. The YJA-Star is active in Turkey (attacks on the Turkish security services) and Iraq (fighting along with other groups against ISIS, protecting the people in Kirkuk, Maxmur, Şengal and other locations).

YPS

Yekîneyên Parastina Sivîl, Civil Protection Units. Youth group linked to the PKK, founded in 2015 to defend the areas proclaimed 'autonomous regions' in south-eastern Turkey. In 2015 and 2016 waged war on the Turkish army in various Kurdish cities in Turkey.

YPS-Jin

Yekîneyên Parastina Sivîl-Jin, Women's Civil Protection Units, women's branch of the YPS.

Zîlan

PKK fighter who blew herself up during a military ceremony in Dersim in 1996. She was the first PKK member to kill Turkish soldiers as well as herself in such an act. She grew to be a legend, especially after Öcalan expressed praise for her. Many PKK fighters continue to choose Zîlan as their nom de guerre.

IRAQ

Barzani

Most powerful family in Kurdistan in Iraq. Founding father: Mullah Mustafa Barzani (1903–1979), father of Masoud Barzani (born 1946), president of the KRG from 2005 to 2017. Masoud is the father of Masrour Barzani (born 1969), who became the Region's prime minister in March 2019. He replaced his nephew, Nechirvan Barzani (born 1966), who became president of the KRG.

KDP

Kurdistan Democratic Party. The most powerful political party in the Kurdistan Region in Iraq, dominated by the Barzani family. Founded in Iran in 1946 by Mullah Mustafa Barzani.

KRG

Kurdistan Regional Government, the government of the autonomous Kurdistan Region of Iraq. Located in Erbil, the capital of the Kurdistan Region.

KRI

Kurdistan Region of Iraq, the autonomous Kurdistan Region in Iraq. Has existed de facto since 1991 and was officially established in the Iraqi constitution in 2005.

PÇDK

Partî Çareserî Dîmukratî Kurdistan, Kurdistan Democratic Solution Party. Political party that falls under the KCK and is thus a sister party to the PKK in Turkey, the PYD in Syria and the PJAK in Iran. The PÇDK stood in the elections in the Kurdistan Region in 2013 but only received 0.1 per cent of votes.

Peshmerga
Kurdish fighters. Currently used to refer to the peshmerga armies of the KDP and PUK, the official forces of the Kurdistan Region, but traditionally the peshmerga are fighters throughout Kurdistan.

PUK
Patriotic Union of Kurdistan. Second party in the Kurdistan Region in Iraq. The PUK is a breakaway faction of the KDP, founded in 1975. The most important founder and for many years the leader was Jalal Talabani (1933–2017), who was also president of Iraq from 2006 to 2014. The PUK is also known by the Kurdish abbreviation YNK (Yekîtiya Nîştimanî ya Kurdistanê).

Qandil
Mountains in the north of Iraq, but also a small village in that region. Outsiders generally use 'Qandil' to mean the entire area of north and northeast Iraq under the military control of the PKK. PKK members use it to refer exclusively to the Qandil Mountains. The rest of the area under their control has names such as Hakurk, Avaşîn, Zagros and Haftanîn.

YBŞ
Yekîneyên Berxwedana Şengalê, Şengal Resistance Units. Self-defence units of Yazidis in the Şengal region, founded by the PKK in 2014 and trained by the PKK.

YJŞ
Yekîneyên Jinên Şengalê, Şengal Women's Units. The women's defence troops in the Şengal region, founded and trained by the PKK.

SYRIA

AANES
Autonomous Administration of North and East Syria, the official name of the Kurdish-controlled regions in Syria, previously named DFNS and Rojava.

DFNS
Democratic Federation of Northern Syria. This area was called Rojava from the time when it fell under Kurdish control in 2012. In 2018, the name was changed to Autonomous Administration of North and East Syria.

Hashd al-Shaabi
Also known as the Popular Mobilization Units (PMU). Shiite militia

supported by Iran and controlled by the Iraqi army.

ISIS

Islamic State in Iraq and al-Sham. Also known as IS (Islamic State) and (in Arabic) as Daesh. Öcalan fighters who combat ISIS in both Iraq and Syria persist in calling ISIS members 'gangs'.

PYD

Partiya Yekîtiya a Demokratik, Democratic Union Party. Founded in 2003. Political party under the umbrella of the KCK and thus a sister party to the PKK in Turkey, the PÇDK in Iraq and the PJAK in Iran.

SDF

Syrian Democratic Forces. Collaboration of Kurdish, Arab and other armed groups who constitute the boots on the ground in the fight against ISIS in Syria. The YPG and YPJ initially provided most of the fighters, but the proportion of Arabs and others has grown over time.

TEV-DEM

Tevgera Civaka Demokratîk, Movement for a Democratic Society. Collaboration between various parties governing the Autonomous Administration of North and East Syria. The PYD is the largest party in TEV-DEM.

YPG

Yekîneyên Parastina Gel, People's Protection Units. Öcalan fighters in (northern) Syria. Founded in 2004 as the armed branch of the PYD. Since the Syrian Civil War and the foundation of TEV-DEM the YPG has fallen under TEV-DEM.

YPJ

Yekîneyên Parastina Jin, Women's Protection Units. Sister organization of the YPG, founded in 2013. Since the Syrian Civil War and the foundation of TEV-DEM the YPJ has fallen under TEV-DEM.

IRAN

HPJ

Hêzên Parastina Jin, Women's Defence Forces, the women's armed branch of the PJAK.

PJAK

Partiya Jiyana Azad a Kurdistanê, the Kurdistan Free Life Party. Political party under the umbrella of the KCK and thus a sister party to the PKK in

Turkey, the PYD in Syria and the PÇDK in Iraq.

YRK

Yekîneyên Rojhilatê Kurdistan, Eastern Kurdistan Units, the armed branch of the PJAK.

Bibliography

The following were my principal secondary sources besides the many articles from online archives of various media outlets, including *ANF*, *Al-Monitor*, *Sabah*, *Habertürk*, *Hürriyet*, *The New York Times*, *The Guardian*, among many others.

Amnesty International. '"We had nowhere else to go": Forced Displacement and Demolitions in Northern Syria'. October 2015.

Aydın, Suavi, and Jelle Verheij. 'Confusion in the Cauldron: Some Notes on Ethno-Religious Groups, Local Powers and the Ottoman State in Diyarbekir Province, 1800–1870'. *The Ottoman Empire and its Heritage*. Vol. 51, *Social Relations in Ottoman Diyarbekir, 1870–1915*, pp. 15–54. Brill Publishers, 2012.

Başaran, Ezgi. *Frontline Turkey: The Conflict at the Heart of the Middle East*. I.B. Tauris & Co. Ltd., 2017.

Bayır, Derya. *Minorities and Nationalism in Turkish Law*. Ashgate Publishing Ltd., 2013.

Biehl, Janet. *Ecology or Catastrophe: The Life of Murray Bookchin*. Oxford University Press, 2015.

Bookchin, Murray. *Remaking Society: Pathways to a Green Future*. South End Press, 1990.

———. *Urbanization Without Cities: The Rise and Decline of Citizenship*. Black Rose Books, 1992.

Bruinessen, Martin van. 'Turkey, Europe and the Kurds after the capture of Abdullah Öcalan'. In *Kurdish Ethno-nationalism versus Nation-building States*. The ISIS Press, 2000.

Çağlayan, Handan. 'From Kawa the Blacksmith to Ishtar the Goddess: Gender Constructions in Ideological-Political Discourses of the Kurdish Movement in post-1980 Turkey'. *European Journal of Turkish Studies*, vol. 14, 2012.

Elçi, Tahir. 'Curfew in Cizre, A survey report of events'. Diyarbakir Bar Association, September 2015.*

* The lawyer and human rights activist Tahir Elçi was murdered on 28

Geerdink, Fréderike. *De jongens zijn dood, een journalistieke reis naar de kern van de Koerdische kwestie in Turkije*. Uitgeverij Spectrum, 2014. Translated in English as *The Boys are Dead: The Roboski Massacre and the Kurdish Question in Turkey*. Gomidas Books, 2015.

General Command of the People's Protection Units. YPG Statement in Reaction to Amnesty Report, as published on KurdishQuestion.com, October 2015.

Gurcan, Metin. 'In struggle against PKK, Turkey takes flight'. *Al-Monitor*, 2016.

Günes, Cengiz. *The Kurdish National Movement in Turkey, From Protest to Resistance*. Routledge, 2012.

Human Rights Watch. 'Mounting Security Operation Deaths: Scores of Civilians Among Hundreds Killed in Southeast'. December 2015.

———. 'Turkey: State Blocks Probes of Southeast Killings', July 2016.

Jones, Dorian. 'Kurdish families claim kids kidnapped by PKK'. Free Speech Radio News website (fsrn.org), 9 September 2014.

Jongerden, Joost and Ahmet Hamdi Akkaya. 'Springtime: The Kurdistan Workers Party (PKK) and the Quest for Radical Democracy'. In *The Kurdish Spring: Geopolitical Changes and the Kurds*, edited by Mohammed M.A. Ahmed and Michael A. Gunter. Mazda Publishers, 2013.

Karaveli, Halil, 'The Coalition Crumbles: Erdoğan, the Gülenists, and Turkish Democracy'. *The Turkey Analyst*, 2012.

Karayılan, Murat. *Bir Savaşin Anatomisi. Kurdistan'da Askeri Çizgi*. [In Kurdish.] Internal PKK publication, 2010.

Mandıracı, Berkay. *Turkey's PKK Conflict: The Death Toll*. International Crisis Group, 20 July 2016.

Marcus, Aliza. *Blood and Belief*. New York University Press, 2007.

Öcalan, Abdullah. *Democratic Confederalism*. Transmedia Publishing, 2015.

———. *Prison Writings. The Roots of Civilization*. Transmedia Publishing, 2015.

———. *War and Peace in Kurdistan: Perspectives for a Political Solution of the Kurdish Question*. Transmedia Publishing, 2014.

Weiss, Michael and Hassan Hassan. *ISIS: Inside the Army of Terror*. Regan Arts, 2015.

November 2015 when he read out a press release in Sur, Diyarbakır, in which he spoke out against the violence in the city. The minimal investigation into the murder has revealed nothing as yet. No one has been arrested, nor any suspects identified. May he rest in peace.